Sign up for our newsletter to hear
about new and upcoming releases.

www.ylva-publishing.com

## BOOKS IN THE SERIES
# GIRL MEETS GIRL

*Never-Tied Nora*

*Not-So-Straight Sue*

*Fenced-In Felix*

# FENCED-IN FELIX

A DRIFTER AND A RACEHORSE
TURN THE OUTBACK UPSIDE
DOWN.

# CHEYENNE BLUE

# ACKNOWLEDGEMENTS

Writing can be a painful process as well as a glorious one, but when you have a great team at your back, it really helps to make the difficult things easier. The team at Ylva are awesome in this respect. Huge kudos and thanks go to them: Astrid Ohletz, Sandra Gerth, Jove Belle, and their team of copyeditors and proofreaders. Thank you.

The team at Streetlight Graphics has once again designed a cover that I love. When they put that string of beads in Josie's hair, I knew I had to write them into the story.

I had some extra help with this one from my friend and fellow author Katharina Marcus, my "horse beta", who speaks the language of horse fluently. She checked my horse facts and terminology. Thanks, Kat.

As always, love and thanks to D, my cheer squad of one, who didn't complain when I spent way too long doing edits when we were on holiday.

And finally, to the Aussie outback, in all its dusty red glory. It will always hold a piece of my heart.

# CHAPTER 1

"Hey, Felix!"

The shout rang loudly in the stillness that was Worrindi's main street in the middle of the day.

I turned. My friend Narelle stood in the doorway of the weatherboard post office, waving a piece of paper in the air.

"Your parcel's here! Don't go home without it."

I lifted a hand in acknowledgment, and she darted back inside.

My parcel. Anticipation thrummed in my chest. I'd been waiting for my new signage and brochures for over a month; the next baby step on my new venture.

Even as I marched purposefully down the main street, my thoughts raced. If I was quick, I could collect my parcel, pick up some groceries, and maybe treat myself to a beer before I had to hotfoot it home to Jayboro Outstation. I ducked into the store. Although it was big by Worrindi standards, it barely qualified as a chain store. "Small town, small store." That's what Narelle liked to say, usually after she'd arrived at a community get-together and discovered someone else was wearing the exact same shirt as her.

I needed curtains. Not something I bought everyday—indeed, the old Queenslander where I lived alone had had the same curtains hanging at the windows for the last twenty or so years.

"Faded like last year's rodeo queen," Mum used to say. "Imagine how much faster they'd fade if Queensland joined the twenty-first century and brought in daylight saving!" Her old joke, the one she used to trot out every year when the rest of Australia moved the clocks forwards an hour to summer time but Queensland stayed resolutely put.

But these curtains weren't to replace the ones in my house. No, with luck, those would last another twenty years. Until recently, I'd barely used them anyway; living in the outback meant there were few people to see into your house, and fewer still who would care if they could. I was always up by daybreak, even in the summer when the sun crested the horizon by four, thanks to that same lack of daylight saving. No, these curtains were for the same project as my signage and brochures; my brand new tourist cabins that sat in a scenic spot in my campground. If I could find some blue and yellow curtains to match the doona and sheets on the bed, then I could open the first cabin for visitors today.

"Today," I whispered to myself as I walked into the store and surveyed their meagre stock. Today could be the start of something big. All I needed were customers. But first, curtains.

I was in luck. At the back of a shelf, I found some curtains with bright yellow sunflowers on a blue background. The print was big and bold, and while it was a bit louder than I would have liked, it would save me a trip to the Isa—Mount Isa, the large town four hours' drive away.

In the spirit of optimism, I bought four sets, enough to curtain both cabins—the one that was finished and the one that was a timber shell awaiting fit-out whenever I got enough money together. But if I didn't buy them now, I'd be lucky to find matching ones a few months down the track, when the second cabin would hopefully be open.

I headed back to where my ute was parked in the shade and put the curtains inside. Next priority was the post office.

Narelle was selling stamps and postcards to a couple of tourists. I waited as she chatted with them about the opal quarry and the camel farm—two of the region's biggest tourist attractions.

When the tourists left, walking out into the sunlight with leaflets clutched in their hands, Narelle turned to me.

"Wait a sec," she said and disappeared out the back. She returned in a couple of minutes, manhandling a large, flat parcel. My new signage. It was bigger than I'd thought and would take some manoeuvring to get it onto the back of the ute. I'd have to tie it down to keep it from getting slapped onto the bitumen if the wind lifted it out of the tray.

Narelle propped the parcel against the counter and disappeared, only to come back a second time with a box. From the way she was puffing, it was heavy. "Your brochures. How many did you order?"

"Maybe a few thousand. It was cheaper that way."

"A few thousand?" Narelle's voice lifted in amazement. "Just how many people are you expecting?" She held out her hand. "Give some to me, and I'll put them on the counter. You heard those tourists; they quizzed me as to where they could find the real outback experience, not the made-up show that some of the bigger towns put on."

"They'll get real all right at Jayboro." I ripped open the parcel, and Narelle handed me scissors to get into the box. It was sealed tighter than a fish's bum hole. Finally, though, I pulled it open and scooped out a bundle of brochures.

"Nice." Narelle nodded approvingly. "Some fancy designer did you a good job with those."

On the front was a photo of a group of tourists in akubra hats sitting around a campfire. One of them held a guitar, and the brilliant outback sky blazed with stars above their heads.

*Experience the real outback at Jayboro Outstation.*

I smiled. The brochure looked fantastic, and no tourist would realise that the happy "campers" around the fire were my friends, Sue and Moni, along with a few borrowed jackaroos from the main Jayboro Station. Nor would they know that Moni couldn't play a single chord on the guitar she held. The brochure gave the feel and the atmosphere of the outback, and that would hopefully be enough to entice them in.

I handed a wad of them to Narelle. "I'll give you a beer bonus if you send them my way."

"I was hoping you'd say that." She put the brochures prominently on her small front counter.

I dropped off more brochures at a couple of other businesses in town, run by people I could count on to promote a local venture. Worrindi was a small town that struggled at times, as it was bypassed by the major highway and didn't have the striking attractions of bigger towns like Winton and the Isa.

I went into the mechanic's, which was always busy with tourist vehicles choked with the dust of outback roads, and gave some to Bazza behind the counter.

"That ute of yours doesn't sound so good, Felix," he said. "Heard it missing on a cylinder as you pulled in. Is it hard to start?"

"Took three tries this morning."

"Might just be a dodgy ignition lead. That's nothing much. If you leave it with me now, I'll take a look just as soon as I've finished with this beast." He nodded in the direction of a huge four-wheel drive. Its roof rack, awnings, and paraphernalia—all coated with red dirt—proclaimed it to be a tourist vehicle.

"Thanks. Be good if that was it. Keys are in the ignition."

"No worries."

I went to the grocery store for some supplies and arranged to pick them up once the ute was fixed. Then I wandered back to see if Bazza was finished.

He was talking to the owner of the four-wheel drive and shot me an apologetic glance. "Can you come back in an hour, Felix?"

I gave him a thumbs up and went back to the street. I was done with errands. Now I had the perfect excuse for a short bit of Felix-time, something I seldom seemed to have.

A few doors up, the wide and welcoming veranda of the Commercial Hotel beckoned. I could kill two birds with one stone and see if the publican would put my brochures on the counter, plus I'd have a beer at the same time. I grabbed more brochures from the ute and headed for the pub.

Even though the lunch rush was over, there were a few people rubbing the long bar with their elbows. I recognised some locals, and there was also a handful of tourists enjoying a beer or browsing the historic photos on the wall.

The barperson was new. She was a short woman with a mop of unruly curls that bounced on her shoulders as she moved. A string of white and turquoise beads glinted in her hair, and she wore a tie-dye T-shirt with a pair of very tight denim shorts. She was maybe thirty, but it was obvious from her economical movements as she poured pots that she was experienced at bar work.

I deliberately picked a spot close to the tourists and waited while the barperson served more people. Her tight shorts rode up as she stretched up to snag a packet of chips from the top of the wire rack to reveal more of her muscled thighs. From the appreciative glances, it seemed that cheese and onion was the most popular flavour of the day.

Finally, she came over. "What can I get you?" Her smile crinkled fine lines at the corners of her eyes, and her skin was tanned, the year-round tan of someone who spends a lot of time outdoors.

"A pot of light, please." An imp of mischief made me add, "And a packet of cheese and onion chips."

The view as she stretched up to the top of the rack was once again nothing short of spectacular. She set the chips and a beer down on the counter in front of me. "Five fifty, please."

I counted out the coins and watched as she whirled around to ring up the sale. For the next few minutes, she was busy serving other customers. She wasn't graceful or pretty. If she were a horse, she'd be a stockhorse rather than a thoroughbred, but she moved with the lightness of one who is comfortable in her skin.

A drifter, I decided. One of Australia's casual workforce, moving from place to place, following seasonal work in small towns. She'd probably learnt of the bar job from one of the city employment agencies, and they'd given her the job over the gap-year students from Europe. She'd probably stay a few weeks, maybe a month or two, and then move on, maybe to pick strawberries near the coast or mangoes up the Top End. But in the meantime, here she was, pouring beer in Worrindi, doubtless staying in one of the tiny rooms above the pub.

Lost in my thoughts, I didn't realise I'd been caught staring until my gaze drifted up, away from her backside, to find her amused smile and direct gaze staring straight back at me.

"Can I get you anything else?"

My breath froze in my throat, afraid she'd be annoyed by my staring. But there was a half smile on her face. She didn't seem too pissed off. I suspected she was enjoying my appreciation. That seldom happened.

I opted for professional—after all, I had an agenda here. "Actually, you might be able to help. I'm Felix, and I run a campground at Jayboro Outstation, about half an hour from here. I've got a couple of cabins available too." Mentally, I crossed my fingers against the white lie. The second cabin would be open soon. "I wondered if it would be okay to put my new brochures on the bar."

She smiled, and the impish mischief of it made her instantly look younger. Maybe late twenties. "Nice to meet you, Felix. I'm Josie. New in town, but you probably already know that if you live around here."

I nodded. "Yeah. I'm used to seeing Chris or Madge behind the bar."

"They're still here, of course, but I'm here as well."

I noticed she didn't say for how long or in what capacity.

"Chris used to have some of my old leaflets somewhere. Maybe you could check with him?"

"No need." She picked up the top one and studied it. "Nice looking campground." Her words were slightly louder, and pitched at the couple of tourists nearby. "Looks like a peaceful place to stop. Do you have powered sites, or is it just tent camping?"

The answer was clearly written on the brochure, but I appreciated what she was doing. "Powered sites, tent sites, and the cabins, which are brand new."

The tourists were openly listening now. With luck, I'd have guests by evening.

"And I lead trail rides," I continued. "I have horses to suit beginners through to experienced riders."

That caught her attention past the little boost she was giving me for the benefit of long ears. "Oh? I'll have to come out. I love to ride, but I haven't had a chance to do so in a while. Be nice to be back in the saddle."

"Please do. The number's on the bottom. I'm sure I can find you something good to ride."

She glanced at me again, and her lips twitched as if in on a private joke. Her eyes were a warm brown, slightly flecked. Intriguing. But I was here to entice campers, not a woman I might find attractive.

She took the brochures and placed them on the end of the bar, next to the collection tin for the Royal Flying Doctor Service. As I sipped my beer, the tourists came up to take a brochure. They read it, folded it, and tucked it in a top pocket.

For the next twenty minutes, I enjoyed the drift of time. Just me and a beer. No horses to feed, no tourists to talk to, no toilet block to clean. I let my mind wander, and if my gaze sometimes followed the tempting outline of Josie behind the bar, well, what of it? There were few enough women around here who even gave the hint that they might not mind the appreciative gaze of another woman.

I was tempted to have a second beer so that I could rest my elbows on the bar and watch Josie's deft movements as she poured beer and bantered with customers. And yes, watch the play of muscles in her legs. But I couldn't linger; I had my ute to collect and things to do back at Jayboro. Always something to do.

I stood, picked up my hat, and took my leave.

Josie waved from the end of the bar. "See you around, Felix."

I lifted a hand in reply and went out into the sunlight.

Bazza had finished with my ute. It was parked in the street, as if its battered and dusty sides weren't good enough to grace his forecourt. I knew better, though; Bazza was simply busy. Indeed, the forecourt was jammed with a fleet of Toyotas, all with interstate plates.

Inside the office, Bazza looked harried. "Needs a new ABS sensor," he said to a grey-haired man who seemed to be the leader of the tourist group. "It'll take two days to arrive, even with express delivery."

The tourist said something I couldn't hear.

"The alternative is I disconnect the sensor, but no, I don't know what that will do to your warranty." Bazza shrugged. "Your choice."

The tourists debated amongst themselves, and Bazza came over to me. "I replaced an ignition lead, and it's going much better now. Keys are in it. You can fix me up next time you're in town. I don't have time to do the invoice right now." He gestured with his thumb at the tourists. "Gotta get this one sorted."

I nodded and thanked him. Worrindi was a few hours' drive from the nearest city big enough to have a supply of uncommon items. Things like car parts didn't arrive in a blink via courier. It was one of the reasons I loved the place.

The new curtains looked fantastic. They were maybe a little long and brushed the floor, but they gave the cabin a lift of colour. When they were closed, the cabin was cosy and welcoming. I opened them again and tied them back with the matching loops. Now all I needed were my first guests.

I stepped outside and saw a dusty four-wheel drive towing a camper trailer at the house, parked near my hand-painted sign that said *Office*. I ambled over. It was the couple from the hotel in Worrindi.

"G'day," I greeted them. "Can I help you?"

"We overheard you talking to your friend in the pub," the woman said. "Can we see your campground?"

I took them down to have a look. The light was starting to drop, and it slanted over the ground in the clarity of evening. A row of galahs sat expectantly on a railing, and overhead, a flock of budgies wheeled in the sort of tight formation that would be the envy of stunt pilots the world over. A couple of red kangaroos grazed in one corner, not put off by the young couple sitting outside their campervan a few yards away watching them. The scene looked peaceful and welcoming, like a magazine picture captioned *the peace of an outback evening welcomes the weary traveller*.

The woman sighed in a soft shudder of breath. "This looks wonderful. Can we stay for three nights?"

I sent mental thanks to Josie, no doubt still pouring beer at the Commercial.

"Of course. Why don't you pick your spot and then come up to the office? I'll fix you up."

# CHAPTER 2

I CAN'T SAY THERE WAS a rush as a result of my new signage, now prominently displayed on the highway by the gravel road that led to Jayboro, but there was a trickle. The couple who'd overheard me talking in the pub moved on to explore the delights of the Northern Territory and were replaced by a German couple and a campervan bursting with gap-year Brits. The teenagers proved my first test of tact and diplomacy, as their idea of a good time involved a staggering amount of beer, loud music, and conversation around an inferno of a campfire. I hated to spoil their fun, but the other campers were complaining. I suggested they shift their camp to the far end of the campground, where they wouldn't have to walk as far to find firewood. Bleary eyed with morning hangovers, they agreed with surprising docility, and everyone was happy.

I spent my days working on the campground as well as preparing the second cabin for rental. I sanded the wooden floors and borrowed one of the hands from the main station to help me fix the kitchen cupboards on the wall.

It was a red-letter day when I rented the completed cabin for the first time to a pair of grey nomads—older people who were spending their retirement travelling around Australia. Although they had a tidy set-up in the back of their four-wheel drive, they liked to allow themselves a little more space every so often—as the woman said with a smile—to make sure they didn't kill each other before they got to Alice Springs. They stayed two nights, and their enthusiastic Facebook posts made me think I might attract some of their friends.

When the sun went down, I'd return to the house where I grew up. It was too large for just one person, but it was still my house, inherited when Mum died. The weatherboard walls held the echoes of my parents, of my bandy-legged father and my crackling-with-life mother. I was born here, and I'd never lived anywhere else. I'd grown up running wild with the rest of the station kids and attending school in Worrindi. I'd sat impatiently on the school bus coming home, feet drumming as I waited to run in the door, drop my school bag on the floor, change into jeans, and get out to the horses. I'd broken my first colt when I was eleven. Won my first barrel race when I was thirteen. On the personal side, my childhood bedroom at the back of the house was where Mum had sat on the edge of my bed and told me about periods and pregnancy, about love and sex. The kitchen was where I'd told her that I would never date a boy because I liked girls. And the master bedroom, where I now slept, was where I'd watched Mum fade away over long months as the cancer ate into her bones.

The bed in the master bedroom was new, but most other things were the same. The en suite bathroom had been enlarged to allow wheelchair access, and the small steps and angles of an old house had been smoothed to make getting around easier. Even though she was gone, the house still held the imprint of Mum and the bouncing gaiety that had defined her life. I'd thought of remaining in my childhood bedroom after she died, but the room was small and the bathroom awkward and old-fashioned, so after a couple of months, when I could enter the master bedroom without seeing Mum lying there like frail cobwebs in the bed, I moved my things. The house was mine now, only mine, and it seemed stupid not to use it to the full extent.

One morning, about a week after my trip to Worrindi, I sat in the old parlour turned office, flipping through my bookings. I had no trail rides arranged, but I still had to check on my horses and on hay. Winter was the dry season in the outback, and realistically, I couldn't expect rain for another few months at least, if then. The horses were already starting to become ribby.

I grabbed my akubra and went out to the veranda to find my boots. The phone rang as I was jamming them on my feet. I raced back inside and grabbed the phone before it could ring out. If only there was mobile reception here, I wouldn't miss so many calls. "Jayboro Outstation, this is Felix."

"Hi Felix, this is Josie. I don't know if you remember me, I'm the—"

"Barperson at the Commercial," I interrupted. I smiled at the remembered pleasure of watching her stretch for the cheese and onion chips. Too late, I wondered what she'd make of me remembering her so well. But I'd never been good at playing it cool.

"Yeah. That's me. You've got a good memory."

A mental image of her legs flashed through my mind. "Suppose it comes of having to remember guests."

"True." Was that disappointment in her voice? "I'm the same. So many people come into a pub, and they all get offended if you don't remember them."

I pressed the phone closer to my ear and glanced at the caller ID. Private number. Oh well.

"But I remember you very well," Josie continued. "For lots of reasons. I've been sending all sorts of people down to your campground. Grey nomads, a few backpackers. I hope at least some of them found you."

"Quite a few have, but they didn't say who recommended them, or I'd have dropped by to thank you."

"You can thank me anyway if you want," Josie said. "It struck me I'm sending all sorts of people out to you, and maybe I could take a look myself. Actually, I know it's short notice, but I was wondering if you could fit me in for a trail ride this morning? I have a last-minute day off."

"That's no problem. There's no one else booked today. What time?"

"I'm sitting in my car, ready to drive away. According to your brochure, I'll be there in half an hour. I don't mind waiting if you're busy, but it would be good to ride before it gets too hot."

"Drive slowly, and that will be fine. It will take me a bit to get the horses ready."

"Thanks. See you, Felix."

The phone went dead. I hurried out of the house. In truth, I wouldn't be ready in half an hour, but I hadn't wanted to put her off. Halfway to the barn, I realised, too, that I had neglected to ask her about her horse experience, the sort of ride she wanted, or how long she wanted to go for. She'd mentioned being able to ride, so I figured she'd want something with a bit of liveliness to it. I went into the home paddock with a couple of halters and looked at my small herd. Patchwork should do her nicely; the piebald mare was a lively but obedient ride with a surprising turn of speed and agility on her. She'd been my last barrel racing pony before I'd stopped competing to care for

14

Mum. And if Josie was riding Patch, I'd need something equally speedy to keep up with her, or she'd leave me floundering. I slipped the halters on Patch and a young stockhorse, Ben, and led them back to the barn.

I liked to check on the campers in the mornings to make sure everything was okay, but today, the rounds would have to wait.

I was brushing Ben's tail when I heard a car. A door slammed, and then footsteps came down the barn aisle.

"Felix?"

I straightened from Ben's rear end and smiled. "Hi, Josie. Nice to see you again."

Her smile could have been merely friendly, the practiced smile of a bartender, but I thought there was an extra curve to it, more than she needed for the appearance of friendliness. It crinkled her eyes.

She looked good. My gaze flicked up and down. I told myself it was a professional assessment to make sure she was suitably dressed for the ride, but deep down I knew better—I just wanted to check her out. She was appropriately, if eccentrically, dressed. Her jeans were close-fitting and would protect her legs from rubbing on the saddle, but they were mauve, and she'd paired them with a lime green singlet and akubra hat. But her boots were well-worn and sturdy and obviously hadn't been new for a long time. They were flat-heeled leather, the boots of a stockman.

Ben, the big sook that he was, ambled over to the bar and pushed his nose against her shoulder, leaving a damp mark on the singlet. She rested her palm against his cheek and worked her fingers up to scratch him behind the ear. He closed his eyes in pleasure and dropped his nose down to rest between her breasts. Lucky nose.

"Am I riding this one?"

"No. Ben's a pussycat, but he pulls like a train. I'm sure you'd prefer your arms remained attached. You're riding Patchwork. She's in the next stall."

Josie paced down to where Patch looked over the bar, ears pricked, ready to meet a new friend.

"Aren't you the pretty one?" Josie crooned, her voice low and sweet. "Aren't you the dainty girl?"

"Don't let her looks fool you. She's fast as a bullet and gutsy as they come. She and I won the open barrel racing competition three years in a row at the Mount Isa Rodeo."

"I'm honoured you're letting me ride her."

"I figured if you've ridden a fair bit, you wouldn't appreciate one of the quieter horses. Patch will give you a good time." I finished tacking Ben, pushed the bar across, and led him out into the aisle.

Josie followed suit, and led Patch out. She handled the mare with confidence; obviously, she was used to horses.

We mounted, and I led the way out of the yard, along the beaten path that skirted the edge of the campground. A couple sitting outside their caravan lifted a hand as we went by, and Josie waved back. "I sent those two here," she said. "Must have been three days ago. I guess they like it."

"I hope so."

We rode side by side, far enough apart that I could make sure Josie was comfortable in the saddle. She rode in a loose manner, not quite slouched Australian stockman style but not upright English, either. I guessed she'd grown up with ponies, learnt at a riding school somewhere, and then relaxed into a more casual style. But she was easy on the horse, with light hands, and Patch, by her pricked ears and free movement, was clearly fine.

Josie was also comfortable with silence, something I appreciated. My love of quietness came from growing up in the bush, where low population density meant that I'd often been alone. Had Josie also grown up somewhere rural? I stole a glance at her. Her mop of curls exploded out from underneath the riding helmet, beads glinting in the sunlight. This particular piece of scenery was clearly new to her, but as she glanced around, it was obvious she was familiar with the outback.

Then she looked across at me and grinned. "Do you have any idea how good this is after a week of serving beer to sweaty station hands and dusty tourists?" She continued without waiting for my response. "Bloody good. It's been months since I've been on a horse." She patted Patch's neck. "And this mare is a darling."

"She is. And you're handling her nicely."

Patch sidestepped a lizard and snorted, and Josie momentarily swayed in the saddle. I revised my opinion slightly. Despite Josie's comfort on the horse, maybe she wasn't as experienced as I'd thought. But it could also just be that she hadn't ridden for a while.

"Thanks. How many horses do you keep here?"

"Half a dozen, all for trail riding. A couple of quiet ones for beginners. A couple of ponies for kids, and these two."

"I have a horse down in South Australia. I haven't seen her in months, of course. I miss her."

That explained her ease around horses. "What's your horse like?"

"She's a thoroughbred, an ex-racehorse. Feisty and utterly beautiful. She didn't do well at the track—not fast enough."

"You must miss her."

"Yeah. But I move around a lot. It's hard to do that with a horse in tow. I'd love a dog, but even that would be hard.

17

A lot of the jobs I take come with accommodation—like the Commercial—and they're usually reluctant to have a dog. Maybe I should get a caravan and be self-sufficient, but I don't think my old car would tow it."

"Where do you keep your horse?"

"In South Australia, at a friend's place." Josie shut her mouth abruptly. The sentence clipped off as if she wanted to say more but didn't.

"Is that where you're from?"

"Yeah. Small town north of Adelaide. Not outback, but still fairly rural. I learnt to ride there as a kid, getting lessons in exchange for mucking out at local stables. I left when I was seventeen, been moving around since."

I wondered when she'd stopped off long enough to acquire a horse, but figured it wasn't my business. Josie had doubtlessly had some extended times in one place.

She nudged Patch closer to me, and the horse obliged, shifting close enough that Josie's stirrup banged against mine. "Worrindi is a good place, though. Think I'll stick around a while. Chris and Madge are decent people, and I like working for them. That isn't often the case with these sorts of jobs. Got sick of working for dickheads a long time ago; that's one of the reasons I move so often. They also pay me fairly, and I've got a reasonable room upstairs. And now that I've met you, I know where I can come on my days off." She looked at me sideways from under the helmet. "That is, if you don't mind and you've got a spot for a rider."

"Of course not. I don't mind if you want to call at the last minute, as you did this morning. As long as you're not offended if I'm fully booked—although that doesn't happen often."

She blew out a gusty sigh. "That's great. Thanks, Felix."

18

We'd moved away from the fence as we rode, and the expanse of land unfurled beneath our horses' hooves. "Want to go faster?" I asked.

In response, she nudged Patch forwards, and the willing mare leapt into a fast canter. I followed but held back to let her set the pace. Dust billowed as Josie and Patch increased pace. Patch was a competitive horse, and she responded as much to my horse at her flank as to Josie's urgings. Josie sat the pace well. The dust blew into my face, and I urged Ben forwards into the clearer air, which only spurred Patch on. Neck and neck, we raced along the red ground, sand and dust in our faces.

"Slow," I yelled at Josie. "Soft sand ahead."

She obeyed and steadied Patch, turning her in a wide circle to reduce speed.

I came up alongside her again and slackened the reins to let Ben stretch and cool. It was still very early, only around eight, but the sun was already warm. Momentarily, thoughts of the camp kitchen that needed cleaning and the second cabin still needing work intruded, but those thoughts left my head for the pleasure of the here and now.

"You live here alone, Felix?" Josie glanced at me sideways as we ambled along.

"Yeah. Since my mother died a few years ago."

"No partner?" That same sideways look. "Seems to me, going by the propositions I've had in the Commercial, that there's no shortage of willing blokes around."

I wondered whether to set her right about my sexuality. Normally, I figured it was no one's business except my own, and it never came up with any of the passing tourists. But Josie had said she'd be back.

"Plenty of blokes," I said. "But they're not my type."

19

"What is your type?" There was a smile in her voice, along with something more, the tiniest edge of interest, of flirtation.

"Someone who likes the outdoors, down to earth, practical. Honest."

"That's it? You're not asking for Brad Pitt?"

"And female. But they don't need to look like Angelina Jolie." I concentrated on Ben's ears rather than Josie, in case she would withdraw.

"I thought so. No wonder you live alone. Not many pickings around here for us."

She'd said "us".

"Not much. But that's fine. Even if I lived in the city, I wouldn't be one for the pubs and clubs."

"Me neither." She stretched out a hand towards me, and I took it. She clasped my fingers briefly, then released. "It's nice to talk to you though, Felix."

I wondered what she'd heard in Worrindi, if that was the reason for seeking me out, but she pre-empted me. "No one said anything, in case you're wondering. I figured I'd read you right when you dropped off the brochures at the pub. And the good people of Worrindi think I'm just very picky."

Small towns could be difficult for anyone growing up different. It had been okay for me—I'd been lucky—but I'd heard stories from others that made it clear that wasn't always the case. My friend, Sue, lived a few hours away in a place that was even smaller than Worrindi. She'd grown up in the outback, and she'd told me her story; her experience hadn't been nearly as positive as mine. She'd denied her sexuality for ten years before she couldn't repress herself any longer. And I'd been the person to break her same-sex drought.

20

"Worrindi's okay," I said. "Most of them know I'm a lesbian. Word travels fast around here. We may be spread out in the outback, but the bush telegraph works well."

Josie grinned. "They haven't spread the word about me yet. My life's an open book—apart from all the secrets."

I grinned back. "If you're around for a while, you'll have to meet my friends Sue and Moni. They're four hours away, but they sometimes come up for a weekend."

The shared knowledge of sexuality had advanced our tentative friendship.

"I'd like that."

The horses moved apart as they picked their way over a rough piece of ground, and we were silent. Josie stared at the horizon, and there was a stillness about her, an aura of contentment. I glanced at my watch. We'd been out for nearly two hours. We hadn't fixed how long the ride would be before we left, but we'd ridden in a wide circle and were now about twenty minutes from the barn, approaching a point where we could either head back along the fence line or take a loop out the other side. I looked over at Josie. If she hadn't ridden for a while, those two hours would be enough, or she'd be as stiff as a plank tomorrow. And I had a cabin to work on.

"By the time we get back, we'll have been out for two hours. Are you happy to leave it at that?" I asked.

"That's fine. I realise I messed up your day by calling at the last minute. I'm glad you were able to fit me in."

"No worries. But now I've got to clean the camp kitchen and do other chores. Nothing very exciting."

"Would you mind if I took a look around? I'd love to come for another ride, maybe next week, if that suited you. I was thinking I could bring my tent and stay over if I can swing two days off in a row."

Warm and nebulous feelings of anticipation surged through me, pleasure that Josie wanted to spend more time out here. But then, she probably wanted simply to get away from the pub and Worrindi. Living on the premises as she did, she was always on call. Part of the problem of working bar in a small town was that most everyone knew you, and even when you were off duty, the perception of availability continued. I concentrated on her face as I replied, "There's some good tent sites closer to Birragum Creek. Quiet. You'd be surprised at how many people want to be near to the toilet block."

"Not me. I like my own space. When I'm moving on, I never stop in campgrounds. I just find somewhere quiet and pull over by the side of the road. I've only ever been asked to leave a couple of times, once because I was trespassing and once by the police because I was too close to the edge of town."

"You could just do that here, if you wanted. Honestly, you don't have to stay in a campground. The whole outback is one enormous quiet place to pull over."

She laughed. "Are you putting me off?"

"No! I'd be delighted if you stayed over. But don't feel obliged."

"I'd like to. It's lovely here. With the added bonus of a hot shower. At least, I assume it's hot?"

"Of course."

We'd reached the barn as we chatted, and I led the way around the back. I dismounted and loosened Ben's girth. Josie followed suit, but her movements were slower. She'd be quite stiff come morning. I led Ben into the barn, and she followed with Patch.

The ride was over, and I had a million and one things I had to do. Still, I lingered.

"Big barn," Josie said. "Stalls for twelve. Were there more horses at one point?"

"We had more when my parents were alive. Their horses, my two ponies. The main station also kept some here from time to time. We often had a couple of youngsters for breaking. I still take one occasionally, but I haven't had any for a while."

Josie stood with her hand on Patch's neck, the light filtering in through the gaps in the timber. She'd removed the helmet, and the sunlight turned her riotous hair into a halo of light. She wasn't beautiful, in her mismatched old clothes, but she was intriguing. Part of me—a rather large part—was delighted I'd be seeing her again.

The silence stretched. I couldn't keep staring, so I jammed my hands in the pockets of my jeans. "Come up to the office, and we can settle up for the ride."

"The ride. Right." There was a definite hint of amusement in her voice.

I straightened my shoulders. Yes, I lived in a remote area, where the possibilities of finding a lover were Buckley's and Nunn, to use the well-loved expression. But it didn't mean that because a fellow lesbian had appeared in my life, we were automatically going to fall into each other's arms.

I led the way to the office. It was at the front of the house and opened to the veranda, which made it easier for campers and tourists to find me. In the early days, before I'd got better signage, I'd been surprised in the shower by a wide-eyed pair of Spanish backpackers. Maybe they'd thought it was a quirky Australian custom to greet visitors wrapped only in a bath towel, but the next day, I'd gone into Worrindi and bought the biggest office sign I could find.

Mum's desk dominated the room; it was where she used to do the accounts. Now, it was where I attempted to do the accounts. Each year, I dreaded tax time.

I sat at the desk and pulled out the cash box. Josie followed me in and looked at the array of photos on the wall. I knew what they were: my parents when they were young; Dad bull riding at the Isa rodeo; Mum barrel racing or working with a young horse; the two of them at the local picnic races, all dressed up in their finery. A couple of me as a child, earnest, with long plaits and a gap in my front teeth. One of me with a pony that I remembered well as it was such a bugger of a thing. Another with the first colt that I broke. A third of me and that same colt at the Isa show, clearing a fence by most of half a metre.

"Your parents?" She stared at a photo of Mum and Dad.

"Yeah. My father was head stockman at the main Jayboro Station. When he retired after working for Jayboro his whole life, the owners gifted him this house and the land that the barn and campground are on. Now they're mine."

"Decent of them." Her gaze switched to a photo of me and Patch. "There's a lot of good people around here." She swung around to face me. "That's becoming a rarity. Sometimes it seems everyone's just out for what they can get, and they don't care who they shaft in the process."

Her voice was light. If she'd been shafted, she obviously hadn't let it get to her. I watched the subtle play of muscles under her tanned skin, revealed by the scooped back of her singlet. Maybe she sensed my gaze as she turned and caught me staring. I averted my eyes, but her lips twitched as she said, "How much do I owe you?"

I told her the amount and waited as she pulled a battered coin purse from her jeans and counted out some crumpled notes.

"Thank you."

"Can I call you when I know my next days off? Chris and Madge are great, but it's hard for them to know in advance sometimes."

"No worries. I can generally fit someone in at short notice." I blew my breath out. "Even if I wish that wasn't the case. It would be great if I were fully booked."

"One day. The word on the street is that outback tourism is booming."

"The street being Worrindi's main drag?"

"Yeah. But it is on the up. All the grey nomads on the move, people in their four-wheel drives escaping the pressures of the city."

"Maybe I should offer them a Back-to-Basics experience. They could sleep in my unfinished cabin and clean my toilet block. That would clear their head."

"Can't see that one taking off somehow." She picked up her hat. "I won't hold you up. Those toilet blocks are singing your name. I'll have a wander around, then head away. Thanks for the ride. I really enjoyed it."

"Me too." The words were out before I could consider how they sounded—overly friendly for what was basically a customer. But I had enjoyed the ride—and Josie's company.

She smiled, jammed the hat on her head, and disappeared out into the sharp daylight.

I opened the cash box and placed her money inside. I couldn't sit around. I had a camp kitchen to clean.

# CHAPTER 3

A WEEK WENT PAST AND, to my surprise, the new cabin was rented for five of the seven nights. Feedback from guests was generally positive: they loved the peace and location. Acting on a couple of suggestions, I started offering a dinner pack that guests could cook in the camp kitchen, as well as a couple of different breakfast packs. It hadn't occurred to me that the people who usually stayed in towns wouldn't have food with them. It meant I had to have more provisions on hand, but it made me a tidy profit.

I also needed to get the second cabin up and running—and soon.

It was now midwinter and the height of the outback tourist season. The days were pleasantly warm and sunny, the nights chilly enough that a campfire was a pleasure. Even the flies, one of the major annoyances of outback life, were few. This was potentially my busiest time of year, and I hoped to make enough to tide me over the summer months, when the heat and flies would become unbearable, and the wet season could make the roads impassable.

It was also a good time for trail rides as the campers didn't have to get up at an unearthly hour to make it bearable. But in summer, even if the trail rides dried up, the horses still needed attention. They didn't go off to the coast with a surfboard; they were still here and still needed care and fodder.

I sat in the office one evening, surrounded by the photos of my parents, and calculated how much it would cost me to get the second cabin open. It wasn't a fortune; compared to the loan I already had from the bank, it was a very low amount. But I was reluctant to borrow more, if indeed the bank would stump up the finance. I was trying to set aside money to meet the loan repayments over the summer. A little more on top of that would be a huge struggle.

"What would you do, Mum?" I lifted my glass of water to her in the photo.

I knew what her answer would have been. She would roll up her sleeves, find another hour in the day to work, and eat meatloaf for dinner for the fifth time that week without complaint, because it was cheap and easy to do.

I resolved to get the second cabin open as soon as I could. Tomorrow, I would ring Matt at the main station and see if I could borrow his floor sander. I'd pick it up on the way to Worrindi to buy stain and varnish for the floorboards. I'd also see what furniture I could find in town. A trip to the Isa and the bigger stores would suck away a day.

If I got lucky, if I put in the work, maybe I could get the second cabin open in a couple of weeks.

I rose and headed for the door. It was late by my standards, nearly ten. The phone rang. For a second, I considered leaving it, but habit won out. Calls late at night in the outback were seldom trivial. But although I'd expected it to be a neighbour, someone from Jayboro Station, I recognised Josie's voice immediately. It was brisk, like her manner, and from the background noise, she was in the Commercial.

"Hey," she said, and I liked that she felt she knew me well enough not to say who was calling. "I gotta be quick. I'm working, and they're screaming for beer here. You'd think there was a drought." Her amused snort echoed down the line. "But I was wondering if you could fit me in for a ride early tomorrow? I could be with you at seven. I can't stay over as I have to work tomorrow night, but I'd love to come."

Mentally, I shredded the day I'd planned and refused to let myself think it was because of her. I'd do it for any tourist. A couple of hours trail ride money would help the finances. I'd go to town later.

"Sure," I said. "The earlier the better."

"No worries. I'll see you tomorrow. Looking forward to it." There was a pause, and her next words were obviously directed to someone in the bar. "Hang on, Ty. Your beer's coming. We won't run out in the meantime." To me she said, "Gotta run. See you."

I was left staring at the phone in my hand, the dial tone buzzing.

The next morning, one of the campers stopped me as I took my usual walk through the campground on the way to the barn. "Hi Felix, I was wondering if you had a spot on a ride this morning?"

I didn't know much about Dan. He was a solitary traveller, and he and his small campervan had been a fixture at the lower end of the camp area for the past few days. He seemed to spend most of his time writing on a laptop or watching the birdlife through binoculars. From what I'd seen of his van whenever I stopped for pleasantries, it was a home-made set up, with a single platform bunk and plastic containers for storage. I had him pegged as doing some sort of paper-pushing job or maybe something technical that didn't require many people skills.

I thought fast. "I have one other person coming at seven. If that's not too soon for you, I can take you then. Otherwise, I'm afraid it will have to be tomorrow."

He gave a short nod and turned away into the van, leaving me to wonder if I'd offended him somehow. But he was back quick-smart with what looked like a bicycle helmet in his hand. "Thanks. I'm ready. I'll come now."

I eyed the helmet, which was covered in plastic ties that stuck up and were supposed to stop magpies swooping. Clearly, he was a total beginner.

"No rush. What sort of riding experience do you have?"

"None," he admitted. "Is that okay?"

I hoped Josie wouldn't be too mad, but I'd successfully taken people with disparate abilities before. I summoned my most reassuring smile, the one I used for worried mothers when I took their small children for an amble around the paddock. "Perfectly fine. I have a couple of quiet horses. I'll see you over there."

Over at the barn, I grabbed three small buckets of feed, put them in the stalls, and opened them up. My small herd was gathered around the gate, like people waiting to board a bus. I opened the gate a crack and managed to let through the three horses I wanted: Patch, Ben, and a quiet mare called Smoke. The remaining three horses jostled at the gate, annoyed that they had missed out. But I only had enough to feed the horses that were working that day.

I'd brushed Patch off and was starting on Ben when I heard footsteps. I peered underneath Ben's belly as I brushed

29

his forelegs, and saw mauve jeans walking towards me. I straightened. Josie walked down the centre aisle. She stopped at Patch's stall to whisper nonsense to the mare.

I stepped out from behind Ben's bulk, and she caught sight of me. an unguarded initial smile lit her face, and she tilted her head to one side.

"Hey." It wasn't my most inspired opening, but the pleasure on Josie's face robbed me of anything more eloquent.

She came closer and rested a hand on Ben's neck. It was a casual, comfortable gesture. "Hey yourself." She yawned. "Sorry. Had a late night last night. We close when the last person leaves or midnight, whichever comes soonest, and last night it was midnight."

"A ride should wake you up."

"That's why I'm here. Am I riding Patch again?"

I nodded. "You seemed to enjoy her last time. We have another person with us today, one of the campers, Dan. He's a total beginner, but I'll make sure you get some faster time."

"No worries. I didn't expect I would always be the only one." She paused. "Nice as it was."

Her riot of curls caught the sun slanting in through the gaps in the barn wall.

"I'll just finish up with these three. If you want a coffee to wake yourself up, go over to the camp kitchen. You'll find some instant there and milk in the fridge." Part of me hoped she'd stay and chat, but she nodded and disappeared in that direction.

Left alone, I was able to finish the three horses. By the time she returned, I was helping Dan onto Smoke. He was obviously nervous but determined not to show it, and his fingers wound into Smoke's mane, clutching harder as she shifted her weight. I adjusted Dan's stirrups and showed him how to sit.

30

Josie saw that I was busy and went over to Patch, checked the girth, and mounted. I had to leave Dan for a minute while I mounted Ben, and Josie moved over on Patch and chatted to Dan. The bartender at work. She obviously had the people skills to put them at ease. Dan's shoulders relaxed, and he loosened his death grip enough to give Smoke a tentative pat.

I led the way out of the yard and along the fence line to where the creek cut a winding course through the parched ground. It was dry, of course, and would remain that way until the summer rains came. I'd picked this way as beginners tended to feel more secure when there was something on one side, even something as insubstantial as two strands of barbed wire held up by rotting fence posts. But that line gave them some security, an artificial marker in an open landscape. And it was true. The horses plodded along like docile cattle, and if anything were to spook them—usually wildlife—then there was only one way for them to turn.

I glanced back. Dan was tipped forwards in a precarious position over Smoke's neck. Josie rode behind, reins in one hand, the other resting in, to what was to the casual eye, a loose position on her thigh. But I could see that she was ready to react if necessary, to lean forwards and grab Smoke's reins.

She didn't *have* to take on the role of Tail-End Charlie, but I was glad she had.

I halted Ben and waited for Smoke to catch up. "You're doing well, Dan. Try sitting back in the saddle a little more. You'll feel more comfortable if you do."

He nodded and obeyed, smiling as Smoke responded and relaxed. Josie came up on his other side, and we ambled along, three abreast. I pointed out a mob of kangaroos grazing on the meagre vegetation on the far side of the creek. Dan must have felt confident enough to look around, as he pointed out a fairy wren hopping through the tangled branches of a mulga tree.

There was no chance for private conversation with Josie, but, I told myself, that was fine. This was my life, my business. Ensuring the likes of Dan had a good time so that they wanted to come back, maybe instil some small appreciation for the outback and its people—well, that was my purpose here. It wasn't to develop a friendship with an intriguing woman. It wasn't to flirt, no matter how much I wanted to.

Half an hour into our gentle ride, I pointed out a wider loop to Josie. "If you want to go at your own pace, keep that fence line on your right. Dan and I will cut across the middle, and you can catch up with us."

Josie grinned. "I'd like that."

She turned Patch and urged her away from us. Patch laid back her ears and jibbed, and it took Josie a minute or so to persuade her to leave. But once away, she pushed Patch into a floating canter, and I took a minute to admire how the coloured horse moved over the land. Josie urged her on, and her neck lengthened. Josie sat easily, relaxed in the saddle. I wished I was with her, racing along like that.

I turned to Dan. "How d'you feel about a trot?"

Dan nodded and gripped the front of the saddle.

Josie caught up with us when we were nearly back at the barn. Her curls were more disordered than ever, and Patch was damp with sweat. Both of them had obviously enjoyed themselves.

She ran a hand down Patch's neck. "This lady moves like the wind."

"Especially when her head's towards the barn."

Josie grinned. "There is that." She jogged up alongside Dan and I. "Enjoying yourself, Dan?"

Dan looked more relaxed. He sat more easily, and Smoke's steadiness had given him confidence. "Yeah."

Back at the barn, though, he was noticeably stiff as he slid from Smoke's back.

"Here." I took her reins. "Go for a walk. Loosen up a bit. You can settle up with me later."

"Thanks." He patted Smoke's neck. "I enjoyed that. A first for me. Hopefully not the last, although not for a few days."

I had two horses to do to Josie's one, so she finished first. She came over and rested her arms on the edge of Smoke's stall.

"You've got plenty of space here. You could have half a dozen more horses."

I bent to brush dust from Smoke's foreleg. "Barn space, yes, but the land is poor. It barely supports the six I have now."

"How many have you had in the past?"

"Nine was the maximum, back in the days when I took youngsters for breaking. But that was during the good years, when we had proper wet seasons."

"Word is this year could see some good rains."

"Let's hope. Can never rely on it though. I've seen the land go for years without real rain, and I've seen it under a metre of flood water."

I straightened. Josie leant on the door, fiddling with the thong on her hat.

"I want to ask you something," she said. "Not sure what you'll say."

"Oh?" I tried to appear open. In truth, I had no idea what she wanted.

"I like it in Worrindi. The pub's a good place to be. Nice people." Her mouth crooked up at one corner. The motion was fascinating. "Believe me, that is not always the case." Her

33

fingers worried at the thong on the hat. "Anyway, I thought I'd stay around. A while. Maybe a lot longer, if it works out. I told you I have a horse?"

I nodded, my gaze on the restless movement of her fingers.

"I'd like to have her near. I was given her. Otherwise there's no way I'd have bought a horse, not with my lifestyle. But she's mine, and I'd like to have her somewhere close. Her name's Flame."

*Flame.* It conjured up a picture of a delicate, feisty horse, quick as lightning with movements of fire. But as tempting as the picture was, I knew I had to say no.

"She sounds like a beaut horse. But honestly, Josie, I don't think I can have her here. I just don't have the grazing. Most likely, I'm going to have to buy hay before long, and that's very expensive."

"I'll pay for her agistment—I didn't mean for you to keep her for nothing. I've thought about what I can afford." She named a figure that was generous.

The money was tempting. With the extra, I could finish up the second cabin.

I shook my head. "That's a good offer, but it's more than you'd pay at other places. But I still don't think I could do it if I have to buy hay."

"If it comes to that, how about I purchase the hay for her?"

I ducked down to Smoke's forelegs again to give myself time to think. The dollars marching through my head beat a compelling rhythm, but before I fell on Josie's neck shrieking "yes!", I had to give this more thought.

"I'm a thirty-minute drive from Worrindi. It would cost you to drive out here, and you may not be able to come that often. I'm sure there is somewhere closer to town where you could keep her. If you want, I'll ask—"

"No." She leant forwards, and her face took on a strange intensity. "I want her to be here with you. If you'll take her, that is. She's special. I don't want to trust her to just anyone. I can pay, if that's what you're worried about."

"It's not. I trust you." And I did. I wasn't just saying the words. For all her nomadic ways, Josie seemed like someone I could rely on. Maybe I'd wake up one morning with a horse that didn't belong to me and no way of contacting the owner and no money coming in—I'd heard of that happening to others—but I didn't think so.

"I can give you a month up front. I'll transfer it to your bank if you agree."

It was a lot of money for someone earning minimum wage less board in a pub. Maybe she had money put aside.

"If you take her, I'll know she'll be well looked after. Cared for. So many places just throw a horse in a paddock and forget about it until the next bill's due." Her head ducked, and she glanced at me from under her hat. "And it would give me an excuse to come out here. To see you."

It wasn't fair of her to play the flirtation card with someone who was obviously interested.

I stood up again, with Smoke between us, and rested my hands on her withers. "Look, I'll think about it, okay? I can't give you an answer now. I need to think about grazing, hay, and things like that." *And about you wanting to see me again.* "Will Flame be okay in with the others? I don't think it will work if she has to be by herself."

"I'm sure she will be. Thanks, Felix, for at least thinking about it."

"I'll let you know."

She nodded, and with a quick smile, she walked off.

I watched her go, watched the sway of her backside under those mauve pants, and tried not to think about the fact that she wanted to spend time with me.

That evening, I sat in Mum's office and juggled numbers in my spreadsheet. If I had an extra guaranteed income coming in, I could put a lot more into the cabins. It would make a difference. I could go out tomorrow and buy everything I needed for the second cabin from my savings and, hopefully, recuperate it over the next few weeks.

I removed the money Flame would bring in from the spreadsheet and looked again. Sure, I still had the money I'd set aside to cover repayments in the wet season, but if I used that, then I lost the buffer of safety. I would be flying too close to the wind. If the wet season closed the roads, then I was done like a dinner.

There was no doubt about it; the money that Josie would pay for boarding her horse would be good.

I drummed a pen on the desktop. Josie must want Flame here very badly. There were cheaper places closer to Worrindi, places that were easier to get to. But if Josie wanted to spend time with me, as she'd said, she didn't need to bring her horse from South Australia to do so. She only had to drive out for a ride or invite me into town. We weren't friends, not yet, but the seeds of friendship were there.

But all that was irrelevant. What mattered now was that if I took Flame, then it would be a boost to my business and my finances. Josie's reasons, whatever they were—well, they were her concern.

I picked up the phone before I could change my mind and called the Commercial.

She answered the phone on the sixth ring, just as I was about to hang up.

"I'll take her." Too late, I realised I should have said who was calling, what I was calling about. But it didn't seem to matter.

"Hi, Felix." There was laughter in her voice, and in the background, the clink of glasses and loud voices. "You're talking about my horse?"

"Yes. If you're happy to put her in with mine and pay for any extra feed, then I'll take her."

"I'm glad. She'll be in good hands."

"I'll do my best."

"I know you will." A purr reverberated in her voice. "I'll call you when I've arranged transport."

The conversation ended, and I hung up feeling as if I was on the edge of something I couldn't control.

# CHAPTER 4

Flame arrived the next week. Josie called me from the pub the day before she arrived with an apology for the short notice.

"Are you coming to greet her?" I asked.

Josie's hesitation was palpable. "I can't. It's too short notice, and Madge has to go to the Isa for something, so I have to work. Sorry."

"A pity. But I'll manage."

"I'm sure you will. I'm sorry I can't be there, but I should be able to get down in the next day or so."

"Flame and I will be waiting."

There was warmth in her voice as she replied, "I'm looking forward to it."

*Flame.* Yeah, that was it. She was looking forward to seeing her horse.

Josie's mare arrived in a rickety truck, one designed to carry cattle, not horses. She was tied to the slats, and someone had put a makeshift partition between her and the rest of the empty truck. I walked up the ramp and untied her, noting that whoever had secured her didn't know much about horses. The knot was as far from quick release as anything I'd seen.

Flame wore a rope halter and a rather tatty New Zealand rug—a weatherproof rug that was popular in the southern states. One of the straps was broken and dangled down between her hind legs. She was rather unkempt-looking, and I wondered where she'd been while Josie was travelling. From what I could see of her under the rug, she was a bright chestnut. A thin stripe ran down her face, and she had two white socks at the rear.

She was pleased to exit the box and clattered down the ramp behind me to stand in the yard, head up, sniffing the wind. Ben, who was in the barn, neighed a greeting, and she responded. I turned to ask the driver where her tack was and other such things as her grooming kit, but he lifted the ramp and walked around to the cab.

I followed, towing Flame, who didn't show any inclination to get close to the truck again. I didn't blame her.

"Hey," I shouted, over the noise of the engine. Flame pulled back against me, and I had to shout louder. "Where's her tack?"

The driver shrugged. "Dunno. I was just given the horse. There's nothing else."

That didn't seem right. Josie couldn't ride her in a halter. It must be somewhere. "Can you wait a minute while I make a call?"

The driver shrugged again. "Don't see what good that will do. I was given nothing except the nag and what it stands up in. If there's supposed to be anything else, it's been left behind."

He had a point, so I circled Flame around some distance from the truck and waited while he pulled away in a cloud of exhaust and a whoosh of air brakes.

Flame seemed unsettled, so rather than put her in a stall or out in the paddock with the others, I took her for a walk. She was sweating in the heavy rug, so I stripped it off and left it on the rail. Without the cover, she was even more unkempt-looking, as if she'd been left in a paddock to fend for herself for a long time. Obviously, Josie's friend who'd supposedly been looking after her hadn't paid too much attention. She was a bit too ribby, her coat was dusty, and her tail was so long it brushed below her hocks. All in all, she didn't look to be much of a horse. But then Ben neighed again, and her head came up. Her whole posture became one of alertness, and her muscles quivered.

Suddenly, she was beautiful. Her arched neck and blown nostrils showed the delicateness of the thoroughbred, a throwback to the Arabian horses from which they were bred so many generations ago. Flame quivered again and struck the ground with a hoof. I gave her a bit more rope, and she spun in a tight circle, her tail a banner floating over the dusty yard.

Oh yes. Get a bit of condition on her, give her some care and attention, and this horse would be a beauty. I wondered how she'd gone in her racing days. Not too well, I assumed, or she'd still be running, or else retired to stud as a broodmare.

I walked her around the yard a couple of times and then out to the paddock to take a long circuit around the edge of the campground.

The campers were all new, none of them had been trail riding with me. Maybe seeing a striking horse would be the push they needed to make a booking.

Flame settled as we walked, and after forty minutes or so, I took her back to the yard and put her in the stall next to Ben with fresh water and a small amount of my precious hay.

I returned to the house and made a mug of coffee before settling myself at the desk. I sat back in the chair, propped my feet in their odd socks on the desk, and rang the Commercial.

"She's here," I said when Josie answered. "She's a beauty. Lifted the class of my yard."

She laughed. "I doubt it. Not if Patch is there."

"She was a bit wound up after her journey, but I've got her in a stall next to Ben, who's a steady influence. She'll be fine."

Josie sighed. "I can't wait to see her."

"One thing, though: there's no tack with her. Only a halter and a rug. No saddle, bridle, no grooming kit or anything. Were you expecting that stuff to come too?"

Josie was silent. "I didn't specifically ask for it. Guess I just assumed it would come with her. That's going to be difficult."

"I'll see what I have lying around that will fit, but I'm sure you'll want her proper gear sent up."

"I'll try and contact my friend."

"When are you next coming here?" There were voices in the background, and the clack of balls on the pool table.

"I have two days off starting Wednesday. I thought I'd bring my tent and camp."

Two days away. "No worries. I'll keep her in tonight and turn her out with the others tomorrow morning."

"Thanks, Felix." There was a pause while she talked to someone. Then she was back on the line. "I have to go. I'll email you later so you have my address. If you reply with your bank details, I'll pay you."

Money. There was definitely more to life than money, but the thought sent a fizzle of relief. In the days since I knew Flame was coming, I'd been out and spent a lot of money getting stuff for the second cabin. My bank balance was getting low. If the wet season came early, I'd be in trouble.

"I'll do that. See you Wednesday."

"See you, Felix." A click, and she was gone.

I took a hefty swallow from my mug and nearly choked when the phone rang. Coffee soaked the front of my shirt as

I answered. It was an enquiry about the cabins. Two couples travelling together, wondering if I had two cabins available from Friday for three nights.

*Why yes*, I told them, I did. As I wrote down their details, I figured it was an omen. Flame must be my lucky charm.

Wednesday morning was busy for me. The first cabin had been occupied Tuesday night, so I had to clean and make it ready. Three people for a trail ride. And as I was getting the horses ready, one of the campers had come over to the barn to tell me there was a snake in the men's shower. By the time I'd persuaded the snake to leave with the aid of a broom and reassured everyone it was unlikely to return, I was already late for the ride. Luckily, the father and two sons weren't put out. Indeed, the teenagers seemed more upset they'd missed seeing the snake.

They were all capable riders, so the two hours went smoothly, ending with a gallop along Birragum Creek before the final cool-down walk back to the yard.

I saw Josie's old red Subaru parked by the barn, but she was nowhere in sight. I figured she was with Flame. She appeared as I was taking all four horses down to the paddock.

"Here, let me." She slipped in between the two ponies and took their reins.

It was a lot easier with only two to manage, and soon they were snorting and moving away from the gate. I saw Flame's bright coat over in the shade of the mulga.

"Are you going to bring her in?" I asked. "We can see what tack I've got that might fit."

She nodded, and we walked across to where Flame grazed.

42

Josie caught her. "Hey, girl," she whispered, running a hand down her horse's neck. "You're looking like you need some TLC. Doesn't look like you've had much love lately."

Flame snorted and pushed her muzzle into Josie's hand and got a peppermint in reward.

We walked back together, Flame between us. Josie rested her hand on the horse's neck and glanced across at me. "Was she okay when she arrived?"

I debated telling her about the rickety cattle truck she'd arrived in. How she'd come all the way from South Australia, a three-day drive, in that thing was a bit baffling. But maybe she'd been transferred from a proper horse float closer to here. "Somewhat upset, understandably so. She was the only horse in the truck. They must have offloaded others earlier."

"I guess." Josie scratched the horse underneath her mane, which was tangled and dusty. "Can I borrow some brushes to clean her up a bit?"

"Sure." I looked across at the horse. Her thoroughbred lines were unmistakable. "You said she's an ex-racehorse? How old is she?"

"Seven. I think."

"When did she last race?"

"I'm not sure. I think she was turned out for a while before I got her. Just a bit slow, weren't you, lovely?" She crooned and rubbed a hand down Flame's shoulder.

A gust of wind blew the sand into a stinging ribbon of grit, and Flame sidestepped, a prancing pirouette with her tail flaring out behind her. Josie's grip tightened on the rope.

Back at the barn, I found some brushes and sorted through my assorted tack. A bridle was easy enough; I had a snaffle bit that should fit and the leather straps would adjust, but a saddle might be a different matter. Flame was narrow, and most of my horses were broader stockhorses, rather than the finer thoroughbred type. Patch was the closest.

I returned to Josie with Patch's saddle and the bridle I'd put together from spares.

"Try this."

She seemed a bit tentative as she palmed the bit for Flame to take, but once on, the bridle fit well with only a little adjustment needed. The saddle, though, was hopeless. Even with a pad underneath, it was too wide for the mare and would rub.

"You could ride her bareback," I suggested.

"Yeah." Doubt threaded her voice. "I've never done it. She can be a handful."

"If you can wait an hour, I'll come with you. But I need to check the campground first."

Her face lit up, and she pushed her hair back behind her ears. "That would be great, if you don't mind."

"I'll be back."

At the campground, I found the man who'd reported the snake in the shower. He was packing up to leave. His wife sat in the front seat of the camper with the windows rolled up.

He gestured with his head for me to walk a few paces away. "We're leaving early. Shirley is terrified of snakes and is afraid to use the shower or toilet in case she finds one." He held up a hand. "I know. You don't need to tell me. Anywhere we go, we're just as likely to encounter one, at least until we're back in the city." His lips twisted ruefully. "But she's never seen one before."

I said nothing. Australia's venomous snakes were legend. But for the most part, if you left them alone and took a few simple precautions, they didn't bother people. The mulga snake I'd shoved out of the shower had slithered off once it was outside.

"Was it venomous?" A quick smile. "On second thought, don't answer that. I've convinced Shirl it was harmless."

I refrained from telling him that mulga snakes were on the list of the world's top ten venomous snakes. I also made a mental note to ask Sue, my lawyer friend, whether I should have some sort of warning for campers.

"I'm sorry you're leaving," I said. "If you stop by the office, I'll refund your money for the unused days."

"Really? I didn't expect that. That's pretty decent of you."

After I'd cleaned the showers, removed a green tree frog from a toilet, and tidied up the camp kitchen, I returned to the office, where I checked out the couple who were leaving early. I'd been well over an hour. There was no sign of Josie, but I figured she was busy with her horse.

I grabbed my hat off the desk, switched the sign to *away* and headed back to the barn. On the way, I saw Flame in the paddock, grazing alongside the two smaller ponies.

Josie was at the barn, but she hadn't been idle. All the stalls had been swept, as well as the aisle. Josie was in the area where I kept the tack. She was listening to news radio and had Patch's saddle in front of her, and she was busy with the saddle soap—something I hadn't had a chance to do for way too long. For a moment, I stood at the entrance, watching the rhythmic motion of her arm as she rubbed. She looked up, maybe sensing someone was there.

"I hope you don't mind that I'm doing this."

"No. Of course not. But you don't have to." I moved into the stall and sat on the wooden trunk that stored brushes and various unused random bits of leather.

"I want to."

"I see you've turned Flame out."

"Yeah. I don't know if the bareback idea is a good one. She hasn't been ridden in a long time, and I don't know how that would go. I'll just wait for her tack to arrive."

I smoothed my palms over my jeans. It was hot in the stall, and I was sweating. "Seems a pity. You've got her here, but you're not going to ride her."

She shrugged. "Yeah, but I'll manage."

I hesitated. "It's a bit hot to go out now, but as you're staying over, why don't you ride with me tomorrow? I won't charge you," I added as she started to protest. "You've earned your ride by cleaning up the barn for me."

"That's not why I did it."

"I know." And I hadn't thought that. Josie struck me as someone who needed movement in her life. A bar job was an active thing, and she had a crackling energy about her. "I've got two people riding, and one of them requested Patch, but you're small and light enough to ride one of the ponies. Do them good to have someone on board who knows what they're doing. They generally get away with murder with the kids, and I'm a bit too heavy to ride them."

Josie's gaze swept over me from my messy, pulled-back plait down to my dusty boots. "You don't look heavy to me. A bit long, maybe. You might have to pleat those long legs of yours around its belly."

I smiled at the image. "Exactly."

She finished Patch's saddle and put it back on the rail and bent to pull the bit from the bucket of water, where she had it soaking. She dried it with a cloth and reattached it to the bridle. "That would be good. I like riding ponies—they're so much fun."

"Is Flame your first horse, or did you have ponies?"

"I rode other people's ponies growing up. Flame is the first horse I've owned. It's scary. Owning something that I'm responsible for."

"You've never had a pet?"

"No. All I own fits in my car. I guess you could say I haven't had a very stable life." She fastened the final buckle. "Not like you: Born here. Live here. Work here."

I pondered her words. From anyone else, I'd be hypersensitive to the tone behind them. So often those words held a trace of condescension or pity. But Josie's words were factual. She was simply stating how it was for me, as opposed to her.

I tried for the same noncommittal tone. "And you haven't had that."

"Far from it. Left at seventeen. Been moving ever since."

There was the same neutral tone in her voice. I wondered at the story behind her words. Sure, lots of kids left home at seventeen, but I got the feeling her reasons were different to the usual university course or a job in another city. "You must have itchy feet."

"Yeah. I did. I do," she corrected. "It's quite hard, though. I don't have a fancy degree or any particular qualification. I can do pretty much anything—if someone gives me a chance. But those sorts of jobs don't pay too well." She rose and hung the bridle on a hook. "I like bar work, though. Talking to different people. Pay's not too bad. Generally, you get a decent enough

47

room and food. Fruit picking is a different thing. A leaky tent shared with five others in a muddy field."

"What else have you done?"

She ticked the jobs off on her fingers. "Nanny—hated that. The kid was a brat, and there was never any time off. Factory work—my workmates were great, the work was dull. I've cooked on stations before—I love that. Done some office work, but they generally expect you to dress neatly and behave a certain way." She pulled a face. "My office jobs have cost me a fortune in clothes. I did some tour guiding when I was overseas. In England, I worked on a tour coach, talking about Stonehenge and Hampton Court. It was fun for a while. I made most of it up as I went along. Not many people ever challenged me on it."

So Josie had travelled outside of Australia, lived in London, at least, and probably other places. Those were experiences and a life I never expected to have. I'd barely been outside Queensland. Hell, I'd hardly ever left the outback other than a school trip to the Great Barrier Reef and another to Sydney and Canberra. More recently, Mum and I went to Perth to see a cousin of hers. That was the first time I'd seen the sun set over the sea, the first time I'd dipped my toes in the Indian Ocean. Those were things many Australians took for granted: the ability to jump on a plane, visit another part of the country, or go overseas. Not for me.

"What made you come here?" I was aware I was quizzing her like a prospective employer, but I was genuinely curious as to her answer.

"Honestly?" She grinned. "I got offered the job at the Commercial. A friend of a friend. You know the drill."

I didn't, but I nodded anyway. I'd never had to apply for a job. I'd always worked for myself—breaking horses, some work on the main Jayboro Station. And then, of course, there were the years when I was Mum's carer.

"I've worked there for six weeks now. I'm still here."

"And now Flame is too."

"Yeah. And let's hope my tack is here soon."

She turned to pick up her hat, which was hanging on a peg. "I better find my campsite. Down by the creek, you reckon?"

"Yeah. It's quiet down there."

"I'll check it out." She shot me a mischievous look. "You know where to find me."

I knew where to find her—but I didn't. I'd seen her set up her little blue tent next to her car and pull out a camp stool. I'd watched without appearing to as she carried a mattress pad, pillow, and sheets into her tent. While I pretended to mend the fence that kept the animals out of my pitiful excuse for a veggie garden, I watched her find a saucepan and heat a tin of something on the gas burner. She pulled a beer out of the fridge and took it back to her camp, where she ate sitting on the stool facing the creek.

My fingers tightened on the fencing wire. I could walk over and join her, maybe take a couple of cold ones with me, sit down and shoot the breeze. It was the sort of thing I'd do with someone who was becoming a friend. But something held me back. Maybe it was that her knowing eyes would see through my attempt at casual friendship and put a different label on it. Maybe "lonely girl."

I didn't want to appear desperate. And I didn't want to intrude. Her job meant she had to talk to people, socialise with and listen to them, even if she didn't want to. I didn't want her to see me like that. So I stayed away, tightening wire, replacing a rotting post. Then, when the sun had nearly gone and a flock of corellas flew past making a hell of a racket, I put my tools away and with a last glance at the little blue tent by the creek, went inside the house and closed the door.

# CHAPTER 5

THE RIDE THE NEXT MORNING went well. Josie, mounted on Budgie, one of my smaller ponies, chattered away to the two women riding Patch and Ben. Both of them were competent riders and had requested a longer ride, so for four hours, we roamed the land around Jayboro. We jumped some fallen timber and had a couple of long gallops across the red dirt.

Josie had an easy, friendly way about her and asked the women what had brought them to the outback for their holiday and, in particular, to Jayboro Outstation. I listened for the most part and took note when they talked about unwinding from the stress of their jobs as nurses in a city hospital and getting back to a simpler time. Also, they didn't have to doll themselves up in the outback, which they would have felt obliged to if they'd had a resort holiday on one of the Barrier Reef islands.

"Here I can wear torn shorts and an old T-shirt, and I don't think anyone cares," said one. "I dressed up to eat at the pub in Mount Isa the other night, and that meant I found a smarter T-shirt. I love the informality here."

"It's totally different to anywhere I've been before," said the other. "It's a different Australia to where we live on the coast. It's nice to get back to basics. Not that your cabin is primitive," she hastened to add. "But it's a novelty for me to sit and watch the stars rather than turning on the TV. To cook a steak in your camp kitchen rather than picking a restaurant."

"If there were things to do in the evening, would you be interested?" Josie nudged Budgie to catch up with the bigger horses. "Like, I dunno, an evening campfire where you could talk to other travellers. Or a nature walk."

"Maybe. If it didn't seem like a charade put on for the tourists. We chose to stay here precisely because it seemed untouristy, off the beaten track."

I stored that information away in my head. Maybe I could offer an evening campfire once a week and a nature walk. Josie was good. I wouldn't have been able to ask in such an artless way, assuming I'd even thought of that in the first place.

Josie pulled back to let the women take the lead and reined in alongside me. "There's an idea for you. Evening campfires. You supply the damper; they bring their own beer."

"Maybe. As long as I don't have to MC a 'spontaneous' evening of bush poetry."

Her laugh rippled out. "Madge tried that in the Commercial. It's a good idea, but all the poets she asked were so used to being underappreciated and told to shut up that once they had a mike in their hand and a captive audience, they *wouldn't* shut up. It went on for *hours*. I was about ready to hit the fire alarm."

"No bush poetry, then."

"Oh, the idea is fine. Madge did it a second time, and she gave everyone a strict time limit of five minutes. That worked better. For all their introspection, it seems once a poet starts reciting, a bomb could drop and they wouldn't notice."

Back at the barn, we dismounted. Normally, I would see to the horses myself, but Josie had other plans.

"C'mon, ladies," she said. "I'll show you how we look after our horses in the outback. After all, a stockman is only as good as his horse, so we do things right. Grab your horse, and follow along."

I stared open-mouthed as Josie led the way into the barn towing her pony, the two women following behind. In thirty minutes, all three horses were turned out in the paddock, and before they returned to their cabin, the two nurses booked another ride for the next day. Sure, they were slower than I would have been, but if I'd had to do all three horses, it would have taken me at least forty-five minutes. This way, I saved a little time and had two very happy customers.

Josie came up to me as I watched them leave. "See? It's not so hard. You're giving people what they want here, Felix."

"You have a knack for dealing with people."

"It's the bartender in me. One part pouring drinks, one part psychologist, one part listening ear."

"It works."

"Does it work with you, though?" She said the words quietly, so softly, I wondered if I'd misheard.

"What did you say?"

This time she was bold. "Just wondering if my charm was working on you too."

Did she mean what I thought she meant? I opted for the neutral reply. "I'm impressed by your skills."

"Only my people skills? What about my purple pants?"

"I thought they were mauve." Too late, I realised my reply showed that I had been looking.

Her quick smile told me that she'd noted that too. "Purple. Better get used to them, as they're the only pair I have. I don't carry many clothes with me, travelling light as I do, and most of my clothes are shorts. No good for riding—the stirrup leathers would pinch."

"Ride bareback and it doesn't matter."

"Me or the horse?" Her retort brought up all sorts of images in my head: a chestnut horse with a rider who was bare of back—and front. One glance at her grin told me she knew exactly what she'd said.

"If I'm bareback, you have to be too. Think about it." She walked off, back towards the campground, and left me staring at the shape her butt made in her jeans.

They were definitely mauve.

The days marched on, and the weather grew steadily hotter and drier. I was now feeding hay to all of the horses due to the lack of grass. True to her word, Josie transferred over the money for Flame's agistment, and after consultation, she added an amount for feed.

Bookings trickled in for my cabins. I'd hoped to have them both booked for two days each week, but so far, they had been booked for four days each week. I had Josie to thank for a lot of the bookings. Customers told me that they'd heard about Jayboro from the girl behind the bar in the Commercial or from the woman in the post office. Even Bazza at the garage had thrown me a bone a couple of times. It seemed I owed thank-you beers in a lot of places.

Josie came up at least a couple of times each week, yet she seldom managed to stay over. And although a month had passed since Flame arrived, Josie—or anyone—had yet to ride her.

Josie's excuse was the lack of tack, which had still mysteriously failed to arrive from South Australia. I'd offered to go out with her a couple of times—me on my steadiest horse, Smoke, and her bareback on Flame. See how she went, I said, a quiet ride.

But Josie shook her head. "I'm just not comfortable riding bareback." She gestured at Flame, grazing alongside one of the ponies. "See how she's filling out? If I ride her, she'll get excited, and she'll drop weight in an instant. She's not a good doer." She grinned. "Not like me." And she slapped her hand on her backside, clad in the ever-present mauve jeans. "Wish I could look as sleek as Flame."

Her words, of course, had the effect of drawing my eyes to her curvy butt outlined in the tight pants, and then my dry mouth couldn't continue the conversation.

I didn't know what to do about Josie.

Not in a business sense. Not in the landowner/horse-owner sense. But she was fast becoming a friend. Our conversations as we rode—both of us on my horses—gradually deepened and progressed. The banter was still there, but often, I would learn a snippet of her life too.

And we flirted.

I was not a natural flirt. The tease, the subtle glances, the light touches, they were all somewhat alien to me. I was a clumsy one, and living alone didn't give me much chance to improve my technique. There simply weren't many people to practice on. The only other lesbians in Worrindi were an older couple—a retired schoolteacher and her "friend". That was how they introduced themselves, but I knew the truth, as did most people in town.

A couple of lesbians had stayed at the campground over the months, but I'd been hesitant to cross that line with them. My friends at Mungabilly Creek, Sue and Moni, had offered to set me up with one of the nurses Moni knew from the Isa, but that was a four-hour drive away and simply not easy on any sort of practical basis.

The last person I'd seduced was Sue, and that was well over three years ago, before Moni had arrived from Texas to take up a position with the Flying Doctor Service. And back then, Sue had been even more of an ingénue in the dating department than me. We had been two clumsy novices falling together.

Josie continued to sleep in her little blue tent on the occasions when she stayed over, and I had yet to invite her up to the house in the evening. I often thought about that—obsessed was probably the more accurate word. If it had been any other friend, I would have said, "Come up for a beer on the veranda." Or I would have invited her to share my meal. But something held me back with Josie. It was a line that, once crossed, could never be taken back. And if she came up once, then it would be expected, the norm. I wasn't sure if I was ready for that.

Josie didn't hint. If she ever saw me taking a stroll around in the evening, as I sometimes did, she'd wave from the doorway of her tiny tent, offer a remark, and then smile and let me walk off.

"You need a dog at your heels," she said once. "You look so alone doing the rounds."

I stared. In truth, I had thought of getting a dog for companionship, but also for the pleasure they bring. There was also no harm in having a dog around to deter snakes and possibly the occasional aggressive client. That had never happened to me, but Narelle had raised it more than once. She, too, thought I should have a dog—something big.

Sue and Moni had a dog, a cheeky little Jack Russell terrier called Ripper, and I'd thought of getting one like him. Indeed, Sue had said she sometimes heard of pups available from the same parents, but so far I'd done nothing.

"A blue heeler," Josie said, her head cocked towards her shoulder, considering. "It would match your hair."

I snorted. "I'm not *that* grey."

"Yet. How about a kelpie, then?"

I shook my head. "Too much work."

"Staffy."

"They abscond. That would be a disaster around here with all the livestock. I need something obedient and good company."

"Definitely a poodle."

I shot her a withering look. "That wiry hair would attract grass seeds like mad. There's a reason most Australian breeds are smooth haired."

"Tenterfield terrier."

"Too small. Great dogs, though."

"What, then?" Exasperation threaded her voice.

"Blue heeler is the best. I've had a couple of them when I was a kid. Fantastic dogs."

"I'll keep an ear out for you."

"I didn't say I wanted one."

"I know." Josie's hair crackled around her head in the dry air. Still no sign of rain. "But there's no harm in looking."

I changed the subject. "How about you and me going out?"

She stared. "I thought you'd never ask. But where would we go around here?"

It was my turn to stare. "I'm talking now. On horseback. Me on Smoke, you on Flame."

"Ha ha…Smoke and Flame."

"Well?"

"I already told you; I'm just not confident riding bareback."

"You ride Smoke, then."

57

She was silent. Then she said, "This is going to sound stupid, but I'd really like to be the one to ride my horse first. Her tack should arrive soon. I can wait until then. I'm sorry, Felix. You probably think I'm making excuses."

I was beginning to wonder. It had been weeks now, and she was yet to get astride her horse. In the meantime, Flame nosed the bare earth in my paddock and ate an awful lot of hay that had to be trucked in from closer to the coast—a long, long way.

But it was her horse. No doubt she had her reasons.

"How about you ride Budgie the pony again, then? He hasn't been out all week."

"Sure. I like Budge. He's fun."

And so Flame grazed on in the paddock, and Josie and I rode out on my horses. There were no other guests riding; it was just her and me.

We rode quietly through the campground and waved at a couple of campers. Everyone else appeared to be out for the day. There were just a couple of tents hunkered down on the dry ground, including Josie's blue tent in its customary position away from everyone else down by the creek.

"Those two." She flapped a hand in the general direction of the grey nomads we'd just waved to. "They're considering doing a farm sit around here. The Mellinses' place. Two weeks to give Rhonda and Harry a chance to visit their grandkids in Perth."

I wondered how she knew so much about people. Those campers had been with me for three days, and I didn't know that.

"They came into the Commercial," Josie continued. "Started asking me about the area. That's how I found out."

There was a pause as she steered Budgie around a stand of mulga. "I reckon tonight would be a good night to try out the campfire idea," she said. "Those two would be in it. Who else have you got here at the moment?"

"Some English backpackers, a couple from Japan, and a pair of grey nomads from Sydney."

"Perfect! Get a fire going at dusk, mix up some damper, boil the billy for tea—do you *have* a billy?"

I nodded. "Somewhere. But we've got no entertainment."

"Try it without. Campfire chats, billy tea, and damper. That's all the entertainment most of them want." Her enthusiasm was contagious.

"I suppose there's no harm in trying. If it's successful, I could make it a weekly event. After all, there's nowhere for them to go after dark."

"I'll help you find firewood after our ride, if you want."

"You don't have to. It's your day off from work. You probably want to lie around with a book."

"In this heat?" She snorted. "If I'm going to be hot and sweaty and outside, I may as well make it count for something."

"I'll need to think about firewood, though. I let the campers collect it from around the campground, but they only have small fires. There just isn't much around."

"There's a bloke that comes into the pub sometimes who sells ute loads of wood. He doesn't charge an arm and a leg. I could send him your way next time he comes in."

"That would be good."

We'd left the campground and were crossing the red open dirt. There were no trees, only the red domes of termite mounds studding the landscape.

"You could also sell firewood." Josie encouraged Budgie to come up alongside my horse. "Campers *like* campfires. And they like being lazy. If you offered bags of wood, ready chopped, I bet you could turn a profit selling it. Do you have a chainsaw?"

I nodded again.

"Well, offer one of the backpackers a couple of free nights' camping if they chop a ute load of wood for you. I bet they'll jump at it."

"I should hire you to be my marketing consultant."

"I'd take the job."

"No pay." I concentrated on Ben's ears. "I barely make enough to support myself and pay my bills."

"Don't worry. I know you don't mean it." She hesitated. "I wish you did, though. It would be nice to live somewhere like this."

"You'd be bored in a month. Let's face it, if an evening campfire is a social highlight, there's not much else to do."

Josie nudged Budgie even closer. "Oh, don't worry. I'm good at entertaining myself, and others. I wouldn't be bored."

I brushed away a fly as I found myself hanging on her next words. When they came, they were low enough that I had to strain to hear.

"Neither would you."

I didn't know what to say. Her meaning was clear. But I'd never been good at flirtation. I tried to think what Moni would say. She always had a quick comeback for any occasion, but my mind sizzled and went white in the heat.

She stared at my face, waiting for my answer, but my hesitation must have given the wrong signal.

She eased Budgie further from Ben. "Don't worry. I'm not about to jump your bones at the campfire this evening." She switched her gaze to the horizon, a shimmering line of heat haze where the red dirt met the blue sky. "Shall we gallop?"

And the moment passed in a thunder of hooves and a face full of dust as Budgie's little hooves leapt away.

# CHAPTER 6

JOSIE AND I DROVE AROUND that afternoon and succeeded in finding enough wood for a fire. As Josie said, it didn't have to be an inferno. Indeed, the evenings were now warm enough that a fire wasn't necessary. It was all about the ambiance.

Luckily, she hadn't taken offence at my lack of response to her flirting. I guess she simply thought I wasn't interested. She hadn't changed in her friendliness nor withdrawn her offer to help at the campfire. But the exchange weighed on my mind.

Because, I *was* interested in Josie. I often thought about her long after she had returned to Worrindi. As I attempted to keep up with the accounts, or as I sat on the veranda with a beer before going to bed, I'd catch myself smiling at something she'd said earlier. She would be good, undemanding company for the quiet moments like this.

But I wasn't sure what to do about my attraction, especially since I'd effectively rebuffed her with my silence.

When we returned with the wood, we built a small fire in the best fire pit, which was over to one side of the campground. It was good too, in that the prevailing winds generally blew the smoke away from the campers.

"Do you have a noticeboard?" Josie asked when we'd finished. "I don't remember seeing one."

"No," I admitted. "Never felt the need."

"What, no rules? No Shut-Up-After-10.00pm sign? No advisories about snakes, or keeping the showers clean, or the dangers of flooded roads? No notices about live music in the Commercial—"

"There's live music in the pub?"

"Girlfriend, where have you *been* for the past few months? There's live music once a month."

"Oh."

"What about letting campers know your trail ride prices, or that you have a book exchange in the corner of the camp kitchen? You *need* a noticeboard."

"When you put it like that, I guess I do."

"Anyway, in the absence of a noticeboard, you're going to have to walk around later and tell each camper individually. No one can resist a personal invitation."

Which we'd done. And then Josie said she was going to have a shower, and I went back to the house to mix the flour and water for damper in a large bowl and cover it with a cloth.

We'd told the campers the fire would be going from seven. That was after dusk for atmosphere but not so late that the early-to-bed people couldn't still be tucked up by nine.

I carried over the damper, butter, a couple of homemade jams from the ladies of the Country Women's Association and a cast-iron skillet for the fire.

Josie eyed my preparations. "Are you going to cook the damper for everyone?"

"That's what I was thinking."

She grinned. "I thought you were a bushie! Come with me."

She led me to her tent by the creek. I figured she was going to get something from within, but we passed on to where the gum trees grew in disarray.

"Look for green sticks," she said. "About a foot long, straightish. Break them off the tree, don't pick up fallen ones. We need one for everyone."

I did as she asked, and we soon had an array.

The fire was quickly alight and crackling with merry warmth. The campers started wandering over in ones and twos, bringing their chairs and beer or wine. Immediately, I could see Josie's idea was a good one. They chatted to each other and swapped stories of where to go and what to see.

Josie nudged me. "The hive mind at work. One big storytelling collective." She raised her voice. "Who's for damper?"

She cut the block of butter into chunks and left it in a bowl by the fire. Then, she picked up one of the sticks and started peeling the bark from it, leaving it green and supple and clean. With swift movements, she picked a ball of dough from the bowl and shaped it like a sausage around the stick, leaving about six inches free as a handle. Then, she squatted and held the stick over the embers.

She didn't have to tell people what to do; she simply led by example. Soon, there was a ring of people busily turning their damper over the embers. When Josie judged hers was cooked, she twisted the damper off the stick so that it came away clean and steaming.

"Pass the plum jam, please, Felix."

Carefully, she filled the hollow area of the damper with plum jam, then dunked it in the melted butter. Her mouth glistened in the firelight as she bit into it with care. "Delicious!"

The idea was a brilliant one. The campers laughed as their damper caught fire or dropped into the flames, and then they ate the blackened dough slathered with jam and dripping with melted butter. It became a shared experience rather than just watching me fry up damper on the pan.

I put water in the billy for tea, and when it boiled, Josie added some fresh eucalyptus to the handful of tea leaves I threw in. "For authenticity," she said.

Now that everyone was obviously enjoying themselves, Josie returned from her position at the fire. We sat in silence, side by side, watching the campers.

"Where did you learn that trick with the damper?" Our chairs were close enough that if I let my hips relax, our knees would touch.

"National Park in Victoria. One of the rangers there. Kids love it, but it seems adults do too."

I looked over to where the Japanese couple were licking butter and jam from their fingers and trying to talk to the retired couple from Sydney. There didn't seem to be much shared language, but there was shared laughter.

My knee wobbled. It would be so easy to let it touch her smooth, brown thigh. I stared at it, rather than look at Josie. "You're very much a people person."

She shrugged. "I just watch and learn."

"No, you've got the knack. Extrovert."

"Don't be fooled. I'm an introvert who does a very good impression of an extrovert. I can talk to people, and I like to do that, but equally, I like to go home and close the door and be alone." She paused. "Or be with someone I'm comfortable with." This time the pause was longer. "Are you like that too, Felix? Do you like to be alone?"

"I'm usually alone." When had my words sounded so forlorn? I enjoyed being solitary. Indeed, it was my natural state, but Josie's words had a resonance to them. I would like to be with someone. Not a campground full of strangers, not friends. One person. Someone special.

I cleared my throat, which had unaccountably tightened. "I should get that poodle."

She laughed, and her knee nudged into my thigh. It was warm. "Blue heeler. Best dogs. But there's alone, and there's the quiet closeness of being with a special person."

I glanced at her. Her face was half in shadow, and the firelight made her wild curls seem alive.

"Are you with anyone?" The question was belated, because I'd already made assumptions about that. Her peripatetic nature made me think she was single, but now she'd been in Worrindi a couple of months, long enough to form a relationship. And flirting with me didn't mean she wasn't attached.

"Nope. Not at the moment. I've had relationships, of course, most of them very short lived."

I was silent. I wanted to ask her more, to find out about the sort of person who could hold her interest, but it seemed too nosy.

She glanced under her lashes. "Go on. Ask. I can see you wibbling about it from here."

I tried for a dignified silence, but curiosity won out. "So what was your last partner like?"

"Girlfriend. I've only ever had girlfriends."

"I didn't want to presume."

"Her name was Lois Lane, and—"

"No way! No one could be called Lois Lane."

"She was. Her parents had a sense of humour."

"Obviously."

The tea had steeped enough by the fire, and I rose to see to it. I hadn't thought to provide mugs—indeed, I wasn't sure I had enough—but the campers had mostly brought their own, and the Japanese couple disappeared and returned with some cups from the camp kitchen.

I poured tea for those who wanted it and explained how it was usually drunk: strong and black, as there used to be no reliable way of keeping the milk from going off. Most swaggies had carried a twist of paper containing some sugar.

When everyone was chatting around the fire again, I returned to my chair.

"Two months. That's how long I was with Lois. She lives in Scone, New South Wales. We split when I moved on."

I filed the information away. I'd think about that later.

"My longest relationship lasted nearly two years. Dee and I travelled together. Picked fruit in the Riverina, travelled the Birdsville Track, then on to Darwin. Worked on prawn trawlers in the Gulf."

"What happened?"

"Dee wanted to settle down somewhere. She wanted somewhere to grow vegetables, to get to know people for more than a few weeks. I wanted to keep moving." Josie cupped her mug of billy tea. "I really didn't get it at the time. Why would anyone want to settle in one place?"

I was silent, not wanting to interrupt her flow of words.

"But now, I'm starting to understand a little. Oh, I haven't decided I'm totally ready to stop travelling, but I can at least see the appeal. Worrindi's a good place; that's why I'm still around."

"That's why you brought Flame here?"

It was her turn for silence. "Yeah," she said eventually. "That's why."

Now that the tea was drunk and the fire had died to the red glow of the heartwood, people started to slip away, back to their vans or tents. Most of them thanked both of us, probably assuming that Josie and I ran this place together. After Josie's contribution this afternoon, I was beginning to think the same.

That left only the English backpackers laughing quietly around the fire. They had stubbies of beer, not tea, so I figured they'd be up for a while.

I looked over at Josie's profile in the firelight. She looked pensive, different to her usual lively self. She stared into the embers as if they held the answer to a major question in her life. The curve of her cheek was gilded by firelight, and that wild hair, shot through with her string of beads, curled underneath the brim of her hat. I wanted to reach out and take her hand and hold it between my palms, just to see what she felt like, to learn what she would do. But I feared the rejection in front of the backpackers.

Instead, I leant back in my chair and looked up at the stars. The Milky Way was brilliant, a long ribbon of stars running across the sky. I cradled my mug of tea and emptied my head of everything except the here and now. It was something Mum had taught me not long after she'd been diagnosed with the cancer that had eventually killed her.

"Live in the moment, Felicity," she'd said. "Don't worry about past mistakes or things you shouldn't have done or said. You can't change them. Try not to worry about things that haven't happened. They may never eventuate. Enjoy every moment. Because then it's gone forever."

I'd been silent. I was a great one for worrying. But if Mum could put aside her fear of dying in order to enjoy the present moment, then I surely could. It was good advice, even if it was hard to put into practice. But I managed it, more or less.

So I relaxed in my chair and enjoyed the night, the background murmur of conversation from the backpackers, and the taste of strong black tea.

Josie was silent. I couldn't know what she was thinking, but I was sure that she, too, was enjoying the moment.

After twenty minutes, I levered myself to my feet. "I better go. Early start and all that." I folded my chair and emptied the last drops of tea onto the dirt.

Josie stood too. "I will as well. I sleep so well when I'm in a tent, but I'm always tired."

We walked in silence away from the fire. There was a sliver of moon, but the stars cast enough light to see. I stopped at the gate to the home paddock. My path took me up to the house, hers down to her tent by the creek.

"I'll see you tomorrow." For a moment, I lingered, my hand on the chain that held the gate closed. "Thanks for what you did today."

She took a pace forwards so that she, too, was by the gate. "It was nothing. Just a couple of obvious things."

"Obvious to you, maybe."

Her teeth flashed white in the starlight. "I was happy to help. I like coming here, Felix. And you let me ride your horses for free."

"You're paying for a horse you don't ride."

She moved closer, and her hand rose to flick the end of the plait that hung over my shoulder in a thick rope.

"That's my problem, not yours." Her fingers closed around my plait, and she tugged. Her intention was obvious.

My breath caught in my throat. How long had it been since I'd been about to kiss a woman? *Too long*, said a tiny voice in my head. Too damn long. Over three years.

I stepped forwards into her space. My hand found her upper arm and traced the muscle lightly.

"And I like coming here to see you." Her words were soft. "I want you to know that, Felix."

"I'm glad you do."

And then her lips touched mine. They were soft and dry and curiously tentative. She seemed unsure of my reaction.

I remembered how I'd inadvertently snubbed her before, so I wrapped my arm around her shoulders and deepened the kiss. It was a kiss of starlight and longing and desire, and the thunder in my blood was a tide of pleasure that I hoped I might soon get to slake.

She responded, and for long moments, we kissed, advanced, and retreated, lips touching and withdrawing. It was tantalising. It was warm. It was anticipatory.

And then she was gone.

One minute she was in my arms, the next she was three feet away, shaking her foot.

"What's the matter?" Even though it was obvious something had happened, I couldn't suppress the momentary pang when I thought she was rejecting me.

"Something ran over my foot. A mouse probably." She shuddered. "I *hate* mice. Comes from sleeping in barns when fruit picking. Rodents *everywhere*."

Neither of us had a torch, but even if it was a mouse, it would have gone.

"Another reason to get a dog, I guess."

The moment when something more might have happened had passed.

"Borrow a terrier, and leave it in the barn."

I thought of Sue and Moni and their Jack Russell, Ripper.

"I will." I didn't know what to do—whether to move forwards and kiss her again, or let the moment slide.

"I better get moving." I opted for the latter. "Thank you, Josie."

Her smile held understanding, and she leant forwards and kissed my cheek. "I hope we can do more of this." With a squeeze of my hand, she was gone, leaving me staring stupidly at the hole in the night that had once held her presence.

# CHAPTER 7

"Felix! How are you?"

The voice on the phone was exuberant, loud, and very American.

"Moni. Long time no hear." I settled back into the chair and picked up a pen to doodle with.

"We're just bonzer. Do you like my Australianism? I learnt that one from a patient."

"I'd unlearn it then. No one says that any more, unless they're about ninety."

"Now that you mention it, he is." Laughter in her voice. For all her strong Texan accent, she was acquiring an overlay of the Queensland intonation. Her sentences tilted up at the end now, and she even occasionally ended a sentence with the ubiquitous Queensland "eh".

"How's Sue?"

"Good. Great. Working hard as usual. And that's partly why I'm calling. We've got visitors coming next week—friends from England. They're in Sydney at the moment, and it's a bit hard for them to figure out when they'll be with us. We'd love to show them the real outback, maybe get them up on a horse. We're wondering if both of your cabins would be free for two nights sometime next week? I'm sorry about the short notice—they're kinda hard to wrestle to the ground and pin down. We can flex the days. At least *I* can, now that I've got a part-time doctor to cover me, and I'm going to force Sue to take some time off."

"Let me look." I drew the diary across and opened it to the next week. "Will your guests share a bed, or will I need a foldaway bed as well?"

"Nora and Geraldine will very definitely share a bed—they're married."

"How about Wednesday and Thursday night?"

"That should work. Can I reserve it for us and confirm tomorrow?"

"No worries."

"I think you'll like them, Felix. I hope we'll get to spend some time with you."

"I'll cook dinner one night. It will be easier than cooking in the camp kitchen." I wrote the booking in as we spoke. That meant that both cabins were booked for six nights out of seven that week.

"Nora fancies herself as a bit of a cook. Sue's got her convinced that she'll have to shoot a kangaroo and throw the entire thing on a campfire. She's up for it, though." There was a voice in the background. "I have to go. My next patient is here. We'll call you tomorrow, hopefully to confirm. Bye, Felix."

The line went dead.

I couldn't remember the last time I'd had four people over for dinner. Certainly not four lesbians. I couldn't ever remember being in the same room as four other lesbians before. Maybe Josie could swing a couple of days off and come down to make it six.

I went out to the campground, passing Flame, who stood alone in the paddock dozing under the scant shade of a gum. Despite the lack of grass, Flame was actually filling out, thanks to a combination of the hay that Josie paid for and the lack of exercise. Her coat was sleek, whereas before it was dusty and staring, and the extra weight made her look like the young horse that she was. On a whim, I walked across to her and ran a hand down her shoulder. She turned her head and pushed her nose into my side, begging for scratches between the ears. I obliged.

Josie had said she was about seven. I cupped her jaw, slid my thumb into her mouth, and pushed down on the bare bit of gum to make her open her mouth. I pulled back her lips and looked at her teeth. It was obvious she was a young horse—her teeth were still a pale yellow, without the browning associated with age. The teeth also met in a vertical line. They had none of the slope that develops in an older horse. To me, she looked younger than seven, more like four or five. I let her jaw go and scratched her between the ears again. She was a sweetie. Saddle or no saddle, I didn't see Josie having any problem riding her bareback, but I guessed Josie knew her horse.

With a final scratch on her poll, I went onto the campground. Both cabins had been occupied last night, and I had new bookings for today. I had a lot to do.

Sue and Moni and their friends arrived around noon. I was leaving the barn when I saw Sue's four-wheel drive pull up in front of the house. By the time I walked over, they were already on the veranda, and Moni was pointing out the campground and cabins to the visitors. Ripper, Sue's little terrier, came running to greet me, going up on his hind legs and patting my thigh with his front paws.

Sue saw me first and came across to greet me, a huge smile on her face. We hugged, and then I turned to Moni and hugged her too while their visitors hung back.

"Felix, meet our very good friends from England, Nora and Geraldine."

They both smiled but didn't try to shake hands. Someone must have clued them in that politeness was appreciated in the outback, but formality wasn't. Nora was tall and lean with short brown hair and a quick smile. Her wife, Geraldine, was stunning. She was shorter and had a curvaceous figure and vivid auburn hair. It was drawn up in a messy bun on top of her head, but when loose, it would probably hang well below her shoulders. Both wore shorts, but while Nora's were topped with a plain navy T-shirt, Geraldine had paired her denim shorts with a beige T-shirt that had a complicated hand-painted design.

"I'm very happy to meet you both," I said. "Come into the office, and I'll get you signed in. Then I'll show you the cabins."

"Is there any chance of a glass of water?" asked Nora. "I'm dying of thirst. We had a little confusion over who was supposed to fill the water bottles before we left Sue and Moni's place."

Her English accent was very pronounced, at least to my ears. The grin she flashed in Sue's direction revealed their easy friendship.

"That would be the same person who was supposed to pack the wine." Sue nudged me in the ribs and stage-whispered, "Her name starts with N. We went back for the wine but still forgot the water."

"And then we went back a second time for Ripper's kibble," said Moni.

"And forgot the water yet again!" Ger chimed in. Her accent was softer than Nora's.

"We're all total eejits." Nora bent to scratch Ripper behind the ears. "But in our defence, Ger and I are utter novices at

74

this whole nothing-for-hundreds-of-miles thing. Whereas these two…"

"Hey! I resent that remark!" Moni stuck her hands on her hips. "Sue and I drink stagnant water from a depression in the rock and dig witchetty grubs with our bare hands for breakfast. Just you wait until tomorrow morning. Those bacon and eggs we packed were to lull you into a false sense of security."

The banter had doubtless gone on since the English women had arrived in the country, and they could probably keep it up indefinitely. They all followed me into the office, and while Sue filled in the paperwork, the others looked at the photos on the wall. I went to get water and handed each of them a glass.

"Is this you, Felix?" Geraldine pointed to a photo of me and Patch barrel racing.

I nodded.

"Sue says we can go horse riding here. Reckon you can teach me to ride like that?"

"Got a couple of years?" Nora slung an arm around her wife's shoulders. "I think you and I will be on elderly ponies so small our feet will brush the daisies. Brush the dirt," she amended.

"Not quite. But I do have quiet mounts for beginners."

"Good. I'm not sure I want to be that far from the ground." Geraldine shuddered, but I got the feeling she was putting it on.

"What happened to your desire to be next year's barrel racing champ at the Isa show?" Moni came up beside me. "Felix has that horse out in the barn, waiting for you to come and ride her."

"She can wait a bit longer." Ger shot me a glance. "Unless she's one of the quiet horses you mentioned?"

"Nope. She's for experienced riders. Sue or I will ride her. Don't worry. They're winding you up. I'll take you out to the paddock later, if you want, so you can meet your horse."

"I'd like that. Thanks, Felix."

Sue had finished signing in, and when the others went back out onto the veranda, she and I had a brief tussle over money.

"Mates' rates," I said. "You're paying half the going price. No arguments."

"No." She tried to shove the cash into the pocket of my shirt. "I accept mates' rates for me and Moni, but you don't know Nora and Ger. Full price for them."

"No way. Friends of yours are friends of mine. Mates' rates for them as well, or I won't invite you around for dinner later. I'm making spaghetti carbonara. Or I will if you take back half this money."

Sue wavered. "That's not playing fair. Seriously, Felix, let me pay full price for them."

"No." I closed her fist around the cash. "You and Moni have done a lot for me these last years. You've been the best of friends. You've helped me out with the right-of-access agreement with Jayboro. Moni answers medical questions when I'm too busy to see my doctor. Mates' rates on the cabins."

"Full price for the trail rides, then." Sue wore her best lawyer face, the one with narrowed eyes and steely voice.

"You can pay full price for the English; you and Moni pay half price."

She capitulated, but only with a parting shot. "Okay, but we're bringing *all* the wine for dinner tonight. And don't argue on that one. You have no idea how much those two can put away!"

"Deal."

We joined the other three on the veranda. "Cabins or horses first?"

"Horses," said Nora. "We're dusty and sweaty, so let's see these dusty and sweaty animals while we're in the same state."

We walked across the paddock to where the horses grazed together at the far end.

I pointed to each horse in turn. "Sue, you want to ride Patch again?"

"Absolutely! She's a fantastic ride."

"Moni, you want to take Budgie?" I pointed at one of the ponies. "You haven't ridden him before, but he's a willing mount for a good rider. And you're light enough."

Moni nodded and went over to the little bay and patted his neck.

"Nora, you'll ride Smoke, the grey over there. She's quiet and well-mannered, and I think you'll enjoy her."

"I will. Whether she'll enjoy me remains to be seen."

"Geraldine, that leaves you with Jetta. She's the chestnut over there."

"The tall one? She's beautiful."

"She has the same colour hair as you." Nora's gaze followed where Ger was looking.

I looked in the same direction. Flame stood alone by the fence, head up, snorting at something on the far side. "No, not Flame. She's on agistment. Jetta is the pony over there." I pointed to where Jetta and Ben stood nose to tail, their tails swishing flies from the other's face.

"I'm a bit sorry you said that." Ger smiled. "I could see myself on Flame, galloping along, chasing kangaroos or something."

"More likely plonk on your nose in the dust while Flame gallops on without you." Moni's gaze was also locked on Flame. "She is a stunner of a horse."

Ger walked towards Flame. She went slowly, her hand held out to the mare. "Hello, gorgeous."

Flame stretched out her nose and touched Ger's hand. Ger sidled closer and patted her neck with a tentative motion. Flame responded by nudging her side.

There was a click, and I looked around to see Moni lowering a camera. "That's one for the family album. Ger, you and Flame have identical colouring."

"Flame's nose is smaller, though," said Nora.

Ger glared. "Thank you, lover. Lucky we're not talking about the size of feet."

Nora went over, and Ger wound her arms around her wife's neck. It was obvious that the teasing was a long-established part of their relationship. They kissed, and Moni's camera clicked again.

"Can you send me those photos later?" Ger asked. "I'd like to email the one of me and Flame home to my family, see if they can tell us apart."

We walked back to where Sue had left her car, and I squeezed into the back seat with Nora and Ger for the short drive to the cabins. I left the four of them settling in, with instructions to come up to the house later for dinner.

For once, I had nothing pressing to do, so I headed home. I wanted to call Josie. I'd told her that the four women were visiting and had asked if she thought she could get time off.

I rang her mobile, but it went straight to voicemail, which either meant she was working or out of range. I rang the pub, and she answered.

"I've been meaning to call you," she said the moment she heard my voice. "I've got tomorrow and the next day off. I can come down early. Will your friends be riding?"

"That's great! And yes, they'll be riding. So if you're early enough, you can come with us. You'll have to ride Diesel, though. He's all that's left, unless you're going to ride Flame."

"I hope old Diesel will be able to keep up."

"We won't be going fast. Nora and Geraldine have never ridden before."

"I'm looking forward to it." Her voice bubbled with anticipation. "It will be one glorious lesbian fest."

"Pity you're not here tonight. I'm cooking spaghetti carbonara, and the others have brought more red wine with them than is found in the bottlo at the Commercial."

"I hope it's better quality. Save some for me—I'm sick of drinking the crap that comes out of the casks of house wine."

Somehow, I'd had her pegged for a beer drinker.

"Can't promise."

The murmur of voices in the background rose to a clamour. "I have to go," she said. "See you tomorrow."

I didn't want to intrude upon the others, so I passed the time catching up on the accounts. I was glad I did; the cabins were proving more popular than I'd thought. Even allowing for the wet season, at this rate I'd be able to get the builder back from the Isa to build the remaining two cabins a lot sooner than anticipated.

There was a scuffle of feet at the door, and Nora came in. "Hi. Am I disturbing you?"

"Nothing important. Is there something I can help with?"

Geraldine also entered. "We went for a walk. The other two are getting loved up in your cabin. You shouldn't have put in such a good bed."

"Glad you like it."

"We've just found out the hard way that there's a reason why no one else is out walking at this time of the afternoon." Geraldine's pale skin was flushed bright red in the heat. "Sue said you had wi-fi here. We were wondering if we could impose and use it to send a couple of emails and photos to family back home?"

"No worries. You can use this desk. I'm going to feed the horses."

"Thanks." Nora moved to the desk and set down the laptop she carried. "Do I need a password?"

I wrote it on a scrap of paper for her. "I never used to need a password, being the only person around here, but one day, I found a couple of backpackers sitting in their van piggybacking off my wi-fi. I wouldn't have minded, but they were downloading movies or something. Blew my data allowance for the month."

"We won't do that. Sue's already warned us."

Her fingers were deft as she booted up and opened her email. The photo she attached was the one Moni had taken of Ger with Flame. It was a great shot. Ger's hair was escaping from the messy arrangement, and she was standing in front of Flame, who looked every inch the dainty thoroughbred. Behind them, the expanse of red dirt stretched to the horizon. It was the sort of photo to hang on a wall, captioned *woman and horse in outback landscape.*

Nora saw my glance. "Ger's very photogenic, isn't she? Unlike me. I'm always squinting, or my eyes are closed, or I'm chewing with my mouth open and you can see my tonsils."

Ger came up behind her wife and wrapped her arms around her shoulders and rested her chin on the top of Nora's head. The pose was one of unselfconscious love and intimacy, and for a moment, I envied them. I wanted the kind of connection with another woman they had, the kind Sue and Moni had.

I had to swallow before I could continue. "I'm the same. We should take one of us together and see who looks the worst."

Ger grinned. "Nora would win." She released her wife. "She looks the worst in photos of anyone I know." She glanced at the screen. "Who are you sending the photo to?"

"Parents—yours and mine."

"Can you send it to Young Seánie as well?" Ger looked at me and added, "He's one of my brothers. He follows the horses—reckons he's got a foolproof betting scheme." She turned back towards the screen. "Tell him it's me and some famous racehorse that he needs to bet the house on."

Nora grinned and typed even faster. "I never let an opportunity pass to get one up on Young Seánie. He's rather…"

"She wants to say 'aggressive', 'argumentative', or 'downright stroppy'," said Ger. "But she's watching her words."

"Young Seánie is the belligerent type." Nora finished in a flurry of fingers and hit *send*. "I've told him Flame is a certainty for the Melbourne Cup this year."

I grinned. "That's only the biggest race in Australia. If he follows the races, he'll know she's not a contender."

"Doesn't matter. It will get him searching madly for her, trying to see if it's a legit tip." Her eyes crinkled in amusement. "He'll blow the internet trying to find out about the horse." She closed her laptop. "That's all. Thanks, Felix."

"Now that you know the password for the wi-fi, feel free to use it anytime. You'll get a connection on the veranda if I'm not around."

I left them to their own devices and went down to check on the horses. Geraldine was right; it was indeed a hot day.

It wouldn't be long before the only tourists that came were the hardy or the insane. My little herd would grow sleek on wet-season grass and lazy from having little to do. But in the meantime, business was good.

# CHAPTER 8

DINNER THAT EVENING WAS A relaxed and happy affair. The others had brought a selection of dips, cheese, and crackers that we nibbled on while I prepared spaghetti carbonara—in truth, the only dish I could make with ease. They had brought beer as well as half a dozen bottles of red wine.

When I protested the amount of wine, Sue just grinned. "Wait until you see what Nora can put away. She was my drinking companion when I lived in London. Led me well and truly astray."

"You didn't take much leading." Nora swirled the wine around in her glass. "But honestly, I've tried, and I just don't enjoy beer. So red wine it is."

I was drinking wine too, and it was a very pleasant change to my normal beer.

Sue was right—those six bottles of red wine were not going to last the evening unless we slowed down.

I concentrated on chopping bacon and mushrooms as the fast-paced conversation swirled around me. I knew Nora and Sue had been best mates in London. But it seemed Moni had also met Nora when she was on a trip to Europe—the same trip where Moni had first met Sue. I'd heard from them how they met and fell in love, a tale that spanned three continents and Sue's coming to terms with her queerness. I looked over at my friend. Sue had always presented to me as a self-confident, capable person. I could never quite reconcile the Sue I knew with the person who'd spent ten years successfully denying her sexuality to her best friend, Nora.

"The first time I took Sue to the Pink Parrot—that's the dyke pub I used to frequent all the time," she told me in an aside, "she got hit on by the sexiest, most desirable, most unattainable woman in the whole of southern England."

"Hey," said Geraldine, in mock affront. "I was never in the Pink Parrot. And I never went after Sue—no offence, Sue."

Sue sighed theatrically. "I only have my dreams of you, Ger."

"All right, the *second* most desirable, second most unattainable woman in the whole of southern England," Nora amended.

Geraldine and Moni both grinned, and I envied their easy camaraderie.

"I'd been pursuing this woman on and off for *weeks,* and she wouldn't give me the steam off her piss," said Nora.

"Does piss steam in a warm climate?" Geraldine wondered aloud.

"Of course not. Elementary physics," said Moni. "But you're welcome to go outside and conduct your own experiment."

"Anyway," said Nora, "Sue and I were sitting in the Pink Parrot, chatting over a glass of wine. Sue had just started at my work, so I didn't know her very well, but to me it was *obvious* that she was one of us."

Sue took a gulp of her wine. "Really? How so?"
"Short hair."
"It's easy to wash." Sue patted her cropped hair.
"Short fingernails."
"I can't stand the feel of fingernails on the keyboard."

"No makeup."

"You fall for those old clichés?"

"Okay, okay." Nora threw up her hands. "It's true. I could be describing my sister, Theresa, who is as straight as Heathrow's second runway. But there is that indefinable *thing*, you know? That look, the voice, the aura. That sense of knowing. You all know what I mean, don't you?"

I did. And the way the others were nodding, they obviously did too.

"Anyway," Nora continued, "there I was, with my new work colleague from Down Under. I thought I was doing her a favour by showing her the best places to go. And she gets an obvious come-on from the woman I've been drooling over for *weeks*. I'm a good friend, so even though my heart was breaking—"

An amused snort came from Geraldine. "Puh-lease. Your heart was never in danger until you met me."

"—I made an excuse and moved away to give Sue space. And I'd gone two paces, if that, and I hear—"

"Sorry, I'm straight!" chorused Moni and Geraldine.

Sue smiled, an abashed grin. Any embarrassment she might have felt over the tale was obviously long gone. "What can I say? I have no excuse. I should have grabbed her and run off to the back of the pub."

"Grabbed who? Nora?" Moni rose from her seat and picked up the bottle of wine to top up everyone's glass.

"Strangely, no. I already got the sense Nora was going to be my very, very good friend. The other woman. I can't remember her name."

"Lex." That earned Nora a dig in the ribs from Geraldine.

"Sue did have an excuse, though," said Moni. Her quiet tones cut through the chatter. "And it's amazing she's emerged from those days as nearly normal as she is!"

Her grin encompassed me, and I remembered Sue's story of bigotry and shame in a too-small Queensland town. She had told me the bare bones of her story in matter-of-fact tones a few months after she and Moni had got together.

"A toast to Sue." Geraldine raised her glass. "Bringing the gay to outback Queensland."

We raised our glasses and clinked.

The camaraderie of the evening was infectious, and I wished Josie were there. She would be able to hold her own with the quick wits around me, but also, she would enjoy the company. I would have enjoyed hers. For all the inclusiveness, it was hard being a fifth person around two very tightly bonded couples. Small, unconscious gestures of intimacy marked their interactions—entwined fingers, sentences finished for the other. When we finally sat down to eat, Moni knew how much parmesan to put on Sue's pasta, and Nora ate the red onion out of Ger's salad. The small knowledge of closeness.

The food brought calm to the evening. We took our wine and full stomachs to the veranda, pulled the chairs closer together and sat under the ceiling fan.

"This is my favourite time of day." Sue set her glass on the table and tucked her legs underneath her. "I love the peace."

Nora glanced across at her friend. "To my ears, it's eerily quiet. I've never been anywhere where the silence is so total." She switched her attention to me. "Do you mind being alone? It's even quieter here than Mungabilly Creek."

"I'm used to it," I said. "I'd find it hard to live in a city. I've only ever spent a couple of nights in Brisbane and Sydney. Of course, that's also why I'm alone. I have few chances to meet someone living here."

"Do you want someone in your life, Felix?" Ger's words were quiet, and she regarded me steadily.

"I'd like it, of course, but I've accepted that my chances are slim." Josie's sharp, intelligent face flickered at the edge of my mind.

"Not impossible." Moni propped her chin on her hand. "Let's think. Who is there?"

Four pairs of eyes stared at me in assessing fashion. As much to distract them as anything, I said, "Actually, I've met someone. She's a friend at the moment, but I'm hoping." The memory of Josie's lips teasing mine and the strength of her grip on my upper arms flashed in my head.

"A tourist?" Sue swirled the wine in her glass.

"No. She works in the pub in Woorindi. She's been here a few weeks. Flame is her horse."

"If she brought her horse, she must be planning on staying around. It's not like taking Ripper along."

Ripper, who was curled up between Sue and Moni, looked up at his name.

"I hope so." I didn't want to say much more about my thoughts where Josie was concerned. It felt too new, too nebulous to be sharing my hopes, even with friends. "You'll meet her tomorrow. She's coming to ride with us."

"I'm looking forward to it." Genuine support and friendship emanated from Sue. "I promise not to give her the third degree."

"Please don't. It feels premature even mentioning it to you."

"We'll behave. Promise." Moni seemed delighted that there was even the possibility of someone for me. "If she's around tomorrow night, she can sample Nora's attempt at outback cooking." Moni's eyes were wide and free of guile.

"A client gave me a kangaroo for the freezer," Sue said. "Nora wants to cook."

"I've never cooked on a campfire," said Nora.

"So will your friend be here for Nora's exploded potatoes and charcoal steak?" asked Ger.

"Yes, she's got two days off in a row, so she'll bring her tent."

Nora sipped wine. "Campfire cooking can't be that hard. It's hardly survival stuff. I found a recipe. Even brought some ingredients over from the coast in anticipation of cooking kangaroo. I wasn't sure if you could get saffron out here."

"Fair bet you can't," I said. "I've never had saffron and kangaroo on the same plate." In truth, I wasn't sure what saffron tasted like. It wasn't something I'd ever seen stocked in Worrindi.

"Maybe I should serve it on a banana leaf or something?" Nora wondered.

"Good luck getting that here."

"Sue wouldn't let me build a campfire in their backyard. She said to wait until we came here, where there's nothing I can burn down." Nora grinned at her friend. "Her faith is touching."

I left most of my wine in the glass. I seldom drank wine, and it was going to my head. Maybe that's what had made me open up more than usual and mention Josie. Or maybe it was just the company of two good friends. Nora and Ger seemed nice as well. It was a pity they didn't live closer.

In the ten days they'd been in Australia, Nora and Ger had seen more places than I had in my thirty-eight years. They talked about Sydney, the Harbour Bridge climb, and the lesbian bars in Newtown. I'd been to Sydney once in my life, and I'd never been to a lesbian bar. I'd only visited the Great Barrier Reef briefly, where they were headed next to go snorkelling. And the nearest I'd come to Melbourne, their final destination, was watching the Melbourne Cup on the TV each year.

Josie had probably been to all those places and more. One day, I vowed, I would see more of Australia. I'd go to Sydney for Mardi Gras. I'd visit Melbourne and experience its cafés and laneway culture. And then I'd come home to Jayboro Station, where I belonged, and where I would always live.

It was early when Josie's car pulled into the yard. I'd been up for an hour, enough time for a coffee and a stroll around the silent campground. Josie's suggestion of a dog was a good one. I'd thought about creeping into Sue and Moni's cabin to see if Ripper wanted to come with me, but that would have meant waking them.

I exited the barn and saw Josie getting out of her car. Her mauve jeans were paired with an orange T-shirt, and her hair stuck out in a wiry mass.

"Hey." She shut the door quietly, in consideration of the sleeping campers, and waited.

She opened her arms when I went up to her, and I kept walking straight into them. She smelt of dust and coffee, and when I kissed her, she tasted of the same.

"Thought I'd come early to help with the horses."

"I was just about to get them in."

I grabbed the halters from the barn and we walked to the paddock. All seven of them were dozing in a tight huddle. With Josie to help, it didn't take long. Flame followed us across the paddock, and when she realised she was left behind, she trotted in a tight circle, her head up and her tail streaming out behind her, whinnying her displeasure.

I stopped for a moment to admire her clean lines. "You'll really have to ride her one day," I said. "The poor girl is bored senseless."

"Yeah. One day soon. Not with too many other people, though."

"How old did you say she was?"

"Seven, I think."

"I looked at her teeth, and they aren't discoloured yet. I think she's closer to five."

Josie fiddled with Budgie's halter rope and smacked him on the neck with it when he bared his teeth at Jetta. "I don't think she's that young. I was told seven."

"Then you haven't had her very long?" I frowned. I thought Josie had said she'd owned her a while.

"A bit less than a year."

Something didn't quite add up, but I figured Josie was just mistaken on her age. "She must be older than she looks, then."

"Yeah. So, I'm riding Diesel? That will be different."

I ran with the change of subject. "I'm sure he'll appreciate having a decent rider for once."

Josie looked back to where Diesel plodded behind the others, his halter rope over his neck. He'd never needed leading. "I'll be nice to him."

With Josie to help, all six of them were ready in record time. We walked over to the campground and met Nora heading for the amenities block. She waved. "Ger's gone to check her email on your veranda," she called. "Hope that's okay."

I gave her a thumbs up, and we continued to the house.

"Coffee?" I asked Josie. It struck me that she had yet to set foot in the house other than the office or the veranda.

"Yes, please."

Ger sat on the veranda, typing with two fingers on a tablet. She looked busy, so I took Josie into the kitchen through the other door. I filled the kettle and found the better of the two

90

brands of instant coffee I used. Josie looked intently around the room as I spooned coffee into three mugs. I wondered what she thought of my shabby kitchen and old-fashioned house. I'd had a couple of the interior walls removed so that Mum could get around in her wheelchair, and put in a wide shower that could accommodate it, but there hadn't been the money to update the decor. Consequently, there were ragged, unfinished edges, and the interior timber frame was visible in several places.

I made three mugs of coffee and handed one to Josie. "You can see the rest of the house later. Come and meet Geraldine."

We took our coffee outside. Geraldine looked up. "Sorry I ignored you when you came in; I wanted to reply to my brother before he went out."

I handed her a coffee. "Sugar's inside if you want it."

She breathed a heartfelt sigh. "Thank you. I've been dying for a cup."

"Ger," I said, "this is Josie. Josie, this is Geraldine."

I watched Ger's reaction to Josie. Her smile was spontaneous, and she nodded. "I'm happy to meet you. I heard about you last night. And I met your horse. She's beautiful."

"Thanks. She is a sweetie."

"I bet she's glorious to ride. All that free-flowing motion."

"Yeah. But I can't ride her at the moment. Her tack is stuck in South Australia."

"Hopefully it will arrive soon." Ger sipped her coffee, and her eyes closed in appreciation before she took a bigger gulp. "Nora took a photo of me with Flame yesterday and sent it to my brother to stir him up. She told him that Flame was a hot tip to win the Melbourne Cup this year. We wanted to drive him crazy—you don't know Young Seánie. I figured he'd be up all night scouring the internet and trying to place a bet on a non-existent horse. He's just replied to Nora's email."

"Did he bite?" Josie sat opposite Ger.

"Did he ever! It worked better than I could have imagined. He's just accused me of being a horse thief! Look." She turned the tablet so that we could see the screen. "He sent a link to an article about a racehorse. She's unbeaten in her last seven starts, and she won the Jackson Plate a few weeks back. Is that a big race?"

"Yeah. Not as big as the Melbourne Cup, but still pretty important." I studied the picture. The horse was shown in the winner's circle at Caulfield. She was chestnut, like Flame. She had a thin, white stripe down her face like Flame. Very similar.

"Apparently, this horse, Fiery Lights, was put out to pasture after the Jackson Plate to rest up for a while before the Melbourne Cup. But she's been stolen—taken from the paddock the week after the race. Young Seánie's joking about having to bail me out of an Australian jail. Which will make a change from me having to bail him out of a London one." She grinned. "Please, Josie, can I take another photo of me with Flame? I'll tell him she's a hot tip, but that I'm sworn to secrecy and can't tell him any more. That will send Young Seánie bonkers—he'll be *convinced* it's Fiery Lights."

"Of course."

"If I can get him to place a bet on Fiery Lights winning the Melbourne Cup, it will be epic. He'll murder me when I get back to London." She looked thoroughly delighted by the idea.

Josie picked up the tablet and looked at the photo of Fiery Lights. "She's very similar, isn't she? Maybe Flame's stripe is a little thinner."

I looked again. To me, the two horses looked uncannily alike. "Fiery Lights is unlikely to ever turn up again except in a can of dog food. Poor animal."

Ger got to her feet. "I'm off to see if Nora's out of the shower. What time are we riding?"

"Forty-five minutes suit you?"

"I hope so. If Nora's alive, that is. The other two were already up when I came over here."

Josie and I sat on the couch vacated by Ger and watched her bright hair as she crossed back to the campground.

"She's lovely." Josie turned to face me.

"She's taken. Her wife, Nora, is bigger than you, so be careful."

"Ger isn't my type. Oh, she's simply beautiful, all right, but I prefer a taller woman. More mature." Her gaze swept over me from head to toe. "With salt and pepper hair, and who knows how to sit a horse."

Her voice had a low, caressing tone, silkier, different to her usual pragmatic voice. I wondered what that voice would be like whispering in my ear. Or in the low moan of sexual pleasure.

Desire washed over me, and I could only stare at her, mute, with the images in my head.

"Know anyone like that?" Josie edged closer, so that our knees touched. "A woman like that would be hard to find, harder to woo, impossible to keep."

"Why impossible?" My voice croaked, as sexy and seductive as a cane toad in a drainage pipe.

"A woman like that would probably not be interested in a drifter who lives in one room above a pub and who owns nothing that doesn't fit in her car."

I picked up Josie's hand, closed in a fist, and cradled it in my larger one. I turned it palm up and unclenched each finger in turn so that her palm was exposed, as if I were Madame Tara the gypsy palmist.

I traced her lifeline. It was long and deeply etched. "You own a horse. I don't see her fitting comfortably in the passenger seat."

Josie's hand twitched in mine. "Yeah, her."

I tapped her hand. "Your heart line's broken. That means you'll have at least two relationships."

"I've already had one." Abruptly, her fingers clenched, trapping mine within. "If I could find that salt-and-pepper-haired woman, if she were interested in a woman who only has one pair of long pants to her name, then maybe I'd have a second one."

I freed my fingers from her clasp, only to encircle her wrist and tug. "If the pants were mauve, that could be a deal breaker."

"I'll dye them red. Then there's only the problem of having nothing to my name."

"Don't forget that famous racehorse you own," I teased. "Your Jackson Plate winnings will buy you most of Worrindi, if you wanted it."

"I'll breed her. Imagine the foals she'd have."

"The winner of the Melbourne Cup in 2024."

"Born and bred on Jayboro Outstation."

"We'd be on the map. I'd have to build more cabins to accommodate the buyers from the Middle East."

Josie was silent. Her fingers twisted together where they lay on her jeans. Our coffee cooled beside us. "I like you, Felix," she said. "A lot. More than I should."

That little twist of desire robbed me of any answer. When I could speak again, I said, "There's no predetermined level of attraction. We can take it how it comes."

"You're right. I'm used to seeing the end of a relationship before it's even started. I'm used to moving on—chasing a job, a new town, sometimes even a new country. To think of a relationship with no predetermined end is a new experience for me. I've never been anywhere before where I've considered stopping."

"You're still thinking of staying around?"

Her brown eyes were huge. An early fly buzzed in my ear, but I ignored it and focussed on Josie's answer.

"Yeah. I don't plan on leaving. Worrindi—here—well, it's wormed its way in."

I wanted to kiss her, and even the knowledge that in a few minutes we'd have to be over at the barn to take the Londoners out for their first ever horse ride didn't dampen my ardour. I shuffled forwards on the couch. Josie's breath puffed on my face. I moved closer still, and her eyes drifted shut. Anticipation, I hoped.

My lips touched hers, and I took her lower lip gently between my teeth. She smiled against my mouth, and then I kissed her, my mouth on hers, her lips parting under mine, our tongues together.

She was the first to move away. "We have horses to ride."

# CHAPTER 9

Nora and Geraldine turned out not to be natural riders. Nora, who seemed such a supremely confident person, morphed into a Nervous Nellie once mounted on Smoke. She was so uneasy, I took her and Ger into my schooling ring before I took them out, which was something I seldom needed to do. Nora's back was so rigid and her muscles so tense that she bounced precariously, even at the walk. Smoke, though, in her time, had seen the nervous, the tentative, and the downright terrified. Her ears flickered back and forth as she read her rider. Nora and Smoke walked slowly around my schooling ring. The reins hung in loops, and Nora held on grimly to the pommel with both hands. Smoke stopped, turned her head, and nudged Nora's foot with her grey nose. 'Hey,' she seemed to be saying, 'it's okay. I'll look after you.'

Indeed, Nora seemed to get the vibe, as she managed a chuckle and loosened one hand from her death grip long enough to stroke Smoke's neck.

Geraldine did better. Her pony was closer to the ground, which probably made a difference. Although she looked nervous, she held the reins with both hands and listened to the basics that I told her, enough to make horse and rider feel comfortable and safe.

After fifteen minutes, I judged our beginners were okay to take outside. The others scrambled for their mounts while I waited with the Londoners. Josie brought Ben over for me, and the six of us ambled out of the yard.

I rode next to Nora, who gave me an embarrassed grimace, very different to the relaxed person of yesterday.

"Thanks," she said. "I can't believe how difficult this is." She glanced over at Sue and Moni, who were riding side by side a small distance away. They were relaxed in the saddle, reins in one hand, eyes gazing over the landscape. "The rest of you make it look so easy."

"We all grew up with horses. If I visited London, you'd laugh at my terror of the traffic."

Nora's fingers loosened a little from the front of the saddle. "After this, I'm never going to laugh at anyone for anything again."

"Not until the next family breakfast, anyway," said Geraldine from my other side. "Family is fair game in our world. Teasing is too mild a word for it. Imagine if they got wind that our Nora was a scaredy-cat on a horse."

"Don't you dare." Nora's answer was half-hearted, but she smiled at her wife. "By the end of our stay here, me and Smoke will be cantering across this paddock like something out of *Gunsmoke*. But without the cacti."

She took one hand from the saddle, looked across at the others, and made a deliberate attempt to copy them. I rather thought that in a couple of days, she and Smoke would indeed be cantering across the landscape.

Josie, who rode the far side of Geraldine, jogged up closer. "Which way are we going?"

Which way were we going? My thoughts spun away from the ride and my guests. Which way were Josie and I going? All the way to the bedroom?

Ben must have sensed my inattention, as he took that moment to put his head down and buck, a tiny lighthearted movement that dislodged me only a little, but made Nora grip Smoke's mane. Smoke, the sensible old lady that she was, merely laid her ears back at Ben as if to say, 'Watch it, mister.' I controlled Ben again and circled around to my place between Nora and Ger.

"How about Nora, Ger, and I take the shortcut and the rest of you go the longer way along the creek? You can go faster."

I waited until the other three had ridden off and then took the shorter route. Nora was more relaxed with fewer horses around. Ger, too, was settling in and seemed quite comfortable, even when Jetta jogged to keep up with the horses' longer strides.

"This is amazing." Nora still had her grip on Smoke's mane but now managed to look around. "It's so beautiful in a sparse kind of way. I'm not sure I could live here, but Sue and Moni wouldn't live anywhere else, so I guess we'll be visiting a bit over the years."

"It's the colours I notice." Ger jogged up on my other side. "They're so crisp and clear. That blue sky. The red dirt, the grey-green of the gum leaves. It's strange, being able to see to the horizon. At home, we're lucky to see to the end of the street."

"What have you been doing since you've been with Sue and Moni?"

"We've been to Mount Isa—the Isa," Nora amended. "Done the mine tour, been fishing. Been opal fossicking. I found a really pretty piece. I'm going to get it made into a ring for Ger. Mainly, though, we've been catching up with Sue and Moni. A lot of sitting around and eating and drinking. Oh, and they have karaoke in the Royal Hotel in Mungabilly Creek now. We nearly shut it down with our awful singing. I miss having Sue around. She was my best friend in London. A fecking good friend at that." The slightest twinge of an Irish accent coloured her voice as she said "fecking." "I don't think she'll ever move back, though. And I don't think the people of Mungabilly Creek would let them leave—the town doctor and the lawyer. Hard to replace."

"They're both very good at what they do," I said. "Sue's helped me out with a few things, and while I see a doctor in Worrindi, I know people who go to Moni."

"Maybe Sue could give me a job," joked Nora. "I'm a paralegal. Surely she wants someone to do her drudge work."

"And I can design you some modern and eco-friendly cabins," Ger said. "I'm an architect. Not that yours aren't lovely," she hastened to add. "They're so very perfect for here."

"Maybe I'll take you up on that one day."

We'd crossed half the paddock while we'd been talking. "How d'you feel about going a little faster? A gentle trot?"

Ger nodded, and while Nora looked a little doubtful, I could see she wasn't going to be outdone. "Sure," she said.

"If you want to stop, just say." I pushed Ben into a gentle jog and looked to see how they were doing.

One minute, Nora bounced around, looking as if a collision with the ground were imminent; the next, she took a deep breath, and the tension left her body. Suddenly she was relaxed. For the first time, she looked comfortable on Smoke.

The mare's ears pricked, and she snorted as if to say, 'That's more like it.'

Ger, who seemed quite comfortable, smiled as if she had expected no less from her lover.

When we slowed to a walk again, Nora patted Smoke.

"What happened?" I asked.

"Interpretive dance."

My look of bewilderment must have been obvious. Nora grinned.

"About a year ago, Nora and I took an interpretive dance class." Ger came up on my other side. "It was my idea, something I'd wanted to do for a long time."

"Because you look fecking *gorgeous* in bare feet, floating around in chiffon with your hair loose down your back, whereas I look like a dysfunctional giraffe in my scruffy track pants and one of my brother's T-shirts."

"But then," Ger continued, "the instructor talked about relaxing and not thinking about what you were doing. She said to blank the mind and forget about what we'd learnt and what our feet were doing and especially not to think about how we looked. It was like a switch tripped in Nora's head."

"I thought about white noise," Nora said. "Static. Nothingness, and then I let the music in. Nothing else, just the notes and rhythm. Suddenly I was moving, and I didn't worry about what an eejit I looked, nor that I was ungainly and didn't know what I was doing. I was still not nearly as good as Ger, but it was better. My limbs knew what to do. And that's what I did just now. Before, I was too worried about falling off, of hurting Smoke, and about trying to get it right. Then I just blanked it all out and pretended I was falling asleep. And it worked!"

We were nearly back to the home paddock. I heard the sound of hooves and turned in my saddle to see the other three coming at a fast canter. They slowed to a more decorous pace before reaching us.

"Hey," said Sue. "Look who's a lot more comfortable now. I thought we were going to have to leave Nora to be dingo food."

The rest of the ride passed quickly. With so many people helping with the horses, we were done in record time.

"I think I need a hot bath and a massage," groaned Nora.

"Can't help with the hot bath, but I have massage skills." Ger held up small hands.

I watched with a sort of longing as Nora took hold of Ger's hands, drew her close, and whispered something in her ear. I suspected it was something about Ger's skill with her hands, as Ger reached up and kissed Nora, grabbing her butt and pulling her close.

Sue and Moni had their heads together too, but it had more of the look of conference. "We're going to Worrindi to get food for Nora's great campfire cookout this evening," Moni announced. "We've brought the kangaroo with us, but we'll get some other meat and spuds and whatever else we can that will be edible when Nora's finished with it."

"You mean I don't have to wrestle a goanna onto the flames?" Nora blinked slowly as if mentally adjusting to the idea.

"I might have lied about that." Sue looked smug.

"In that case, I'll come to Worrindi too, now that you're not going to make me do a Bear Grylls impersonation on the way," said Nora.

"I didn't say that," said Sue. "Do you have any tiger snakes in your freezer, Felix?"

"Sorry," I said with a straight face. "Only a couple of king browns. You'll have to trap a tiger snake on the way to town."

The horrified expression on Nora's face made me burst out laughing.

It seemed very quiet when the others had gone. Josie went to see Flame, and I did a quick clean of the amenities block and went around the few other campers to make sure they were okay.

I mentioned to them that there would be a campfire that evening and that they were all very welcome to come and cook their dinner on the communal fire, as well as share billy tea and damper. Josie was right; this was as good idea. I hadn't repeated it when I was by myself, because I just didn't have the sort of effervescent people skills needed to make the evening a success. But seeing how they all responded with enthusiasm, I figured I would have to give it a go.

Josie was still down in the paddock with Flame. I could see her mop of hair and mauve jeans as she stood in the shade with her horse.

I went back to the house and caught up on a couple of email enquiries about the cabins. On a whim, I searched the stolen racehorse Fiery Lights. I found a different picture of her. As before, she really did look the spit of Flame. This photo showed all of her, and she had the same two white socks on her hind legs. I enlarged the photo—maybe the markings were not exactly the same, but they were pretty close. The article said there was no trace of her—a lead on a horse in Western Australia had turned out to be false.

For a moment, I entertained the idea that Flame was Fiery Lights. But that would mean Josie was lying about Flame being her horse, was lying about wanting her near. No. I shut down that line of thought. Flame was Josie's horse, and the similarity was just a coincidence. After all, most thoroughbreds had that fine-boned look about them. And what person in their right mind would keep a valuable racehorse on some of the poorest, most drought-prone pasture in Queensland—indeed, we were in the middle of a drought. And then there was the possibility of flooding that could endanger all stock. No, you'd have to have a 'roo loose in the top paddock to consider it. If you wanted to hide a racehorse, you'd keep it somewhere on the coast, where the grass was lush and green and the horse would blend in with many others. You'd dye its markings. You wouldn't keep it at Jayboro Outstation.

I'd moved on from searching racehorses on the internet and was halfway through an email to the builder to get a quote for the third and fourth cabins when I heard the hollow thud of boots on the veranda. Maybe a new customer, although I hadn't heard a vehicle. It was Josie who walked into the office.

"Am I interrupting?"

With the light behind her, her hair was a wild and static cloud.

"No. Definitely not." I wanted to hold her, kiss her, remind myself of what we had started so recently.

She moved forwards. "I like your friends. They're good company. But I'm rather happy they've all gone to Worrindi for a bit."

"Oh?" I knew why she said it. It was there in the half smile, in the easy confidence she wore as easily as her orange T-shirt.

"Are you busy?" She advanced a half pace and placed her palms flat on the desk.

I turned back towards the screen. "Emailing a builder. Then I have to mix up damper, collect firewood, and find some pots and pans that Nora can't destroy on a fire."

"Sounds like a relaxing arvo." She leant in so that her chin rested on top of the computer monitor, and my eyes flicked away from the screen again, back to Josie. Finish emailing the builder, or kiss the woman in front of me? It was no contest. With a small sigh, part longing, part anticipation, I pushed the keyboard aside and stood, placing my palms flat on the desk opposite hers. Our fingertips brushed. Our faces were level.

"That's better." Amusement percolated through her voice. "I thought I'd lost you to a hairy builder named Clarkey with a plumber's crack the size of Carnarvon Gorge."

"His name's Macca. But you're right about the rest."

"What, that I nearly lost you?" She rocked forwards on her hands so that her lips touched briefly on mine. I forgot to breathe.

"No. Not that." A slow burn started deep in my belly.

"Then why don't you finish that email, and then I'll come and help you with the firewood?"

I nodded, caught in the spell she was weaving—the heat of the day, the heat between us, the slow movement of the ceiling fan. The air was thick and heavy. It was too early in the season for it to rain, but the bigger part of my brain wasn't thinking of the weather. More importantly, more urgently, I wondered if Josie would kiss me again. Kiss me properly.

She rocked forwards again, pressed a kiss to my left cheek, and then moved back. The second time, her lips touched my right cheek before retreating. A third time, and they grazed my forehead.

Josie's lips tilted up. She had mischief in her eyes. "I wonder where to kiss this time?"

Oh God. A thousand possibilities shifted through my mind like the flick of playing cards in the hands of a gambler.

*Anywhere*, I wanted to shout. *Anywhere that is my skin, where I can feel your lips.* And at the end of that wild shuffle of images, were the ones that I couldn't talk about out loud just yet, as we were not at that level. Her lips on my breast. My nipple. My belly.

Lower.

As if she read my mind, her gaze passed over my lips, down to the V-neck of my shirt. She must be able to see my bra in the gap, see my breasts. It took all my willpower not to look down to check. And then her gaze moved lower, down to where my crotch pressed against the edge of the desk.

It was as if she had touched me. Desire flared urgently in widening ripples from my crotch up to my belly, down to my thighs, which were suddenly trembling.

"Here, I think." The final kiss. She rocked forwards one last time, and this time, her lips lingered on mine when they touched. She exhaled slowly, and my mouth opened under hers, and we were kissing, really kissing, with tongues and with breath and with the intermingling of sighs.

The angle of our bodies meant we needed our hands to brace ourselves across the wide desk, but in that moment, the melding of our mouths was enough. The kiss ended, not instantly but in a slow part and return, and we touched again before we finally both retreated.

I stared at her, lost for words. I wasn't sure any kiss had ever made me so liquid with longing that all I wanted to do was sink to the floor and take her in my arms.

"Finish your email," she said, in a voice that was part croak. "Can I get a glass of water?"

I nodded, unsure I could trust my voice.

She disappeared through the other door that led into the house, and I returned to my email. What had I been writing about? Oh yeah, whether Macca's price still held if I got the remaining two cabins built when he was next available. I typed slowly, my mind still spinning with Josie and all that she suddenly was. I wasn't a fast typist at the best of times, but now my fingers fumbled on the keys, and I made mistake after mistake.

I hit *send* on the email just as Josie reappeared through the door with two glasses of water in her hands. She gave one to me, and even though it was warm from the tap, it was refreshing and just what I needed to soothe my suddenly dry throat.

I shut down the computer and moved over to where she stood looking at the photo of me grooming a pony in the barn.

"I'm looking at your history. It's here on this wall, right back to when you were a tiny little girl." She pointed at a photo of me and Dad. He was mounted on a rangy stockhorse, and I was sitting in front of him, hands clutching the horse's mane, a big smile on my face.

I moved behind her and wrapped my hands around her waist. It meant I had to stoop, but that put my chin on the top of her head. Her hair tickled my face. "Don't you have photos like that?"

"No. Not really."

"Any brothers or sisters?"

"No, I'm an only child. I'm guessing you are too."

Her hair tickled my chin. "You're right. Mum had problems with my birth, and so I'm it."

"It must be nice to see the pictures every day. To be surrounded by your family and their love, even if they're not around anymore."

There was a wistfulness to her words. I took these photos and what they represented for granted. I was lucky.

"I don't see my father at all," Josie said. "There seems little point. He's happy with his bottle and the races, and the life he has. I didn't see where I fit, so I stopped bothering."

I was silent. Families are only really known from the inside, and I didn't have the words to respond.

"Firewood." Josie's abrupt change of subject was clear; she'd said too much. She took my hands from around her waist, kissed my fingers, then let them drop, and turned to face me.

"I heard from the bloke in the pub," I said. "He delivered a ute and trailer load of firewood. It's underneath the house so the campers won't help themselves."

It didn't take us long to set the fire, so we left a note in Sue and Moni's cabin for the four of them to come over for sundowner drinks when they arrived back and went to the house to mix up the damper.

It took all of five minutes, so I collected two beers from the fridge, and we sat on the veranda. It was a rare moment for me when I had nothing to do. No horses to tend, no campers to pander to, no cabins to clean or fences to fix. Just me and Josie and a cold beer.

With my feet on the railing, I sipped in silence. Eventually, a cloud of dust approached the property that would either be tourists hoping for a campsite or Sue and the others arriving back. As they got closer, my friends drove slowly past the house, and Moni yelled out of the window, "Back in a few. Gotta put the meat in the fridge before it walks there of its own accord!"

I lifted my beer in acknowledgement, and the Toyota disappeared in the direction of the campground.

The clumping of feet on the veranda announced their return. I got up to offer beers. Everyone took them except Nora, who produced another bottle of red wine.

"What meat did you get?" I asked.

"Lamb chops and crocodile skewers." Moni took a long slug of her beer, her throat working as she swallowed.

"*Crocodile?* In Worrindi?" Although crocodile was sold in gourmet places and city restaurants, I'd never seen it in the Worrindi supermarket.

Sue pressed the toe of her boot into my ankle. "Yup, weren't we lucky?"

"You were."

"Nora has to cook it."

"I went to the library and searched for recipes," Nora said. "It was hard to find one that will work on a campfire, but I settled on a marinade of ginger, garlic, and sweet chilli. I think that will work."

"I've heard it tastes like chicken," said Ger.

I suspected an elaborate wind-up, so I said no more. Moni started talking about a band playing in the Commercial this Friday and did I ever go. The conversation flowed while we drank our beer.

Nora put down her glass with a thud. "I'm off for a shower before I do my gourmet chef stint. See you later."

The others were quick to follow, leaving Josie and me alone again on the veranda.

"I should shower too." When Josie pulled her T-shirt away from her skin, she revealed a strip of pale flesh. I tore my eyes away from the sight.

"No point going now," I said. "There's only two female showers." My own shower was a few steps away. Really, it seemed silly to make Josie wait. "But if you want, you can use the one here."

She tilted her head to regard me. "You don't mind?"

"No." I pushed down the thought of Josie naked in my shower. The inch of flesh I'd just seen on her belly was only a teaser.

"Then that would be great. Thanks. I'll go and grab my stuff."

She leapt down the steps and disappeared back to the campground. I used the few minutes she was gone to take a quick pass through my bedroom and bathroom, shoving dirty clothes out of sight and even giving the shower a quick wipe. I'd just returned to the kitchen to continue my tidy up when she returned. I showed her the bathroom. "Grab whatever toiletries you need."

She placed her bathroom bag on the counter and pulled out shampoo, conditioner, and soap. "Thanks, I'm good." A disposable razor followed. I thought of that razor sliding over the smooth skin and firm muscles of her calves and tried not to think of what else she might be shaving.

I returned to the kitchen and attempted to clean up, but my mind wouldn't relinquish the image of Josie in my shower. It wasn't made easier by the memory of the last woman who'd been there—Sue. Back then, I'd walked in and joined her, but Sue had made it obvious that she'd welcomed it, and I'd known from the outset that we would only have a night or two together.

With Josie, I wasn't so sure. Yes, we'd kissed, but we also had a business relationship. The money she paid me for Flame was important, and I didn't want to make her uncomfortable by mixing business with pleasure.

My feet dragged on the floor as I moved from the sink to the bench, washing, drying, and putting away items. The shower was loud, and my imagination stuttered on the thought of Josie in there, her brown curls flattened by the water, the soap slick against her skin. I clenched my fist on the tea towel. No. Don't go in there.

The sound of running water stopped. She would be towelling dry, wiping my faded old towel down her body about now. Maybe she was studying my meagre collection of toiletries, maybe taking a squirt of my supermarket-brand body lotion, smoothing it on areas dried by the sun. Or maybe she was the sort who moisturised everywhere. Then she would brush her teeth and tug a wide-toothed comb through that mass of hair. Maybe she whistled under her breath as she got dressed.

Desire hit me hard, a wallop, a clench, a thunderstruck moment. I stood at the bench, the tea towel still twisted between my fingers.

"Those dishes won't dry themselves." Mum's voice resonated in my head, but still I remained rooted to the floor.

I don't know what would have happened if there hadn't been footsteps on the veranda. Sue appeared with Ripper at her heels.

"Nora sent me," she said. "She wants to know if you have any sesame oil she can use."

My blank stare must have been answer enough, as Sue said, "I thought not. Nora wants it for the marinade for the 'crocodile.' She'll have to manage without. If she makes it through the evening without setting fire to herself, it will be a bloody miracle." Sue's gaze snapped to the doorway behind me, and she said, "Hi, Josie."

I turned. Josie was in the doorway, drying her hair on my old towel. She'd changed out of her mauve jeans and now wore the pair of brief shorts I'd seen the first time I met her in the pub.

"Can Nora actually cook?" asked Josie, who had obviously caught Sue's remark. "Or should we have a frozen pizza backup plan?"

Going by the way her lips twitched, Sue had obviously made her own interpretation of Josie's presence in my shower. "She can, actually. Pretty well. But that's in a kitchen with modern appliances and a gas cooker where you can control the heat. She's never cooked on an open fire before. It could be interesting."

I gestured to my pantry. "Take what you want. I'm going to have my shower, then I'll come over."

I left them to it.

# CHAPTER 10

By the time I got to the campground, the others already had a roaring fire going. Nora presided over a camp table full of chopped vegetables and mysterious spices that drew my attention, and she opened the lid of an esky at her feet to show me containers of meat.

"Kangaroo steaks with onion, saffron, chilli, capsicum and lime juice." There were also lamb chops and some skewers that looked like chicken, although Nora said they were crocodile kebabs. In addition, she was preparing coleslaw, and foil-wrapped spuds were already roasting on the edge of the fire.

Moni came up and handed me a beer. "Our master chef's waiting for the fire to burn to embers."

Ger and Josie were deep in conversation on the far side of the fire, and some of the other campers wandered over with chairs and drinks.

Considering Nora was working with unusual ingredients on a camp table, she seemed well in control. She crushed garlic with the back of her knife and added it to a bowl with a good splash of soy sauce, powdered ginger, and a dollop of honey.

"This is for the crocodile kebabs." She took a mouthful from her glass. I was learning that Nora and wine went together like, well, kangaroo and saffron. Whatever that was.

"You must cook a lot at home." I took a swig of my beer. "Do you need a hand?"

"I'm fine, but thanks for asking. I like to cook. I've never cooked kangaroo or crocodile before, though." She whisked the marinade with a fork, then peered suspiciously at me. "I know it's really kangaroo, as I was at Sue's when this big dusty station hand appeared in a ute with a dead kangaroo on the back and asked if we wanted any. Mrs T, Sue and Moni's housekeeper, had skinned it before you could say 'roadkill', and Ripper had eaten...well, *something*. But these crocodile skewers... The internet says that crocodile meat is firm and fine grained. This looks like chicken to me. And it wouldn't be the first time my dear friends have tried to pull a fast one."

I kept my face neutral. "You're asking the wrong person. It's too expensive for me to eat."

"So you don't have a Crocodile Dundee type with corks around her hat and a machete in her belt to hunt one for you?"

"Not around here." I waved a hand at the dry landscape. "You have to go north to the Gulf to find them."

"Hmmm."

"But just because it wasn't shot here, doesn't mean it isn't croc." I pointed to the salad. "Most of our foodstuff is trucked in. It's cattle country around here, not mung bean farms."

"Good point. I'll just have to trust them. Can you take my photo?" She nodded at her phone. "No phone signal, so I may as well use it as a camera."

I took her photo with Moni's akubra on her head and a pile of steaks in front of her, the dry landscape behind.

"Thanks." She studied the result. "*Survivor*, here I come."

There was now a small group around the fire. Sue had raked out some embers for people to cook on, and a couple of the other campers were already grilling chops. The smell of barbecued meat made my mouth water.

Nora was very efficient as she lined her steaks up on the griddle, and they were soon sizzling. Only one steak fell into the dirt.

I did the rounds of the campers who had come to join us. I didn't want them to feel unwelcome. I'd been outside of enough cliques as a child to know how that felt. I wanted guests to have a good experience at Jayboro, and including them in the activities was a good start.

Josie was ahead of me, though. It seemed as though she could talk to anyone: the couple from somewhere in America, the family with young children who had taken a year out of their lives to go around Australia, the backpackers from some Eastern European country who spoke little English. My own attempts were stilted compared to her ease.

Luckily, Nora called that the food was ready, so I didn't have to struggle for too long.

There was enough for everyone, and even though I hadn't said to the campers that there would be food, Sue took plates around to everyone at the fire.

It was good. It was better than good. The kangaroo steaks—which could have ended up dry if not cooked correctly—were melt-in-the mouth tender. Nora hadn't gone overboard with the chilli—it added a bite to the taste and no more.

Moni put down her empty plate and sat back. "That was amazing, Nora. Can you stay with us forever and cook?"

Nora flapped a hand, although she was obviously pleased by Moni's words. "Mrs T might have something to say about that."

"You'll have to give me the recipe for the marinade on the chick—er, the crocodile." Sue covered her slip well, but Nora was onto her like Ripper onto a bacon rind.

114

"So it *was* chicken! You had me convinced." She stuck her hands on her hips and glared, but her lips twitched. "Good try." She picked up the steak that had fallen in the dirt and threw it at Sue, who dodged. The steak landed at Ripper's feet and the next minute was spent prising it out of the dog's eager jaws. After all, as Sue said, chilli and Ripper didn't agree, and it would be better for everyone if he didn't eat it.

I glanced around at the campers, wondering what they would make of the banter and fireside laughter, and found they were all smiling. Even the young backpackers from Eastern Europe looked like they were enjoying themselves as they nibbled the pieces of chicken from the skewers.

My plate was empty. I left the fireside laughter where Sue was trying to persuade Nora that *chickodile* was a legitimate food, which was so tasty that Aussies kept it for themselves. I took my beer and walked into the darkness away from the fire. The glow dimmed behind me, and I kept going until the chatter was muted. I leant against a tree and rested my head on the trunk.

It was going well. The outgoing visitors had brought life and laughter to my little corner of the outback. The campers seemed to be enjoying themselves. And Josie… Josie had stirred me from my steady comfort zone and had encouraged me to try new things for the business. The guests' laughter wafting back from the fire right now was proof of her good instincts.

I wasn't really a people person. My friends were all a lot more outgoing than me. The proof of that was in their success at including a disparate group of people and making them welcome. I was more of an introvert, happiest by myself or talking with friends. More of a listener than a talker, more of an observer than a participant. Even last night, in the company of friends, I'd listened to the banter between the others and hadn't joined in much. I was probably in the wrong job. Horse training, with its solitude, was more up my alley. No people skills necessary.

However, for better or for worse, I was running the campground, and I was making a go of it. Maybe I needed to be dragged out of my comfort zone occasionally.

Something rustled behind me, and I glanced back, expecting to see a dingo, or maybe a 'roo, but it was Ripper who came leaping over. He seemed delighted that he had found me, and I looked around to see if anyone was with him.

It wasn't Sue or Moni who stepped across the sand, but Josie. Ripper ran in circles around her as she got closer.

She came to a stop in front of me. "Am I interrupting?"

"No. I just wanted a few moments by myself. I'm not used to so much company these days."

"Oh. Then I'll leave you to it. Sorry." She turned to go, and only then did it sink in that my words must have been taken as a rebuff. I took a couple of paces and grabbed her wrist.

"No, I didn't mean you. Please stay. If you want to."

She glanced at my fingers, still encircling her wrist, and I released her, but she didn't move away.

"It's beautiful here in the darkness. Even Worrindi isn't this silent."

I nodded. "I was thinking."

"About what?" As she came closer, there was a faint tang of wood smoke from the campfire in her hair.

"About how unsuited I am to be running this campground."

"I think you're doing a great job of it. Look back there." One arm waved in the general direction of the fire. "Happy campers. The cabins get more bookings every day. You run trail rides a few times a week. You must be doing something right."

"Yeah. And that's great. But the outgoing person who walks up to the campers and starts a conversation? That isn't the real me. The real me is a person who lives alone and can go days without talking to another human."

"Is that what you want to return to?" She moved closer and placed her hand on my forearm, where it hugged my waist. "Sure, you're an introvert, but most introverts still need some sort of interaction with others."

"No. Yes."

Josie looked puzzled. I wasn't surprised. I was confusing myself. "I enjoy the company of others. Sue, Moni, the two from England. And I really enjoy your company. But all of you... Well, you're a natural at conversation, at banter, at jokes. I think you could strike up a conversation with a rock."

Her teeth flashed white as she replied, "Well, only if the rock sat on a barstool and complained it was out of work and its partner had left it."

"There. That's exactly what I mean. A quick response. You set people at ease. You came here, and in no time you organised the campfires and encouraged people to come trail riding. I've lived here all my life, and I can't see what's under my nose. I'm just wishing I were more like you and the others. Confident and outgoing. If I were, my business would fly along."

"Oh, Felix." She shifted closer, and her hands settled on my waist. "And here I was, envying what you have with every fibre of my being. Wishing I were more like you, with your quiet confidence and sense of belonging." Her lips twisted. "You don't get it, do you? These faults you've listed, well, that's what people love about you. That's why you have campers coming and staying, even in the stinking weather we've got right now. You're genuine, Felix. Honest and steady. Like that rock you mentioned. And it shines out of you, and people come flocking. Those campers? They're all looking for the real outback, the one of *Waltzing Matilda,* red dirt and blue sky, and wide horizons. They're not looking for the staged tourist experience. They're looking for you. And you, exactly as you are, are part of that experience."

Her words made me pause. Maybe the negatives I'd perceived were some of the drawcards.

Instead of dwelling on that, I focussed on Josie's earlier words. "Would you really want to live somewhere as quiet as this?"

She was silent. "Yeah. I would. I've never really felt I belonged anywhere. Not with my father, such as he is, and not in any of the towns and cities we moved to when I was a kid. Not any of the places I visited overseas, either. I'm not saying I belong here, but I would give it a fair crack at staying." She heaved a sigh. "Maybe one day."

For a moment, we were silent. I loved Jayboro's isolation and quietness, but at times, I was lonely. What would it be like to have someone to share that life with? Someone who loved the outback as much as I did? Sue and Moni had found each other; they were my marker as to what was possible. Maybe. One day. But equally, they were very lucky to have made their relationship work. Who would there be for me?

Someone like Josie. The thought popped into my head. Here was a lesbian to whom I was attracted, standing in front of me and saying that she wanted nothing more than to live somewhere like Jayboro. It seemed like fate. But I was more cautious than that.

Josie wanted this right now; next week or next month, her wants might be different.

And Jayboro was mine. Handed down to me from my parents. It was my little patch of land, carved out of the main station and given to my father when he'd retired. I had Buckley's chance of finding another tiny patch of land here outside of a town. Most of the land was held by the stations, huge parcels normally measured in square kilometres. There were stations that were larger than small European principalities, larger than whole counties. If I were to leave Jayboro for any reason, I would battle to find anywhere comparable.

Sue had mentioned that to me once when she was talking generally about the division of assets when relationships failed. She'd warned me to think of that if I found a partner.

It was way too early to think about Josie moving in with me, and even if she did, I didn't think she was after what I could give her in a monetary sense. No, that wasn't relevant. But did she see me as anything more than a convenient lesbian, someone who owned land she could escape to from Worrindi, somewhere she could board her horse?

"You're here now," I said. It was a mundane comment, neutral. It didn't offer anything or any encouragement for us together.

"Yeah. And I think I'm pretty lucky at the moment. A job I enjoy. You here to visit. Flame."

Maybe, having Flame here was part of that security. Riding her—or not—wasn't as important as knowing her horse was nearby. What did I know? I'd lived here all my life. It was hard for me to relate to Josie's peripatetic lifestyle.

"I'm glad you're in Worrindi." I meant it. Life was brighter with Josie in it.

Her hands still rested on my waist, and I moved closer to enfold her in my arms. She fitted snugly under my chin, and her head rested on my shoulder. With her arms curved around my back, we stood for long moments in the darkness, pressed tight together. There was a burst of laughter from the campfire and then Ripper's little sigh as he sat next to me and pressed his body against my leg.

Josie raised her head, and the invitation was obvious. I bent to kiss her. The kiss was not one of passion, more one of exploration. Of warmth and getting to know her. Of promises, maybe, and a shared enjoyment of the night and where we were. Her tongue came out, touched mine, and then we were really kissing. Still not a kiss of passion, but one done for the pleasure of kissing without the expectation of more.

Eventually, I raised my head. "We better get back. The others will wonder where we are."

Josie moved away and picked up my hand. She threaded her fingers through mine. "I don't think they'll wonder."

She was right. When we reappeared at the campfire, hands linked, there were a couple of knowing smiles. I was glad they didn't give us the third degree.

What I was building with Josie still felt too fragile to sustain much teasing.

# CHAPTER 11

It was a late start the next morning, but the others were keen for another trail ride. Even though it was hot, the six of us went out for a gentle hour's ride.

Nora seemed more and more comfortable on a horse, so much so that she wondered aloud whether she and Ger could take lessons when they got home to England; maybe go on a trekking holiday in Scotland.

Josie didn't mention riding Flame, and I didn't suggest it but merely threw her a halter and said that Diesel had enjoyed having a better rider for once.

The others had to leave that day, but before they did, they cleaned their cabins so that I didn't have to. I protested, saying it wasn't necessary, but they did it anyway. Ger came over to get the clean linen, and they made the beds up for the guests arriving later and checked on what else was needed.

"Maybe we should run a B&B in Mungabilly Creek." Moni stuck her hands on her hips and looked around the immaculate cabin. "This doctoring and lawyering business is getting old. We could convert the house, have three guestrooms. Mrs T could cook breakfast."

"She wouldn't be happy with that," Nora remarked. "She reckons it's hard enough taking care of you two messers."

"Stick to being a doctor," Ger said. "And Sue has to stick at being a lawyer so that she can employ Nora if we come back for a six-month visit."

"Are you going to?" I asked.

"Thinking about it. We're having a great time, although realistically, we're both city people, so if we did come back, we'd probably work in Brisbane for a stint."

"Maybe we'll come back for the Melbourne Cup and see Fiery Lights win by three lengths!" Ger dug Josie in the ribs as she spoke and laughed at her own joke.

There was a beat of silence, and then Josie chuckled, but there was an edge to it, the sort of laugh someone gives when they're uncomfortable.

I looked over to where Flame grazed in the paddock. With the extra hay Josie was supplying, she was filling out and was now sleek, whereas before she'd been too thin. She looked every inch the classic racehorse.

"We have to go if we're to get back to Mungabilly by dark." Moni stepped forwards to hug me and reached up to kiss my cheek. "Thanks, Felix. It's been great. Love the new cabins."

She released me, and Sue took her place. "Hope it continues well with Josie," she whispered in my ear under the guise of a hug. She squeezed my hand and moved on to say goodbye to Josie.

The two Brits also hugged me. "We've loved visiting," Ger said. "I hope we'll get to see you again."

"I love it here," Nora said as she, too, kissed my cheek. "Think of me the next time you buy chicken in Worrindi."

"Chickodile," said Sue.

I stepped back with a grin as Nora whirled around and started chasing Sue while the others laughed. The chase ended abruptly when Nora cornered Sue against the fence and stuffed gum leaves down her shirt.

"Don't mind the children." Ger grinned. "You'd think they were thirteen, not thirtysomething."

And then they all climbed into Sue's four-wheel drive and were gone in a flurry of waving hands, Ripper's barks, and shouted goodbyes.

Josie and I were left alone. Suddenly, it seemed very calm. I'd loved having the others visit, but the silence was appealing.

Josie was also quiet. Her hands rested on a fence post.

"Need any help with anything?" she asked eventually. "I have to be back in Worrindi by early afternoon, though."

"Nothing you'd want to do. I have to clean the amenities block and the camp kitchen and empty the rubbish bins."

"Who do you think cleans the toilets at the Commercial? I'm not above such work, Felix."

She meant it. Sincerity infused her voice.

"Thanks, but I can do it. I'll be done soon, though, so why don't you come up to the house in an hour or so and we can have a sandwich?"

"Sure. I think I'll take Flame for a walk. Poor old lady looks a little bored."

"Any news on when your tack might arrive?" I asked the question idly, but the answer was suddenly all-important.

"No. I can't contact my friend. I think she might be away."

"If you want to wait until after lunch, I can walk alongside if you want to ride Flame bareback."

"I think I'll have to leave after lunch. Thank you, though."

"It seems silly, Josie, having her here and not riding her. Are you sure you wouldn't like me to try her first? Maybe if I ride her and get out all those kinks and hijinks from her not having been ridden for so long, you might feel more at ease."

"Maybe the next time I come up. I'll see if Madge will give me another two days together next week. Maybe then."

"Maybe." I hesitated. Words I shouldn't say hovered on my tongue. It really wasn't my business. As long as Josie paid her agistment fees, what concern was it of mine what she did with Flame? "That's what you said before. I'm wondering if there's something you're not telling me? Some other reason you don't want to ride Flame?"

"Is that what you think?" Her gaze slid away to lock on Budgie and Smoke grazing side by side. "No. I'm just a little nervous. You've seen me ride your horses. You can tell I'm not that capable a rider. I don't want to get ignominiously dumped on my arse in the dirt."

"Don't want to get those mauve pants dirty?"

"Purple. They're purple." She peeped sideways at me. "I'm trying to impress you, Felix, in case you haven't noticed. Trying to fit in with your life."

There was enough of a smile in her voice that I couldn't tell how serious she was. But the thought that she wanted to fit in with me was heartwarming. Was I falling for Josie? I knew that I was. But was I falling for her enough to ask her to stay, with all that entailed? *Whoa, Felix*, I thought. *Whoa girl. Just because she's the first single lesbian who's come your way for a long time, doesn't mean you should be booking her a U-Haul. Or a horse float.*

And there was still something that didn't quite add up about Flame.

We parted company. Me to the joys of cleaning the campground, plus a round of the few campers who were there. I offered a cheery hello, checked that they were okay, offered tourist advice if anyone asked, and made sure they were generally comfortable. I'd found that by doing this, someone often decided to stay an extra night or two or book a trail ride.

Maybe Josie was right. Maybe my quiet approach was the way to go out here.

"We enjoyed the campfire last night." The Americans, Suze and Larry, had chatted with Moni last night and shared stories about America.

"I'm glad. We organise them once a week or so, whenever there's enough campers to make it worthwhile."

"We're on our way down to Brisbane for a few days," Suze said. "We're going to meet up with a couple of friends, and then we'll be touring. If we come back this way in a few weeks, do you think you'd be able to arrange one for us? Our friends would love it."

"Sure, weather permitting. It will be the height of the wet season then. You might not get through, and the heat will be intense. But if you make it, I'll do it for you."

"That would be great. We'll do our best. We had a great time last night." She grinned. "Was it really crocodile your London friend was cooking?"

I grinned too. "Chicken."

"Figured. We do the same in Arizona and tell our visitors they're eating rattlesnake. No rattlesnake I know has two breasts, two wings and tasty thigh meat."

"I better get on." I lifted my cleaning gear. "Things to do. Take a card when you leave and give me a call when you know you'll be back this way. It will be my pleasure to have you stay again."

"Thanks, Felix. And please thank your…partner? Girlfriend? I'm sorry, I'm an old fuddy-duddy and I don't know the preferred word."

"Josie?"

Suze nodded.

"Josie's not my partner. She's a friend."

"Oh. Sorry. I should have kept my mouth shut."

"No worries." I gave Suze a reassuring smile so she knew I hadn't taken offence and left with my cleaning gear.

The amenities block was already sparkling clean. I suspected Sue and the others had been through there too. Both cabins would be occupied again tonight. They were going so much better than I'd hoped. Maybe this time next year, there'd be four cabins standing there. Not in a row; that was too ordered and smacked of the type of commercial campground that my guests seemed keen to avoid. Maybe up on the slight rise. That would also put them further out of reach of any flood—although if there was a wet season like that of 2011, nothing would save them from going under. Even my house, nearly two metres in the air on stilts, had had water lapping mere centimetres under the floorboards and brown snakes climbing up onto the veranda to escape the flood.

I bagged up the rubbish and went back to the house to prepare the promised sandwich. Over in the paddock, Josie's mauve pants stood out like a beacon as she led Flame around the perimeter. Flame ambled along like a compliant old nag. I really couldn't see her giving any trouble to a rider, even bareback, but then horses were unpredictable creatures, as my dad had been fond of saying. He should know. Over the years, falls off those unpredictable creatures had broken more than a dozen bones in his body.

Back at the house, I made some simple sangers with sliced bread from the freezer, ham, and tomato. I put them on a plate with the last of Nora's coleslaw from last night and carried it out to the veranda to wait for Josie.

She appeared around the corner of the veranda a few minutes later. Her face shone with sweat and her curls clung damply to her forehead.

"Tell me again why I'm working in an outback pub at the hottest time of the year and spending my time off outside in the heat?" She slumped in the chair opposite me and lifted her hair from the back of her neck.

"Because you're proving how well you fit into my life." I grinned to take the seriousness out of the words. "And this *is* my life. Heat and dust and floods and snakes and lack of air con."

"Oh yeah. There is that." Her gaze switched to the sandwiches. "These look great, and I'm starved."

I went back to get iced water and glasses. When I returned, she was midway through a second sandwich, and she paused long enough to gulp water.

"Thanks." She lifted the sandwich. "This is nice of you. I have only some odds and ends in the fridge in the camp kitchen. Nothing as good as this."

"Anytime. You help me all the time."

"I like to, Felix, really. I'm not one to sit around doing nothing, and that's exactly what I'd be doing if I stayed in Worrindi on my days off. I'd prop my elbows on the bar and drink beer until I drowned in it." She picked up a piece of tomato that fell out of her sandwich and ate it anyway. The five-second rule. "Thank you for inviting me up to meet your friends. They're such lovely people. Lots of fun." She touched my arm. "Nice to be around queer people. The people in Worrindi are great, mind you. Great and straight."

I chuckled, and she continued. "I like the sense of belonging I get around other lesbians. Shared experience maybe, I don't know. But I can see you know what I'm talking about."

I nodded. I did know only too well. Apart from Sue and Moni, there were very few lesbians around. Maybe they all left, went to the city. Maybe there were a few still closeted. But whatever the reason, in this isolated area, there was little chance for interaction.

Sometimes, I thought about looking further afield, at a bigger place. Even the Isa would offer rich pickings compared to here. There was a wider world out there. Maybe I should seek it out.

But the thought of bar hopping, looking for a partner or a one-night stand, filled me with dread. No worries if it worked for others; I certainly wasn't judging. I'd had the occasional one night stand when I'd got lucky. But it wasn't really me.

No, any relationship I had, if I were lucky enough to get that far, would probably have to be with someone who enjoyed rural life as much as I did.

I'd been silent with my thoughts while Josie polished off her sandwich, and mine was nearly untouched.

"You okay?" she asked.

"Yes. Just thinking." I took a bite of my sandwich. Josie's expression was one of interest. "Thinking that maybe I can get a start on the third cabin soon. I was thinking of putting it a bit further away, on the rise. Better view, and the guests might like that."

Josie nodded. "Less chance of getting flooded too."

So she was attuned to the land enough to realise that. Most city people didn't think of that. They saw the wide brown outback and thought it was always like this. They focused on the "drought" and forgot the "flooding rains" part mentioned in one of Australia's popular songs.

"That too," I said.

"If you faced the cabins to the northwest," Josie said, "away from the campground, the view would be better. It would compound that whole remote feel. The two existing cabins overlook the campground, which is lovely most of the time. But if there were a huge motorhome parked in the middle, it would really spoil the view."

"I thought it might be too hot with a westerly aspect."

Josie gestured to the veranda we were sitting on. "This return veranda includes a westerly side. You just walk around to the part that's coolest. If you could stretch to putting an L shape veranda on the cabins, north-west and north-east, it would give people a choice, and the shade from the roof would help keep the cabin cool."

She had a good point. I was so used to how things were that I hadn't thought what a small change like that could mean. Once again, Josie's fresh eyes had come up with something obvious that I'd failed to see.

"That's a great idea."

"Glad you like it."

I took another bite of sandwich. "You have the best ideas."

She shook her head, but I continued. "I mean it. Obviously I am completely lacking in imagination."

She moved in front of me, placed her hands on my thighs and leant forwards to kiss me. The kiss was long and soft and slow and started a lazy burn of arousal in my belly. Josie pulled away. "I have absolutely no doubts about the strength of your imagination, Felix. I just hope one day I get to find out just how creative you can be."

The heat in her eyes could have started a bushfire, and I dragged a deep, shuddering breath.

"One day."

# CHAPTER 12

WHEN I WENT ONLINE THE next morning to check for bookings, I found an email from Sue.

*Hi Felix,*

*Thank you so much for putting up with the four of us. As always, Moni and I really enjoyed seeing you, and I hope we can catch up again soon. We'll bring the campervan next time, when it's just the two of us.*

*Nora and Ger send their love and say that they had the best time. Your cabin was perfect for them: homey enough that they were comfortable, different enough that they felt they had a real outback experience. They loved the campfire too—I do hope you continue with them. They're a great idea.*

*Nora's seen the funny side of the whole crocodile thing, of course. She's not one to sulk! But she says to tell you if you're ever in London, she's going to take you to a restaurant where they serve the world's weirdest foods. I can't remember everything she mentioned, but there was clam juice and squid ink and blue mushrooms.*

*We really enjoyed meeting Josie too. She's lovely, Felix, and if it's going the way it looks to be going, I hope it works out for you. She seems very comfortable in your world.*

*Finally, before I sign off, there's one other thing I said I'd pass on. Ger's brother, Young Seánie, emailed again about Flame. The email was waiting for Ger when we got back to Mungabilly Creek. Young Seánie is a bit of a strange one, and he's big into his internet conspiracy theories. (If you want to waste an hour of your life, ask him what he thinks about the lunar landing. Let's just say he thinks it's Hollywood's greatest production ever.) But he does know his racehorses. He sent a couple more photos of that horse that went missing, Fiery Lights, and even I have to say that Flame is the spit of her. Young Seánie is convinced Flame is Fiery Lights, despite Ger telling him it was all a joke. Fiery Lights is still missing, BTW.*

*I'm not saying Josie's mixed up in anything shady, not knowingly—she doesn't seem the type to me—but do you know that all racehorses are microchipped? A unique identifier. I'm not saying you should be suspicious, but if you could get hold of a microchip reader, you could eliminate any possible doubt.*

*Anyway, now that I've wrecked your day by saying that, I have to go. Moni left early this morning for the Isa—she's attending a rural medicine workshop at her old stomping ground, the Flying Doctor base. I have no idea what they can do in a day, but it keeps her up-to-date. And she's promised to stop by the Asian grocers there and stock up for me. I'm making a slow-cooked beef massaman for Nora and Ger's last night here. It's their favourite, but I'm using kangaroo instead of beef. I've still got kilos of it in the freezer.*

*Moni and I hope to see you soon. And thank you again for your hospitality.*

*Love, Sue xo*

She'd attached a couple of photos of Fiery Lights. I studied them carefully, mentally comparing Flame's markings to those of the missing horse. Same bright chestnut coat, same thin white stripe down her face, same white socks at the rear, but looking at the new photos, I thought that Flame's socks went a little higher. Flame had filled out since she'd been with me, and she now was plumper than the racehorse. I searched the internet, coming up with a database that gave more stats about her. Fiery Lights was a five-year-old. Josie had said Flame was seven, but when I'd looked at her teeth, she'd seemed younger than that.

But really, the whole thing seemed like a bizarre coincidence. Why would a valuable racehorse be hidden in outback Queensland? Unless Fiery Lights was in foal, I suddenly wondered. A foal from such a mare would potentially be worth a lot of money and if the mare was in foal, then keeping her in a backwater where she was unlikely to be recognised would make sense. Flame was looking quite plump, but I didn't think it was the plumpness of pregnancy. I resolved to take a closer look at her later.

Then the phone rang, and my musing was cut short by an enquiry about the cabins from the tourist information centre in Winton, a good six hours away. The lady asked if she could book a cabin for some tourists who were standing in front of her right then with a creased brochure in their hands that they'd picked up in a pub somewhere. Sure, I said, and was able to book them in for a couple of days' time. I also said I'd mail some brochures to the helpful lady in Winton to add to their display racks.

My unease over Flame evaporated in the workload of the day.

The spring heat was growing, and as I'd predicted, I was getting fewer tourists coming to stay. Even fewer motorhomes turned off the highway to follow my sign, and hardly any tent campers. Even at this time of year, it could be stifling, especially in a tent.

With no visitors, I finished my daily chores earlier and retreated to the relative coolness of the office to catch up on accounts. Things were looking positive, more than I dared to hope. I again thought of the builder in the Isa I'd yet to hear back from with a starting date. Hopefully he would respond soon.

It was late afternoon when I finished. On a whim, I decided to go for a ride. Just me and Patch, my favourite horse. I couldn't remember the last time I'd gone out by myself.

I went to catch her. Flame ambled up and nudged me in the side, hoping for a scratch. I obliged, and she closed her eyes in pleasure, lower lip hanging loose. When I stopped, she put her head up and lipped at my hair, tickling my cheek. I patted her neck. She was a beautiful horse, and so good-natured. For a moment, I thought about taking her instead of Patch. But no. Josie had said it wasn't a good idea, and despite my horse sense saying otherwise, I had to respect the owner's wishes.

If Josie was Flame's owner.

If Flame was indeed a too-slow ex-racehorse from South Australia and not the missing multi-million dollar horse Fiery Lights.

That reminded me of my earlier thought that Flame might be in foal. I took a careful look at her. I was no expert, although I did have some idea of what to look for, but to me, she looked like a contented lazy animal with a hay belly on her.

I left her with a final scratch of her poll. Patch was delighted to be caught, and I led her by the forelock to the barn, where I gave her a quick brush and bridled her. I rode her bareback for a change, and soon we were jogging along the fence line towards the creek.

With the fierce heat of the day gone, the landscape had a burnished orange glow from the slanting rays of the dying sun. It was still hot but not unbearably so. A flock of galahs wheeled overhead, their cries loud and urgent. A goanna raced up a tree away from the perceived threat of Patch's hooves, and a mob of 'roos stirred for the evening from their daytime position under a tree in the shade. I came around a patch of mulga to find myself face-to-face with the patriarch, a big red 'roo. He stood directly in my way as he assessed me and Patch. He must have been nearly two metres tall, and while he was unlikely to be a threat, I drew Patch to a halt. She'd seen enough 'roos in her life not to worry, and we stood still and watched the big red as he regarded us, nostrils flaring to catch our scent. After a few minutes, he obviously figured we were no danger, and hopped off back to his mob.

I pushed Patch into a fast canter, and we swept along the track, red sand puffing under Patch's hooves.

It was a lovely time to ride. We slowed to a walk, and dawdled along. I usually rode in the mornings. Out of habit, I acknowledged. No other reason. Now I wondered if dusk rides would be popular with the campers. Not everyone rose early, and there was often more wildlife to be seen in the evenings. I'd give it a go.

It was close to dark when I got back and, after turning Patch out, I went back to the house.

Flame was still on my mind. I grabbed a beer from the fridge and sat on the veranda, looking west to where the desert stretched for ever. Sue's suggestion of borrowing a microchip reader and checking if Flame's microchip identified her as Fiery Lights made sense, but doing that made me uneasy. If I did, it was an admission that I didn't trust Josie. She'd told me Flame was hers. If I tested that, the implication was that I didn't believe her.

But that was exactly what I was thinking. There were tiny things that didn't add up about Josie and Flame. Separately, they were nothing. Together, they cast doubt on her story, especially in light of the photos Young Seánie had sent of Fiery Lights.

I ticked them off in my head: Flame wasn't the seven-year-old that Josie had said—she was closer to five, the age of Fiery Lights. Her tack was yet to arrive, and Josie didn't seem bothered about chasing it up. Maybe there was no tack. Josie didn't want to ride her horse. That was a big one. Maybe she'd been told not to ride the valuable horse. She was paying good money to keep her here in an out-of-the-way place when there were places closer to Worrindi. Places where Josie could visit her more often. I snorted softly. I couldn't fool myself that Josie kept Flame here because of me. I wasn't much of a drawcard, for all that we were forging a rapport and an attraction.

Then the biggest reason of all: Flame's uncanny resemblance to the stolen racehorse.

I wanted to trust Josie. I liked her, and I counted her as a friend. And maybe, one day, we would be more. The potential was there, burning bright between us. But trust was important to me; indeed, a lot of outback Queensland still operated on the old-fashioned principle of a handshake to seal a deal.

I should walk back inside, pick up the phone and call Narelle in the post office. Her husband, Alain, was a vet. He was the person I called when I needed a vet for my horses. He might well have a microchip reader. Maybe he would let me borrow it.

And not ask too many questions, a little voice in my head whispered. Because if I borrowed the microchip reader, if Flame's microchip matched that of Fiery Lights, then I had a big decision to make: would I put friendship and trust over a block of evidence?

I laid my head back on the back of the chair. It shouldn't be difficult. Did I trust Josie? Or at least trust her enough to give her the benefit of the doubt for a little longer? The things I should do rattled around in my head, and top of the heap was the simple fact that if I suspected a crime, I should call the police.

And what about my part in this? If Flame was that racehorse, then I was harbouring stolen goods. Unknowingly until this point, but now I didn't have that excuse. But still I hesitated. Maybe it was the way I'd been brought up, always to see the best in people. All I had was a string of coincidences and supposition. That wasn't enough to make me pick up the phone.

I would leave it another few days, until I next saw Josie. Then I would ask her about my suspicions and see what she said. It may not be the most sensible way; indeed, I was possibly about to be the idiot who tipped off a criminal. But it was the way that I was most comfortable with. I didn't want to go behind her back. Not yet, anyway.

# CHAPTER 13

DESPITE MY RESOLUTION TO LET things sit for a while, I spent the next two days stomping around in a bad mood. The only booking was for one of the cabins—a couple who stayed only a single night, but left the place in a huge mess. Dirty dishes, a frying pan burnt so badly I would need to replace it, and even a tear in one of the sheets.

Obviously, I was a bad judge of people; when they'd arrived, I'd thought they were a sweet young couple.

It was four days before Josie got a day off, and by then I was as jumpy as a bag of tree frogs. Long and complicated scenarios had played out in my head over those four days. Most of them involved the police. But I'd stuck to my decision to give Josie a chance to explain first.

My mood had swung between total belief in what she had told me about Flame and the conviction that she'd played me for a fool and that she was involved in some thieving ring, right up to her pretty neck.

She tracked me down at the barn. Knowing she was coming, I'd brought Patch, Ben and Flame in and I'd brushed all three off before she arrived, so I used the extra time to scrub out the mangers.

"Hi."

Even though I was expecting her, she still took me by surprise, and I startled, banging my head on the ring that was used to tie haynets.

She entered the stall and moved as if to kiss me. I ducked down with the scrubbing brush again. One part of me craved her kisses, but a bigger part didn't want to touch her. Not while there was so much hanging between us.

She rested an elbow on the bar. "I'll tack up. Which one do you want me to ride today? Patch?"

I straightened and put down the scrubbing brush. "No, I'll ride Patch. You can ride Flame." I pinned her with a steady gaze, watching for her reaction.

She smiled. "Felix, no. I'm still not comfortable with that idea. I've told you why."

"Then I'll ride her. It's time one of us did."

"Honestly, it's better that you don't."

I advanced a pace. "Oh? And why would that be?"

"She's difficult. You could get hurt. She's mine, so it's right that I take the risk."

She looked sincere. She sounded sincere. So why was I having trouble believing her? Some of my antagonism drained away, but the kernel of doubt remained, a nugget of worry in my chest.

I took a deep breath and exhaled slowly. Anger wouldn't help. And she was, at this point in time, my friend. She didn't know my inner doubts simply because I hadn't voiced them.

"Thing is, Josie, I'm struggling here. I'm battling to find a reason to believe you. I *want* to believe you, but it's bloody difficult."

She cocked her head and regarded me steadily, but didn't answer.

"The first thing is, I don't think Flame is your horse. I'm not sure whose horse she is, but I don't think she's yours. Why did she come without tack, grooming kit, haynet—any of the normal accoutrements of horse ownership?"

"I told you. My friend sent her and she's not a horsey person. She didn't know—"

"Please." My voice held an edge of pleading. I wanted so badly to believe her. "Just hear me out. Don't make it worse."

I dragged another deep breath. "She's not seven, as you said. She's more like five. If you look at her teeth, you'll see."

Josie opened her mouth as if to deny that, or maybe say she didn't know how to age a horse by its teeth, but she shut it again.

"And you won't ride her. Is it really because you're nervous? Or is that the person who passed her to you to look after told you not to ride her? After all, a racehorse is a difficult ride. And if she got hurt, if she broke one of her fragile forelegs in the rough outback country that she's not used to, then she's suddenly not such a valuable commodity. Whoever went to the trouble of stealing this horse presumably wants her back in one piece."

Josie was pale under her tan, her fingers clenching and unclenching.

"And the final piece? You've probably guessed that already. Her uncanny resemblance to Fiery Lights. Sure, she was a bit run-down when she arrived, but maybe that's because she'd been shunted from pillar to post, being moved around the country until she ended up here in the outback where the odds of someone recognising her are greatly reduced." I looked over at Flame in the next stall. She had her head over the bar, ears pricked, watching us. "So, Josie, what's it going to be? Are you

141

going to come clean, or do you have a good explanation for all of this—a *proper* explanation, one that makes sense of all these fragments."

My voice had risen as I spoke, and it had become loud and shrill. I stopped speaking and waited. Ben kicked the partition impatiently, and somewhere outside, a kookaburra laughed. I waited, but she didn't say anything. Her silence was its own guilty verdict.

"I want to believe you, Josie, I do." I softened my voice. "I think I'm falling for you, but I can't let myself do that if there's some big secret you're not telling me. If Flame is Fiery Lights— even that name is as if someone's playing me for a fool—then I need to know."

"And if she is?" Her voice was hoarse, but she drew her shoulders back and looked me in the eye. "I'm not saying she is, but *if* she is, what then? Will you tie me up with baler twine and lock me in the amenities block while you call the cops?"

"I would have to. If you've stolen her, or if you're harbouring her for someone else, then I have to tell the police. It's my land you're keeping her on. That makes me an accomplice. I live here, Josie. I've never lived anywhere else. I can't just up stumps and move to the next town as you do. My life is here."

Josie slumped against the wall, as if her bones had melted along with her feisty nature. "You're very quick to think the worst of me. You piece together some circumstantial evidence and take the word of some stranger on the other side of the world whom you've never met but who happens to send you photos of a racehorse that looks a bit like Flame. Thanks for the trust." Her voice morphed into bitterness. "Thanks for the friendship. Thanks for believing me."

"You have to give me something to work with." I moved to stand next to her, close enough that I could see the golden colour of her eyes. Close enough to smell her scent, a tang of citrus soap, of shampoo, of fresh sweat from the hot day. Close enough to desire her once more, to make my legs tremble under the weight of my body, to make me want to say *Forget all of this. Forget I said anything. Let's go into the house and make love.* But I couldn't. "Tell me, Josie. Please."

"I can't. I'm sorry, Felix, but you're going to have to trust me."

"Trust you? It doesn't work like that. I did. But if you want me to keep trusting you, I need more. Is Flame your horse?"

She took a step back. "No. She's not. But I can't tell you any more."

"Can't or won't?"

"Please, Felix. I can't just tell you everything."

"Then give me something to work with. Make me believe you."

"You said you were falling for me. Well, to me, that implies you must already believe me somewhat. Give me some time."

"What, so that you can arrange for Flame to be removed, so that you can walk out on your job and disappear? You talk the talk about wanting to settle down, but is that all it was? Just words?"

I had to swallow hard against the acid in my throat. The more I said, the more Josie evaded my questions, the harder it was for me to give her the benefit of the doubt.

"Trust. It's what friends have." Her voice was low.

"Seems to me that old line is used every time a person wants to avoid answering a question. *Trust me.* The ultimate manipulation."

"It's not like that, Felix. It's not."

I linked my hands behind my neck. "Then tell me what it is like."

"I can't. Not yet."

The anger that had cycled through me spluttered into life again. "Then this conversation is over."

I pushed past her out of Ben's stall, uncaring that I knocked her arm as I did. Patch's bridle hung on a hook. I grabbed it and stalked down to where Flame hung her head over the bar. I slipped the reins over her neck and palmed the bit, slipping my thumb into her mouth so that she opened it. When the bridle was on, I led her out into the aisle.

"What are you doing with my horse?" Josie's anger and anxiety were palpable.

I led Flame outside. Her ears pricked and she jogged along beside me. I shortened the reins so she couldn't get away. Finally, the poor girl was going to have a rider.

"Felix, stop! You can't ride her."

I vaulted up. Flame's muscles bunched beneath me and she trembled with excitement. From my position atop her back, I looked down at Josie. "She's not your horse. You said so. And until you give me a better reason than that, I think it's time this girl went out." I nudged Flame with my knees as she sidled beneath me, her ears pricked so hard they nearly touched at the tips. She snorted.

"Let's see how fast this racehorse can go."

I squeezed with my calves, and she danced beneath me. It took all my skill to hold her to a curvetting sideways canter as we left the yard. One large circle in the paddock, and then I turned her head away from the yard and relaxed my fingers. Released, Flame sprang forwards. Her neck stretched, and she shook her head, snatching at the bit. As we swept past the barn, I saw Josie's face, taut with worry.

Flame's stride lengthened as I let her go across the paddock, my anger evaporating with the thrill and speed of a good horse. Flame was a champion. She had to be. Her stride was smooth and flowing, and even without a saddle, I felt secure on her. She was sweating in the heat, her coat shiny beneath my jeans, her neck damp. But her ears were pricked, and her hooves thudded the dry ground in an even, four-beat rhythm.

I should be feeling sadness, sorrow at the imminent failure of what could have been a relationship with Josie. The anger that had precipitated my wild ride was gone, and there was only the exhilaration of the gallop. Flame was well named. She flickered across the red dirt like a bushfire.

And then suddenly it wasn't right. Flame's effortless gallop became a struggle. Her head lowered, and I heard her wheeze to draw breath. I tried to ease her back, but she set her jaw, took the bit between her teeth and ploughed on. Yet, her sides heaved, and the rhythm of her hoofbeats became slower, uneven. She stumbled, and I nearly pitched over her head but regained my seat with a yank on her mane. Still she galloped on.

I had to stop her. Obviously, the weeks of lazing around in the paddock had taken a far greater toll on her fitness than I would have expected. I sat back, tried to collect her between hands and legs so that I could slow her, but she wouldn't have any of it. Her ears flattened, and her neck set like iron. I shortened one rein, drove her in a circle, gradually tightening the circle until she was forced to slow. She dropped back into a jarring trot and, finally, a walk. I drew her to a halt and slid to the ground.

Flame looked in a bad way. Her head hung low, and her wheezing breath sounded loud in the stillness. Her flanks heaved like bellows, and she braced her forelegs as she sucked in air.

"Easy, girl," I crooned to her. "Easy, sweetheart." My hand made long sliding strokes trying to calm her. Her eyes rolled white. I stood with her in the blazing sun, waiting for her to recover. Still she laboured. I frowned; this seemed more than an unfit horse. This was a distressed horse.

I took the reins over her head and encouraged her to move. We were a few hundred metres from the barn. It took a little coaxing, but Flame started to move. At first she was slow, but as we walked, she recovered, and by the time we reached the barn, she was nearly back to normal.

Josie was not in sight. I led Flame inside, topped up the water bucket, and watched as she drank deep. Her extreme reaction to the exercise was both a confirmation and a rebuttal of my suspicions. She was obviously a racehorse. But was there something wrong with the mare, more than simple lack of fitness? And if there was, it had to be recent. Fiery Lights had won the prestigious Jackson Plate only a few weeks ago. Alternatively, if she had a chronic condition, then she couldn't possibly be Fiery Lights the racehorse. She must be simply Flame, the ex-racehorse from South Australia.

Once I was sure Flame was going to be okay, I left the barn in search of Josie.

# CHAPTER 14

Josie's old car was parked in the campground, so she still had to be around. I figured she'd find me, so I returned to the house and booted up the computer.

I brought up images of Fiery Lights. Similar to Flame in some, a spitting image in the others. It was impossible to tell from the photos alone.

There was movement on the veranda, and then Josie entered.

"I've put Flame in the paddock," she said without preamble. "I don't know what you did to her, but she doesn't look too happy."

I glanced at Josie. Worry for the horse darkened her eyes. And the doubts thrown up had made me unsure. Abruptly, I decided I'd level with Josie. But before I could say anything, she came over to the desk.

Her palms rested flat on the timber, and she leant forwards. "Felix, I know I'm being evasive here. I know it looks bad. But while you're right in some respects—Flame isn't my horse—I think you're wrong in others. I was told not to ride her, but I wasn't told why. And I know I'm going to ask a lot here, but I'm asking you to trust me for one more week. I'm going to contact her owner and see what I can find out. Hopefully, we'll be laughing about this next week, and Flame will still be grazing in your paddock. Can you do this? For me?"

I was silent, then I gave her a nod, a slow up and down. "Okay. But I—we—need answers here. Real ones. I rode her, Josie, and she was as fast as the wind. At first, I could see her streaking past the post to win the Jackson Plate, she was that fast, that flowing, that strong. But then she started labouring, her breathing was difficult, and she was in trouble. That's when I pulled her up and led her home."

Josie was silent, but her gaze never left my face.

"Did you know that would happen?"

She shook her head. "No. But then, of course, I've never ridden her. Does she need a vet?"

"I don't think so. Not at the moment. But I'll keep an eye on her. If I think she needs a vet, I'll call one."

"Thank you." Her words were slow and sincere. "You probably don't believe me, but it's that concern for your horses that led me to bring Flame here in the first place." She straightened. "I'm going back to Worrindi. I'm not running away. I don't want to run from you, Felix. And I don't want to leave Flame."

I nodded and switched my gaze back to the computer screen. It seemed safer that way. If I kept looking at Josie, maybe I'd tell her too much. Maybe I'd spill the beans about microchips and how I could find out for sure if Flame was Fiery Lights. I didn't want to tell her that, not yet, anyway. I wanted her to tell me the truth, and I'd already said more than I should.

Out of the corner of my eye, I saw her turn and leave. I stayed at the computer, and thirty minutes later, I heard her car head back to the road. Only then did I stand and stretch, then dropped my head into my hands.

I jammed my hat back on my head and went to check on Flame. She was lying down in the paddock. I crouched next to her. She didn't look distressed, just tired. I stroked her neck. If she had a microchip, the tiny chip, no bigger than a grain of rice, would be implanted at the crest of her neck, under her mane. I could call Alain and beg his microchip reader, or I could call the police and tell them my suspicions.

Flame turned her head and nibbled one of the buttons on my shirt. "You sweet thing," I murmured, rubbing her forehead. "I'll hate to see you go."

Not just the money, but Flame, the horse. The darling of the paddock.

I wouldn't call the police yet. All I had was suspicion, circumstantial evidence, and an unwell horse. Hardly enough to make them rush out and arrest anyone. *Arrest Josie*, a voice whispered in the back of my head.

I straightened and went back to the house to call Alain.

He answered on the second ring. "Felix," he said, his cheerful voice booming down the line. "Nice to hear from you. Narelle tells me you're getting a lot of enquiries for your cabins. Good onya!"

"Thanks. Narelle's been great. I think she refuses to let tourists out of the post office until they take a brochure. A lot of my guests say they learnt about Jayboro from her."

"My darling wife is a pushy one."

"And you love her for it."

"I won't trade her in anytime soon." There was a smile in his voice. "Now, did you call for me or for Narelle?"

"You, actually, Alain. I'm wondering if you have a microchip reader?"

"I do. It normally collects dust in the clinic, and now you're the second person who's asked me that in a week."

Was someone else suspicious about Flame? "Oh?" I asked. I tried to keep my voice neutral.

"There's a dog hanging around town, not a wild one, a stray. Gentle thing. Bazza at the garage wondered if she was with some tourists and got lost. Or dumped. So he had me take a look at her. No microchip."

"Poor thing."

"Anyway, why do you want it, Felix? Are you buying a horse and want to check it?"

He'd given me the perfect reason. "Something like that."

"When do you need it? I'm coming past your door in a couple of days. If that's soon enough, I could drop it off. Or do you want me to take a look at the animal with you?"

"Thanks, but I think I'll be okay." I hesitated. "I did want to ask you about a horse, though. Not one of mine, which is probably a good thing."

"Fire away."

"A thoroughbred. Ex-racehorse."

"Aren't they all. Racing industry needs to look after the animals they let go. But anyway, you were saying?"

"Horse looks fine. Not currently in top condition, but should have some residual fitness. Anyway, I galloped her. She went like the wind at the start, then started labouring. Wheezing. Had to walk her home. Didn't seem like purely an unfit horse to me. Is there something chronic that would cause that?"

"Plenty of things. Recurrent airway obstruction, but I'd expect that to have shown in milder symptoms before then. How old is the horse?"

"Fiveish. Sevenish. Don't know exactly."

"If it's only hard exercise, my money would be on some sort of myocardial disease. Heart disease, y'know. Probably following on from a chronic infection. If that's the horse you'd considering buying, I'd run far, far away."

"Different horse. Would something like that have come on instantly after just one burst of hard exercise?"

"Highly unlikely. Chances are if it's that severe, the horse has had it a while. Maybe it only shows up with a long gallop, but it's likely to get worse, not better."

"Thanks, Alain." I shifted the phone to my other ear. "That's been really helpful."

"Still need that microchip reader, or have I talked you out of the horse?"

"Still need it, if you don't mind. But I have to go into Worrindi anyway. I'm out of milk, eggs and practically everything edible. Can I come by tomorrow and pick it up?"

"Of course. Narelle can take it to the post office, if that's easier."

"Thanks. Tell her I'll come at lunchtime. I owe her beer and lunch for all the tourists she's sent my way."

"I'll do that."

Too late, I remembered that Josie worked in the only pub in Worrindi. Hopefully, she wouldn't be working then.

I said goodbye to Alain and hung up.

I was in Worrindi by noon the next day. True to his word, Alain had left the microchip reader with Narelle. The post office was quiet, so she pulled it out of its pouch and gave me a quick rundown on how to use it. It was as simple as a supermarket barcode scanner, which it basically was.

"Lunch?" I asked her. "My shout."

In answer, she grinned, grabbed her bag and hollered to her assistant that she was off for at least a couple of hours.

Narelle loved her beer, and she also loved the chicken parmigiana that the Commercial did, so there was no point asking her where she wanted to go. There was little choice anyway in a town the size of Worrindi.

There was no sign of Josie behind the bar when we walked in, and I was quietly relieved. I wasn't avoiding her, not exactly, but I didn't particularly want to see her yet. Not until I'd had a chance to scan Flame's microchip.

We ordered and sat at one of the high tables by the window, where we could see the street. The food arrived quickly.

"Hear you've been busy." Narelle dipped a chip into the ketchup and ate with her fingers. "I tell anyone who asks where they can camp to go to Jayboro. Nice to know some of them do."

"Quite a few." I cut a piece of battered fish and put it in my mouth. It was scalding hot, and rather than spit it out again, I took a long draught of beer while Narelle laughed.

"Some of them come back through town after they've stayed with you. I always ask how they enjoyed their stay. Figured you'd like the feedback."

I nodded. The roof of my mouth was already blistering from the fish.

"They love the peace. Love the cabins. They think your dinner packs are overpriced—"

I snorted. "They should try grocery shopping here and see what it costs. And the fuel and my time—"

152

"You're preaching to the choir. I'd love to have city prices. Most of them enjoyed the horse riding, although there was one miserable old bugger who complained about the horse he was given. It sounded like you'd put him on Ben, from what he said."

"Extremely large bloke?"

Narelle nodded.

"I remember him. He must have weighed close to 150 kilos. Ben was the only one up to the weight. He said he'd ridden before, so I thought he'd be okay. He could barely control Ben, so I cut the ride short and gave him half his money back."

"You're too good to people."

"That's the hospitality industry. You have to take what walks in the door."

Narelle cut a huge chunk of parmie and chewed for a moment. "I also hear you've started doing evening campfires. A couple of people said they loved them."

"That's good."

"I heard too that your partner is great at making people feel at ease." Narelle nailed me with her gaze. "Care to tell me who they're talking about? They definitely said 'partner'. Do they mean business partner? Or *partner* partner?"

I glanced around the bar to make sure Josie hadn't bobbed up behind the counter.

"I think they mean Josie, the barmaid here."

"Josie? *Josie!* I didn't know—"

"Sshh."

"She's in the closet?"

"No. I just think she's rather private about her life."

153

"Fair enough. I'd probably be rather private about mine if I had the choice." She drained the last of her beer. "Do you want another?"

"Thanks. Light beer, please."

"That's what I'm drinking. I have to at least pretend to work this afternoon. I can't just fall asleep under the counter."

Narelle returned with the beers and sat back down. "So, as you have no secrets from me—"

"Well, only small ones."

"Small ones are allowed. But as you have no major secrets from me, are you going to tell me about you and Josie?"

I was silent. I'd just lied to my oldest friend. Because I *did* have a major secret I was keeping from her, the possibility I was harbouring a stolen racehorse. That would have to stay a secret for a little longer, at least until I'd had a chance to check Flame's microchip. And after that, one way or another, I'd know.

"Felix?" Narelle leant across the table and poked my chest. "You in there?"

"Yeah. Sorry. I was miles away for a second."

"Thinking about the big secrets you're keeping from me?"

"Now that you mention it…" I played it for a joke, knowing that Narelle would see through any serious denial.

"Tell me about Josie," she prompted. "You owe me the gossip. Nothing happens in Worrindi. Nothing more exciting than Pat's bullocks breaking through the fence and running down the main street. And that happens too often to be classed as major excitement."

"I don't have much to tell you, Els. We're attracted to each other—that I know—but we're not really girlfriends. Not officially. And it's not exactly straightforward."

"Because she's a temporary worker living in the pub?"

154

Narelle's voice had crept up in volume, and it didn't feel right to be discussing Josie while we were in her workplace. "Sshh, keep your voice down a bit. Yeah, that's part of it, falling for someone who'll probably be gone to Tibooburra or Tumbarumba or Thargomindah when she gets bored with Worrindi."

"And that would bother you? You're not up for just a fling?"

"I know it's never stopped me in the past. But maybe I'm getting old and staid—"

A disbelieving snort from Narelle.

"—or, I dunno, maybe I am looking to settle down. I just know I'm not rushing into a fling. Indeed, I haven't. Yet."

"If it helps your thought processes, I hear Josie's been asking around town if anyone has any small houses or granny flats to rent. And I know Madge and Chris love her and would be delighted if she stayed on. Madge said it would be nice not to train up a new backpacker every three months and go through the endless process of them having a fling with someone unsuitable and then leaving when they find they can't avoid them. So maybe she's not as transient as you think."

"She didn't say."

Narelle grasped my hand. "You never know what will happen."

She was correct there. You never do know.

Back at Jayboro, I took the microchip reader and, following Narelle's instructions, I passed it over Flame's neck. Sure enough, there was a chip. I took the reading, and went back to my computer. Using the login that Narelle had given me, under pain of death to delete when I was done, I accessed the online database.

The microchip implanted in Flame's neck was registered as belonging to Fiery Lights.

I rubbed my eyes and peered at the screen again, in case the information had somehow changed. Fiery Lights. Chestnut mare. Five years. Registered owners listed as a Sydney syndicate. The name of the training yard from where she was stolen.

I sat back in my seat. This was getting complicated. I'd been pretty convinced the two horses were one and the same. But Flame's heart condition—if that's what it was—had made me doubt. And now there was this information—what should be irrefutable evidence that Flame and Fiery Lights were one. But how could a racehorse that had won the Jackson Plate only a couple of months ago have such a chronic condition? That didn't add up at all.

It was all too hard, so I did what any sane person would do in the circumstances: I put it out of my head and went to clean the amenities block.

# CHAPTER 15

Josie returned a couple of days later. I'd spent the days in between working: I saw to the cabins, maintained the campground, and tended to the horses; the endless round of work that was my life.

I took Flame out once more and, again, rode her bareback. This time, I didn't gallop but kept her at a steady trot to see how that exertion affected her. She was fine for the first few minutes, but then she started to flag and show signs of distress, so I immediately dropped back to a walk to let her recover.

A few things had straightened out in my head over the two days, the most important being that I couldn't keep this to myself any longer. Unless Josie had some compelling information, I would go to the police.

Josie found me repairing the fence that separated the campground from the paddocks. Jetta, the little greedy guts, had pushed through it in search of greener grass. Not that there was much on either side. The rains had still to come to Jayboro, although there were reports of rain elsewhere in outback Queensland.

"Hi," Josie said.

I straightened. "Hi."

She looked tired, as if she'd had a late night, and there were black circles under her eyes. Despite that, she looked great. Her riot of curls was tied back into a bushy ponytail, and she wore shorts rather than the usual mauve jeans.

"I'm sure you want to talk to me about all sorts of things," she said. "But before you do, can you come with me for a minute? I have something for you. Well, I hope it's something you'll want."

I'd nearly finished the fence. I put down the tools and followed her to her car, which was parked in the shade of the barn. She opened the door, and I saw the dog in the passenger seat. It was a golden retriever, very thin, with a reddish rather than pale coat. The dog's eyes were worried.

"This is Tess. She was either deliberately dumped by a tourist, or she got separated from her people. She's been living rough around Worrindi for a couple of weeks."

"I've heard of her," I interrupted. "Alain the vet mentioned her."

"That would be right. He checked to see if she had a microchip. She doesn't, only a collar tag with her name. No phone number. She's friendly—she's obviously been around people a lot. Had several litters of puppies too, according to Alain, but she's only maybe four or five. He thinks she may have been in a puppy farm, and now that she's bred her litters, they've dumped her. But why dump her out here is beyond us. Maybe she had a home after the puppy farm."

I held out my hand to Tess, who sniffed it cautiously, then gave me a tentative lick.

"Alain has given her shots, cleared up her fleas, given her heartworm tablets, and fed her up a bit. She's ready for a home. You mentioned a dog. I wondered if you would give her a forever home."

Tess looked at me, and I looked at Tess. Already, my heart was melting towards her. Puppy farms often dumped their animals when they no longer served their purpose—just like the racing industry.

"A retriever, though? It's not the ideal dog for out here. They're massive absconders, and there's a lot of stock around. She'd be shot by a farmer if she escaped, or she'd eat poison bait—there's so many wild dogs doing damage that the baiting program is in full swing."

"I don't think she'll run off." Josie petted Tess's head, and the dog pressed into her hand. "She's been hanging around the back of the pub, staying as close as she can to people. Alain said she had bite marks on her hindquarters that got infected. Chances are she's already learnt the hard way about the wild dogs. She dug herself a couple of wallows in the dust at the back of the pub and she slept there. But she made them in a corner where there was a fence on two sides to reduce the chance of her being attacked."

I crouched by the side of the car so that I was eye level with Tess. "Hello, girl. You've had a hard life so far. Would you like to live with me, or do you want a comfortable house in town?"

It was as if she understood me. She stood on the seat and gave a tentative wag of her tail. Then she jumped down and came and sat next to me. My hand automatically reached down to rest on her head. I'd missed the comfort and friendship of a dog.

Josie watched her. "Looks like she's made up her mind."

I walked a couple of paces from Tess, just to see what she'd do. She stood, wagged her tail once, and moved over again to sit beside me.

I always was a sucker for a hard-luck tale. Tess deserved a home and someone to love her. "She can stay, but on the proviso that she's okay with horses and strangers. I can't have a dog that's difficult with new faces. That wouldn't go down well."

Tess gazed up at me as if she were listening.

"And I'm serious about the escaping thing. If she's a wanderer, that won't work. I can't be worrying whether she's out harassing stock or eating poison bait. If she's that sort of dog, she'll be better off in town where someone can keep an eye on her."

"I really don't think she would. She seems to know she's safer around people. She barely left the rear of the pub the past week. Then Alain came and got her, and she's been at the vet's ever since." Josie hesitated. "Felix, I know this is not what you expected, and you're probably still angry with me about Flame. But honestly, I saw Tess, and I thought you were made for each other. I'm not doing this to win you around. I hope you believe that."

I did. The raw appeal in Josie's voice was compelling. And Tess obviously needed a home. Josie hadn't conjured her out of thin air.

"Thank you. She's a sweetie. I hope she's fine here. But Josie, this won't change anything about Flame. You have to let me say what I need to say."

"I understand. I didn't expect it to. I've been thinking too."

"We need to talk, but I'll have to finish the fence I was working on first. Come up to the house in half an hour and I'll put the kettle on."

There was a moment of wide-eyed disbelief, as if she hadn't expected me to be civil, and then she nodded and walked off. Tess watched her leave and took a small step after her. I didn't say anything, just started walking back to the fence repairs. Tess looked at me and then came after me, to lean against my side, right where my hand would find the top of her head.

"Looks like it's you and me, Tess."

The repairs didn't take long. I went back to the house and put the kettle on. Tess had followed me in, and she curled up in a corner of the kitchen, her back to the wall. She watched me with cautious eyes. I would pay attention to Tess later. Right now, I had to talk to Josie. She appeared a few minutes later.

"Can I come in?"

I gestured to the kitchen table where I'd put the mugs of tea.

She sat and picked one up.

"I've been doing some research." I dunked my teabag up and down in my mug. "But before I tell you what I've learnt, why don't you tell me how you came by Flame?"

She was silent for a few moments, then she looked across at me. "It's not a pretty story."

"I still want to hear it."

She sucked in a deep breath and blew it out. Took a sip of her tea. It was still scalding and must have burnt her mouth.

"About six months ago, I was working, cleaning motel rooms in Longreach."

I nodded. The town was a centre for outback Queensland, maybe five hours from Jayboro.

"There was a bloke staying there. He must have been in the same room for over a week. At first, he put the *Do Not Disturb* sign up, and of course, I respected that. Then he switched the sign to tell me to clean his room. So I went in. You know the drill: cart full of clean sheets, those little sachets of shampoo and tiny bars of soap that are never enough. He was in his room still, watching TV. That wasn't a problem. He was harmless. We weren't supposed to go into a room if the customer was there, but really, it was up to us.

"Over the next few days, I'd clean his room, and he'd always be there, watching daytime soaps. We got to chatting. Somehow—I'm not exactly sure how—I mentioned that I'd owned horses in the past and that I missed riding. Barney—at least that's what he said his name was—said that he had a horse too. We talked a bit about riding. He wasn't bullshitting. He obviously knew his stuff.

"After a few days, he said he needed to find somewhere quiet to agist his horse for a few months. He said Flame was down in South Australia, but he wanted to bring her to Queensland and place her somewhere. Then when he took up his new job—something in the Isa—he would come and get her."

She paused and took another mouthful of her tea. Outside, I heard magpies gargling their song, and somewhere there was the sound of an engine revving. I hoped it wasn't a new guest.

"He offered me money," Josie continued. "Quite a lot of money. Certainly more than it would cost to agist a horse. Of course, I guessed it was dodgy. I didn't challenge him on that. When you move around a lot, do the lower paid jobs, you learn to overlook a lot of things." She looked into her mug of tea as if she could drown all the uncertainty and wrong decisions in its depths. "I said I was moving to Worrindi—by then, I'd already got the job at the Commercial. Barney said that was fine. Closer to the Isa, he said. He asked me to keep a lookout for a place for Flame."

My hand shook, and I put my mug down on the table before it spilled. If I'd wanted proof that Josie had an ulterior motive, she'd just provided it. Stupid me had thought she'd liked me. Wanted to spend time with me. I'd just been a convenient place to park a horse. A stolen horse. Everything Josie told me pointed to that.

"Go on," I said, and my voice was hard and flat.

"I'd been in Worrindi for a couple of weeks, and had pretty much forgotten about Barney. He hadn't contacted me again, and I figured he hadn't been serious. It had sounded too good to be true. But then he called me—we'd exchanged mobile numbers in Longreach. He asked if I was in Worrindi, asked if I'd found anywhere for Flame. By then, I'd already met you and knew you kept horses."

"And you thought poor Felix needs the money. She won't ask too many questions."

"I don't expect you to believe me, but it wasn't like that."

I let it pass. I needed to find out about Flame. Now wasn't the time for wounded pride.

"I found I liked Jayboro. I liked coming here. And yes, it was quiet enough that it was exactly the sort of place that he wanted me to put Flame. So I told him I'd take her. He paid me three months' agistment via Paypal. It was a lot of money, Felix. More than I could expect to earn working bar at the Commercial in the same amount of time. Once I saw the money, I stopped thinking about what could be wrong. I know, that's no excuse, but it's the truth. What is a tiny amount of money for some people is a fortune for me. From what you've told me, you've never worked a minimum wage job. You've always had your protected life here on Jayboro." Her lips twisted. "I don't begrudge you that—how could I? But equally, I have to look after myself. And placing Flame on agistment was a big boost."

"How much did you get?"

She named a price that was twice what she was paying me—and I'd thought that was generous.

"He told me to keep her quiet and not to ride her."

"Did he tell you how long he wanted you to keep her?"

"Not really. He's paid another month, though. I didn't hear from him, but the money arrived via Paypal again."

"And you didn't question this? Honestly, Josie, money doesn't come for nothing. You, of all people, should know this. Somebody rocks up, out of the blue, and you just go along with it?"

Her fingers clenched on her mug. "Easy for you to say. Have you ever been poor, Felix? Have you ever sat in a shared backpacker dormitory, or a tent, or your car, and counted your dollars, wondering if you've got enough fuel to get to the next town where there might be a job? Have you ever pinched fruit from backyard trees to get something to eat?"

I was silent. I hadn't. Even when times were tight, I'd always had food and shelter, thanks to my family.

"Sure, there's Centrelink benefit, but it's often more trouble to get than it's worth. I've hardly ever claimed it—usually, I've found a job before I'm eligible for the payment. Judge me if you want, Felix, and I know you are, but even though Australia's the land of plenty, it's still not easy when you're like me. I should have asked more questions, but I didn't.

"You may find this hard to believe, but the first I heard of Fiery Lights was when Ger mentioned it." Her lips twisted. "I don't follow racing. Why should I? Money for gambling is a long way down my list of priorities."

I was silent. Josie's story fit the pattern of Flame being stolen. And being told not to ride her—well, that would fit either way. Don't ride her because she's a famous racehorse and she mustn't get hurt, or don't ride her because she has heart disease and it might damage—or kill—her.

Josie sat opposite me. Her raised chin and hunched shoulders made her look as if she was waiting for the axe to fall or for me to lift the phone and call the police.

I should. I knew I should. But Josie's story had the ring of honesty to it. I could see that happening. And while there was a twist of hurt that Josie had liked me more for what I could offer than for myself, I pushed past it. Whatever her reasons for coming to me in the first place, that was then. The now was that she sat here waiting for me to make a decision. I held her future in my hands. Sue would know what to do. I thought about calling her, but then decided against it. I didn't want to drag her in if I didn't need to. If I called the police, there was a good chance Josie would be arrested for…well, something. Maybe I would be as well. Possibly not horse stealing, but probably some charge of receiving stolen goods. But then again, my decision shouldn't be influenced by Josie's situation.

But it was. I liked Josie. Liked her a lot. And even if she'd come to me initially because of Flame, I didn't think that was entirely the case now. The liking and attraction between us ran both ways. Of that I was sure.

Abruptly, I came to a decision. I would give Josie the benefit of the doubt—for now. I'd tell her what I'd found about the microchip. Maybe she could shed some light on that. Maybe not. But for now, maybe we could work together to solve the mystery.

# CHAPTER 16

JOSIE WAS CLEARLY AS BAFFLED as I was by the microchip. I took her out to the paddock and read Flame's chip once more and showed her on the database that it matched the one registered to Fiery Lights. I told her, too, what Alain had said about heart disease in horses.

"I could call Barney." Josie scratched Flame on the neck, and the mare nudged her in the ribs for more. "Ask him why I can't ride Flame. See what he says."

"And tip him off in the process that you're suspicious? Great idea." I couldn't quite keep the sarcasm out of my voice.

"Not if I put it that I just would like to ride her. After all, he said he wanted me to look after his horse because I knew about horses. It's not so stupid."

When she put it like that, it made sense.

"I'll miss her." Josie watched Flame nose the bare dirt, searching for grass. "I've got fond of her."

"Me too," I admitted. "She's such a calm presence. Although it was different when I rode her. Then she was fired up, ready to gallop. If she's not Fiery Lights, I'm sure she was a racehorse at some point in her life."

"It's just a matter of which racehorse."

The sun beat down. It was baking in the middle of the paddock with no shade. I turned to walk back to the house,

Tess at my heels. So far, the dog had shown no inclination to stray.

There were still no campers, which was hardly surprising. Now, only the hardy or insane were holidaying in the outback.

"I have to go back to Worrindi." Josie turned to face me. "I have to work this evening. I wouldn't normally have come, but I wanted to see you. Wanted to see if we could mend things between us. Can we?"

I moved so that I could rest my arms on the rail of the gate. "I don't know." Tess came to sit by my feet.

"Do you believe me?"

"I don't know," I said again. "I believe you more than I did before. After all, if you were up to your neck in this, you would have just disappeared. With or without Flame. The fact that you're still here runs in your favour."

She nodded, but didn't speak.

"As for us? Is there an 'us', Josie?"

"I thought there was, that we were getting to that point. I thought you were with me on that."

I couldn't answer. She'd lied to me, repeatedly, and I wasn't sure if I could live with that. Trust had been the bedrock of my family and my friendships. Could I sustain a relationship without it?

"Okay, then." Josie turned away when I didn't answer. "I'm going to work. I'll let you know if I hear from the owner or if anything changes. Are you going to call the police?" Her voice was offhand, but the tension radiating from her was palpable.

"No. Not yet. I want to check a few things first."

She didn't ask what, and in truth, I wouldn't have known what to answer. I hadn't made a list or a firm plan. I just wanted time to make what I hoped would be the right decision. Over the years, I'd seen what a too-hasty call to the police could do.

Shit stuck on people, and in small communities, it was hard to shed. I owed it to Josie not to drag her in until I knew it was the right thing to do.

"See you, then." She walked off, and I watched her leave— watched the muscles in her legs, the tight fitting shorts, the sway of her hips and the mass of brown curls bouncing on her shoulders.

My stomach clenched. The attraction was still there. I wanted to kiss her, hold her, twist my hands into her hair. I wanted to push her away, shout at her, sift through her lies.

I didn't know what I wanted.

I turned away. I had things to do before I saw Josie again.

Back in the house, I fed Tess with some of Ripper's kibble that had been left behind, refilled my water bottle, sat at the computer, and opened the search engine. This time, I wasn't looking for pictures and news stories. I wanted rumours, chatter, and the conspiracy theories and gossip found in forums and chat rooms. At first, all I turned up were the news stories. They were basically same as the one Ger's brother had sent across. Fiery Lights disappeared from the training yard in New South Wales, and hadn't been seen since. She'd been turned out in a paddock, and although there was CCTV coverage, one far corner had no camera. The thief must have known this, as apparently there was no footage of her being removed from the paddock. The paddock adjoined an easement. Someone had cut the fence, led her out, and then repaired the fence in a makeshift way so that the other horses wouldn't get out.

The articles talked about her ability as a racehorse, her prospects for the big races in Australia and overseas, and mentioned that her value as a broodmare would continue long after her racing career was over.

I started sifting through the various forums. Most mentions of her were jokes, or speculation, but then an entry on a trail riding forum caught my eye. The poster, who seemed to be female and went under the name Penny Dreadful, talked about a place in Victoria where she rode. She mentioned that the stables adjoined state forest, so there was great riding on the doorstep, and they had good horses for experienced riders. At the end of the post, the poster added that their latest horse was the spitting image of Fiery Lights.

I copied the post into a document, and hunted around some more. Two hours later, my shoulders were stiff from hunching, and I was bursting for a pee, but I'd found two more mentions in forums where people mentioned a horse that looked like Fiery Lights. One was in Scone, New South Wales, which wasn't surprising, as that was close to where Fiery Lights was trained. It was also the centre of the Australian equestrian world. The second was in Western Australia. Someone had posted a picture of a horse who was agisted with their own horse, and made a joke about Fiery Lights. I enlarged the picture, and the resemblance was uncanny.

I went back to Penny Dreadful's post, and saw that if I joined the forum I could send her a private message. I signed up with the username Ripper. I trusted Sue's dog would have no objection. I sent a message, saying that I too had seen a horse that was similar to Fiery Lights and suggested we trade photos.

I sat back and rubbed my eyes. Outside, the light burned bright, and the air was heavy. Something rumbled outside, and I moved to the window to look. A four-wheel drive and a camper trailer had pulled up outside, and a couple of grey-haired people got out and stretched. Potential guests.

Their names were Jane and Robin, and they were grey nomads from Sydney. I showed them to the campground, and they were delighted.

"Unusual time to be on holiday," I said to them.

"We're on our way to the Northern Territory," said Jane. "We're in a program that matches grey nomads with farmers who need a break. We feed the house animals, mow lawns, keep the veggies going, keep an eye on the stock, and in return, we stay in the house for free and experience a different way of life."

Tess had followed me out, and I watched to see how she was with strangers. Although she stayed close to me, she wagged her tail. When Robin crouched and encouraged her over, she went willingly enough and sniffed his hand.

"Has your dog been sick?" he asked as he stood again. "I don't mean to pry, but she's so thin. Lovely dog."

"I've only just adopted her. Poor girl's had a hard time."

"Oh?" He sounded interested, so I told him what I knew of Tess's story.

Jane's lips twisted. "Bastards. How do people do things like this to their animals? I used to volunteer at an animal shelter, and some of the things we saw were horrific. When we wanted to put weight on a dog, we found the best way to go was feed little and often. And, if she'll eat them, bananas are great for building up a dog."

"Thanks for the tip. I'll get some the next time I'm in Worrindi."

Tess returned to sit by my feet, and I rested a hand on her head.

"I think she knows she's found a good home." Robin smiled at me.

They said they'd stay two nights. I took their money and made sure they were set up and went down to the horses. They crowded around the gate when I appeared, pushy little Budgie, top dog in the paddock, in front as always. The paddock was nearly bare. I'd have to move them further away from the barn, which would mean more work when I needed to get them in. I put off that day by feeding them hay. Flame hung back, but I made sure she got her share.

It was quiet. I was fine with being alone for the most part. But having Josie around for the last few weeks, with her good humour, boundless energy, and enthusiasm, made me think differently. Josie had livened up my life—and my business— with her ideas. Left alone, it was just me, quiet Felix.

I went over to the cabins. I didn't have any bookings for them until next week, when I had an overnighter for one of them, but I took a walk through anyway and made sure all was right in case I had any drop-ins. All was perfect: the beds made-up and comfortable looking, the kitchenette tidy, a basket of tea, coffee, and biscuits on the counter. All I needed to do when I had a guest was bring over the perishable items for breakfast, if they were required.

I was killing time. I recognised that even as I fiddled with the chairs on the veranda, twitching them into place. I thought about going for a ride, but it was already too hot. I checked the amenities block and the camp kitchen and made sure all there was clean and tidy. Robin and Jane were setting up their van and didn't seem to need anything, so I went back to the house.

I needed to go to Worrindi. I needed dog food and bananas, among other things, and a proper bed for Tess.

"Want to come?" I asked her.

I'd expected her to be wary, given the upheaval in her life lately, but she jumped into the passenger seat of the ute.

I found everything I needed quickly, including a new collar and lead for Tess for the times she came with me to town. It looked like she was a people dog, the way she had taken to Robin and Jane.

All the strays coming home to roost.

I hadn't intended to go to the Commercial, but as I walked past the door with Tess on her new lead, I glanced inside and saw Josie behind the bar. I kept going, but I hadn't gone more than a few paces before I heard her shout. "Hey, Felix, wait up a minute!"

She waved from the doorway of the pub. I walked back, and she smiled at me before she bent to greet Tess.

"She's looking better already. Look at her eyes. Happier. She's found a home."

"She did well with the campers today. They loved her."

"What's not to love?" When Josie straightened, she was closer to me, enough that I could see the flecks in her eyes.

My fingers clenched on Tess's lead so that I wouldn't curve a hand around the back of Josie's neck and pull her in for a kiss. Josie's kisses. It seemed that I still craved them, despite all there was hanging unresolved between us.

"Did you want something?" My voice sounded harsher than I intended, but the gruffness was the only way I could keep control.

Josie didn't respond to my off-putting tone. "I just wanted to see you. And Tess. I'm glad you and she are getting on well."

I smiled down at my dog. "We are." My tone softened. "Thank you for thinking of me. I'm glad you brought her to me. I'll look after her."

"I know you will." She hadn't stepped back, and I could still see every fleck of colour in her light brown eyes. "You're a good person, Felix."

I took a step away. I couldn't let myself give in to the temptation of touching her. "I'm going to drop by Alain's clinic and find out if there's anything else I should be doing for Tess."

"Wait." Josie glanced back into the bar, checking if she had customers waiting. "I rang Flame's owner last night."

My instinct was to snap at her that it was still a stupid idea, but I said nothing.

"I thought I'd give him an update on his horse. I've done it once before, so it wasn't an out-of-the-blue idea."

"What happened?"

"Got a message from the mobile carrier that the number was not in service. I'm positive it's the number I called last time. I have it saved in my phone."

I didn't know what to make of that. People did change mobile numbers, but I would have expected him to let Josie know his new number.

"I have the day off tomorrow," Josie continued. "Can I come out?"

She sounded hesitant, which was hardly surprising.

I shrugged. "Sure."

And then there seemed nothing else to say, so I said goodbye and continued down the street to see Alain.

Alain welcomed me and, between the two of us, we lifted Tess onto his examination table. Tess seemed at ease there, I guess because Alain had fed and housed her for a while.

"She's looking good, Felix." He plucked a bag of the expensive dog food from a shelf. "Give her this for a while until she's got more weight on her. It's more nutrient dense than the cheaper stuff."

I pulled my purse out to pay, but he waved me off. "You're giving a deserving dog a home. Don't worry about it. You'll have to buy the next one, though."

I thanked him, and we lifted Tess down again.

"Did you find what you needed using the microchip reader?" he asked. "Did you buy the horse?"

I stared for a moment before I remembered that had been my excuse for borrowing it. "No. I didn't." I felt bad at the white lie. True, I hadn't bought a horse, but there wasn't one to buy.

"Did you bring the chip reader back?"

I stared a second time, guiltily remembering that I'd left the reader on my office desk. I hadn't given it a thought.

Alain laughed. "You're so easy to read, Felix. Not to worry. I seldom use it. Just bring it the next time you're in town."

# CHAPTER 17

I CHECKED MY EMAIL THE next morning, and the first one I saw was an email from the trail riding forum, saying I had a private message waiting. There were also two emails from the booking service I used for the campground and one—finally— from the builder in the Isa. My cursor hovered over the four emails. The bookings could wait five more minutes, and the builder had kept me waiting. I logged into the trail riding forum and opened the message. It was from Penny Dreadful.

It was short and friendly, the sort of email one poster would send to another whom they don't really know.

*Hi Ripper,*

*I think there's a few chestnut mares around resembling Fiery Lights. Here's a photo of the one I know—who is called Flame. She's a beauty! Would love to see a photo of your mare.*

*PD*

I stared at the words. The horse in Victoria was also called Flame. Tingles ran down into my belly and coalesced into a rock. That surely couldn't be a coincidence. I opened the photo. It was a bit blurry, maybe taken with a mobile phone, but the chestnut mare had the same thin, white stripe as Flame, the same white socks at the rear. She was slightly stockier, with more bone than Flame, but other than that, she was similar. Uncannily similar.

I didn't reply to Penny Dreadful. There was nothing I could say without getting deeper into it. Instead, I dealt with the two emails for cabin bookings, one for the weekend—the day after tomorrow—the other for a couple of weeks' time.

I opened the builder's email. He said he could come and start site prep in three weeks' time, with the works above ground to follow on a month later. It wasn't ideal, given that the imminent wet season could turn the ground into a morass and wash out any underground work, but it was the best he could do, so I sent an email accepting that.

I went into the kitchen and tidied up, fed Tess, and made a coffee, which I drank on the veranda. The slow turn of the ceiling fan made the heat almost bearable. For a few minutes, I relaxed, listening to the shrieking chatter of corellas as they did an early morning fly-past. Tess raised her head but didn't bark.

Josie arrived when I was in the barn, and the first I knew of her arrival was Tess, who wagged her tail and gave two short barks.

"Hey, gorgeous." Josie stroked Tess's head. "She looks happier each time I see her."

Tess pressed her head into Josie's hand. I envied my dog.

Josie was wearing shorts again, and I realised why. She wasn't presuming we would ride. She'd taken that part of our friendship as being over. The thought saddened me. Riding with Josie had been something I'd looked forward to.

It was on the tip of my tongue to suggest we go for a ride, but I bit it back. Instead, I told her about the forums I'd found and the posts talking about horses that looked like Fiery Lights. I said I'd emailed someone in Victoria who knew of one such horse.

"I had a reply from her," I said. "She sent a photo. The horse in Victoria is the spit of Fiery Lights. And she's also called Flame."

Josie's eyes widened. "Really? That can't be a coincidence."

"That's what I thought. The horse is obviously a thoroughbred. I wish we could get a look at the microchip."

"Could you ask your forum friend to read it?"

"Not really. You don't know who you're talking to on the other side of an email. She could even be your Flame's owner posing as a random person just to see if anyone is suspicious. Plus it's a big ask to get someone to borrow a chip reader and all that."

"We've got a horse called Flame with a chip that says she's Fiery Lights. What if this horse in Victoria has a chip that says she's Flame? What if it's a simple old-fashioned switcheroo? What if it's really Fiery Lights down there in Victoria, and they're going to enter her in some race as 'Flame' at huge odds, and she'll clean up?"

"Possible." I thought a bit harder. "Probable. I think that was done a long time ago, in the '80s, maybe. I think that's one of the reasons microchips were brought in. But if you have two horses that are the spit of each other and you manage to swap the chips, then it would be a lot harder to detect."

Josie leant her arms on the railing, watching as I swept the bedding into a corner of Diesel's stall. "We should go to Victoria."

"What?" I straightened and stared at her, mouth agape. "Go to *Victoria*? Why?"

"With the chip reader. Do you still have it?"

"Yeah, I forgot to give it back to Alain."

"Must be fate. If he doesn't need it back for a couple more days, we can fly to Melbourne, drive to the stables—did your forum friend say which one it is?"

I nodded. "It was in her original post as she was promoting the trail-ride business. It's in the Yarra Valley, about two hours out of Melbourne."

"Easy, then. We hire a car at the airport and drive to the Yarra Valley, find the horse, read the chip in its neck, and then decide what to do after that."

"Fly to *Melbourne*?" I realised how stupid I must sound. Josie wasn't asking me to fly halfway around the world. She was suggesting we take a four-hour domestic flight. Very little advance planning required. "It seems like a lot of trouble."

"You don't have to come if you don't want to, Felix, but I think I will. After all, I'm the one who's likely to end up in trouble for this. I'm the one who took possession of stolen goods—if that's what Flame is."

She stepped aside as I exited Diesel's stall and walked out into the sunlight with a water bucket. Her casual acceptance that she would fly halfway around Australia to clear her name floored me. But then, what was so strange about that? I wasn't so stuck in the mud that I wouldn't do something like this; it was just that I never *had*. The little travel I'd done previously was planned months ahead, and usually by someone else: my parents or the school. All I'd had to do was show up.

But I wasn't Josie. I wasn't free as a bird, a flitter, a drifter. I had responsibilities, and most of them were staring me in the face right now: seven horses, a campground, cabins, a business, campers. And now Tess, who was sitting in the dust at my feet with a hangdog expression on her face.

"I can't. This doesn't run itself." I gestured weakly at the surrounds.

"Would you come if you could?"

"Yeah, maybe," I said. And then, "Yes. Definitely." It was easier to be definite about something that wouldn't happen.

"Okay, then."

I stopped. What did that even mean? Okay that I couldn't come, but she would go? Okay that she accepted my reasons? Okay that she would forget about it? I turned to ask her, but the yard was empty apart from me and Tess.

I stared at the space where Josie had been for a second and then shrugged and continued my chores.

I'd swept the barn, been out to the paddock, checked on all the horses, and made a circuit of the empty campground when she caught up with me.

"That's sorted," she said. "Sue and Moni will arrive tomorrow to look after things here, and we can fly to Melbourne. They're fine for five days. Any longer than that might be difficult for them."

"Sue and Moni? Coming *here*?"

"Yeah. I called Sue. I hope you don't mind, but I used your phone. I'll pay for the call."

"You called *Sue*?" I was beginning to sound ridiculous, but my brain was fixated on Josie's casual usurping of my life.

"Yeah. You said you'd come if you could. And who else would you trust to mind the place for a few days?"

"I wouldn't have asked them. It's too much of an imposition."

"I looked up Sue's number and called. I told her what was going on with Flame and why I was calling. She said, 'Leave it to me.' Then she rang back fifteen minutes later. She and Moni will be here at dusk tomorrow. They can stay until Monday afternoon. They were delighted."

"What about the campers? And I can't ask Sue and Moni to clean toilets!"

"Why not? They clean their own. Just because they're a lawyer and a doctor doesn't mean they don't do manual work."

"They have a housekeeper. Mrs T cleans their toilets."

"You know them better than me, but honestly, Felix, they don't mind. Sue said you'd jib like a horse at a gate. She said to call her."

She fell into step with me as I headed for the house. It wasn't that I didn't believe her, but I'd never left Jayboro in the hands of someone else since I'd opened the campground. I wanted to make sure Sue and Moni knew what they were in for, even if it was only for five days.

Josie perched on the end of the desk as I called Sue.

She answered on the second ring. "Whitely and Brent Law, Sue speaking."

When she recognised my voice, she said, "I've just lost a bet. I said to Moni you'd wait at least an hour before calling. Twenty-two minutes. Not that I was timing you or anything."

"You lawyers are good at timing," I teased. "I know all about your six-minute billing increments."

"Industry standard. Just like you provide fresh milk in the camp kitchen."

In truth, I knew Sue's six-minute increments would often run to double that, and she often undercharged her clients.

"Moni and I will be there tomorrow," said Sue. "I called Moni at the surgery, and she's already arranged for her part-time doctor to cover. I'm not particularly busy; I can swing it. We were thinking of having a long weekend away somewhere.

Jayboro will be perfect—if you trust us with your business, that is."

"There's nobody better." I shifted the phone to my other ear. "But Sue, there's work to do. I have a booking for a cabin. There might be campers, trail rides, horses—"

"Felix, shut up. We'd love to do it. Just tell me what we'd have to do."

I lined up the thoughts in my head. "Well, greet the guests, check emails for bookings, clean the amenities block, clean the cabins, check on the horses, feed them hay daily, check the water trough, oh, and of course, there's Tess now—"

"Tess?"

"I hope Ripper doesn't eat her. You are bringing him, aren't you?"

"Of course. Is Tess human or what?"

"She's my dog."

"Dog. Of course. She's got such a doggie name. Felix, how about Moni and I try and make it early afternoon tomorrow, then you can show us exactly what needs doing."

"Are you sure you don't mind?"

"We'd love to. Honestly. From what Josie said, you have good reason to go. And we get to stay somewhere beautiful, go riding anytime we want, and relax away from the metropolis of Mungabilly Creek and its eight hundred residents. Don't worry about Rip. He's cool around other dogs."

"Come in the four-wheel drive, and you can stay in the house. Unless you want to bring the camper, of course."

"House will be good. Thank you."

I hung up and stared wide-eyed at Josie. I'd never done anything so impulsive before, and the logistics were starting to build a wall in front of my eyes.

She hopped down from the desk. "Great. Now let's book our flights. Can I drive?" She gestured to the computer.

I shifted to one side to allow her to sit. "Be my guest."

She pulled up a chair and started clicking and typing. "It would be best if we could fly from the Isa to Melbourne. I doubt there are direct flights—we'll probably have to change planes in Brisbane or Sydney."

For a moment, there was silence, and then she said, "Hmmm. Now that's annoying."

"What?" I moved closer again so that I could see.

"There's only a flight from Mount Isa every other day. That's yesterday and Friday. But Friday's flight is chockers. Completely booked. Sue and Moni are arriving tomorrow and have five days. If you wait until they arrive, there won't be time to get to Melbourne and back if we fly from the Isa." She clicked and typed some more. "However, if we leave tomorrow morning, we can drive to Townsville by nightfall, get a late flight and be in Melbourne by midnight the same day."

"Sue and Moni won't be here until the afternoon."

"They can let themselves in. You don't lock the house anyway. Leave a note with instructions."

"What if they get delayed? What if there's a problem?"

"Felix." Her exasperated sigh shuddered through the room. "You said you'd come. I would like you to come. Really, what can happen in the six or so hours when the place is unattended?" She scooted her chair around the desk and picked up my hand from where it was clenched on the desk. "I admit my motives aren't pure. We were well on the way to…well, something, you and I. Kisses. And I hoped there would be more. But now, since you don't entirely believe me, that's all gone west. I'm not saying I blame you, but I want to try and get back what we had. You coming with me is part of that. Please, Felix. Say you'll come."

I stared at her light brown eyes, lit with hope and something else, something undefinable, but also promise.

I turned my hand so that I could link her fingers. "I'll come. Book the flights."

# CHAPTER 18

W E  L E F T  A T  D A W N  T H E  next morning. I'd spent an hour typing a long list of instructions for Sue and Moni, but I knew that Josie was right. They would be fine. Tess had seen us off with sad eyes. Given her history of abandonment, she must have wondered if we'd be coming back.

And then we were speeding along the road with ten hours' drive in front of us to Townsville. We'd taken my ute in preference to Josie's old Subaru, and it rattled and bucked its way over the corrugated dirt road out to the main highway. Once it got fully light, I increased speed to ten kilometres over the limit.

Josie sat back and put her feet on the dash and handed me one of the two travel mugs of coffee that we'd made before we left.

She'd returned to Worrindi only long enough to grab some clothes, plead an unexpected emergency to Madge and Chris, and get a few days off. She'd then come back to Jayboro. To save time, she'd slept in my spare room rather than pitch her tent. And so she banged on my door at just gone four, when the dawn was still a faint eastern glow.

Our flight wasn't until seven that evening, but we were allowing for the unexpected. We made good time on the paved road, pushing the ute when it was safe to do so and buying sandwiches at fuel stations, rather than stopping for a proper lunch. Josie shared the driving, which allowed me to watch her under the guise of looking out of the driver's window. She had a slight wrinkle in her forehead above her cheap sunnies, and her hands either relaxed on the wheel or impatiently pushed buttons on the radio to find something to listen to other than news.

We pulled into the car park at Townsville airport just before four, which left us plenty of time to grab a beer and a bite to eat before boarding.

Once on the plane, Josie propped her head against the bulkhead and immediately fell asleep, so I stared across her out the window as the plane lifted off. As it dipped a wing and circled, I had an ideal view of the coast and the blue, blue Coral Sea. Then it headed inland, crossing the outback as night fell.

Queensland's lack of daylight saving put us an hour behind the other eastern states, which meant we didn't touch down in Melbourne until midnight. Neither of us had thought to book a motel, so we took a bus to the city. The friendly driver told us about a backpackers' hostel in one of the city laneways that had twenty-four hour check-in, so we headed there through the throngs of late-night revellers and the tantalising smells coming from Chinatown.

It was years since I'd been in a city that was as big and vibrant as Melbourne, let alone in the middle of the night. The noise, the traffic, the strangeness of it all was fascinating, and my head swivelled constantly as I tried to take it in. Josie seemed relaxed and pushed through the crowds spilling out from the laneway bars with a muttered "'Scuse me, mate." I bobbed along in her wake as she found the hostel, which luckily had two dorm-room bunks available.

By then, I was so tired I just stripped to a T-shirt and knickers and fell into bed, which was as saggy as a hammock and half as wide.

The next morning, we snagged a discount leaflet for car hire from the receptionist and called them. An hour later, we drove away from Melbourne in a tiny, bright yellow car that, after my ute, seemed as small and insubstantial as a matchbox. Josie drove, which I was relieved about, as the early-morning city traffic was fast moving and chaotic. Josie expertly negotiated a hook turn—a road rule peculiar to Melbourne to allow for the trams—and I grinned across at her.

"I am so glad you're driving. We'd be under that tram by now, needing jaws-of-life extraction, if I were at the wheel."

"It's not too bad when you get used to it." Josie crept along in first gear in a line of traffic crawling towards the Melbourne Cricket Ground. "Let's see if we can go a bit further before stopping for breakfast."

I nodded. The instant coffee we'd had at the backpackers' would keep me going for a while longer.

It was just over an hour later when we pulled off the highway into the small town of Yarra Glen. By then, I was starving and bursting for a pee and a coffee. We found a bakery in town and sat outside on a bench to eat some tasty bacon-and-egg rolls.

I found the map I'd printed from the internet and studied it. The map said the trail-riding place abutted the state forest, about forty minutes away. Josie slid back behind the wheel, and we started off again.

"This is rather fun." Josie kept her eyes on the road, but her hand reached over the space between the seats to squeeze mine.

"I feel like I'm in a detective show. You know, where the female protagonists banter back and forth and throw sparks off each other before one of them gets captured by the bad guys and the other saves her skin."

"No capturing," I said. "And I'm not much good at the banter either. But apart from that, well, maybe."

"Those shows generally end with one detective going home to her husband, while the other stares moodily into her scotch in a bar and waits for someone to flirt with."

"No flirting either," I said.

She glanced at me sideways before she returned her eyes to the road. "None? Really? I was hoping that, as we're stuck in a car together, there might be just a little."

I looked out the window to give myself time to collect my thoughts. Victoria's landscape was very different to outback Queensland. It was only October, still spring, and the winter rains had obviously been kind.

"Are you going to answer me?" Josie's voice had an amused lilt to it, as if she knew my inner dilemma. "Or are you going to change the subject and talk about the scenery?"

I faced her again, wishing the matchbox car had a little more room. "We need to sort out about Flame before we can consider flirting."

Her face shuttered over, wiped clean of laughter, so that it was a blank sheet. "Right. The horse is still between us. Trust—or lack of—is still an issue."

"Josie, I—"

She reached back again and this time her fingers clenched briefly on my thigh. "Felix, please. Just for today, just until we see this horse up the road, can we go back to being friends again? Can we flirt, can we imagine the possibilities there might be between us? You're such a straightforward, honest sort of person that I know this is difficult for you. But I wish you'd believe in me again. Just a little."

She stared back at the road, swinging the car around a bend with skill.

I could do that. In truth, I missed the ease between us. I opened my mouth to say that I could, when her phone beeped and the robotic voice of the GPS said, "In eight hundred metres, turn left onto Bluegum Range Road."

Josie slowed. "Not far to go now. Excited?"

"Nervous," I admitted. "We also haven't discussed how we're going to go about this. We can't just waltz in and demand to see Flame and run the chip reader down her neck. They'll be people about, wondering what we're doing."

"Hopefully, we can say we're tourists from Queensland and are thinking of booking a ride, and can we have a look around. It might be as simple as that."

"As long as she's actually there. As long as we can find her."

"Don't overthink it. Sit back and try and look like a tourist who's come to explore the famous Yarra Valley wineries."

"That's not difficult. I've never been here before."

"No? I lived in central Victoria for a while a few years back. Picked grapes. Then I moved up to the Murray River and worked in a dried-fruit factory." She swung left onto a dirt road, following the GPS's directions.

The little car fishtailed slightly as its tyres lost grip. I grabbed the doorhandle to steady myself. Josie slowed, and we bounced over the rougher road. Another right turn, and we drove along a flat-bottomed valley.

"There." I pointed to a sign that said *Trail Rides*. We turned through the gate and came to a stop.

The yard was tidy, although it was somewhat muddy. In the summer heat, it probably turned to dust. There were two lines of six looseboxes facing each other across a yard. A handpainted sign pointed to the office at the end of the rows. There nobody about, but someone was whistling in one of the boxes.

I gripped my bag, and the blocky shape of the microchip reader dug into my hand through the canvas. Without discussion, Josie took one side of the yard, and I took the other. Walking quietly, I peered into each box in turn. The first three were empty, the fourth held the round shaggy rump of a plump Shetland, and the fifth held a thoroughbred, but it was black, not chestnut. Across the yard, Josie gave me a thumbs down and pointed to the path that led alongside the office to some paddocks where horses grazed. I followed her, but as we passed the office, someone noticed us.

"Hello. Can I help you?" A gangly youth appeared in the doorway. His hair hung over one eye, but his smile was friendly.

I stopped. "Hi. We were just passing on our way to the Yarra Valley wineries, when we saw your sign. We're visiting from Queensland. Do you mind if we have a look around? We're staying locally, and it might be nice to book a ride in the next couple of days."

"Sure." He gestured at the yard. "Some of the horses are out, but you'll find a few there, and there's more in the paddock. Have you ridden before?"

Josie came up beside me and slipped her hand into mine. "A bit," she said. "We went trail riding in South Australia, and on the beach in Queensland."

The boy's eyes flicked over our joined hands, and he smiled. "I'm sure we have horses that will suit you. Have a look around and come and see me when you're done. I can book you in."

"Thanks." I forced myself to saunter down the path, resisting the impulse to tighten my grip on Josie's hand and make a dash for it. Once around the corner and out of sight, she grinned at me. "See? That was easy."

Green paddocks stretched in front of us. I could see three horses in one, and by squinting into the bright light, I could see they were two chestnuts and a grey. A second paddock to our left also held a couple more horses, one of which was a chestnut. I gestured to the second paddock. "Those are closer. Let's go there first."

The horses in the second paddock crowded to the rail when they saw us coming, jostling for position in the hope of attention.

"No go," said Josie. "The chestnut's a gelding."

In case anyone was watching, we made a show of petting the two horses.

Josie tugged my hand. "Look, there's a path there that will take us closer to the other horses.

We set off, but the path stopped at a water trough. The horses were closer, but still too far away to make out if either of the chestnuts was a mare with Flame's markings. Josie twitched her head to indicate we should keep going, and we ducked between the strands of barbed wire and walked across the field. It was hot in the sun, and anyone looking from the office would see us. Hopefully, they would think that we were city dwellers who were ignorant of horse etiquette.

The horses saw us approach and walked towards us.

There was a shout from behind. "Hey, wait up. You shouldn't be in this paddock with strange horses."

"Pretend you didn't hear." Josie grabbed my hand again and swung it, to make it look like we were just loved up.

The horses came closer and her fingers tightened on mine. "Look at the one on the left."

It was Flame. At least, it was a chestnut mare who was the spitting image of Flame. Same thoroughbred fine lines, same white stripe. Same way of flaring her nostrils, ears pricked as she approached, neck stretched out in the hope of a pat.

I freed my hand from Josie's and fumbled in my bag for the microchip reader.

"Go around the far side of the horse," Josie muttered. "There's a woman coming up fast. Hurry." The last word was said with some urgency. "I'll try and hold her off."

I ducked around the horses so that the chestnut was between me and the woman.

"Hey," I heard her say. "I'm sorry, but you really shouldn't be in here. It's an insurance thing."

"Hi," Josie said. "We're sorry, we didn't realise we were doing anything wrong. We just wanted to see these three beauties closer. We're thinking of booking a trail ride."

I got the chip reader out of my bag and fumbled with the leather case. Nerves turned my fingers clumsy, and it took three tries to undo the strap. Finally, I freed it and turned it on, waiting impatiently for the digital display to show that it was ready.

"They are lovely," said the woman who had approached. "But these three aren't used for the trail rides. They're all agistments."

"Are they racehorses?" Josie asked. "They look gorgeous enough."

"Thoroughbreds," the woman replied, "but not actively racing. Come with me back to the gate now. I can show you the other horses in the yard."

I aimed the reader at the chestnut's neck. For an agonising moment nothing happened.

Josie started to amble back to the yard.

"Your friend too," said the woman.

The reader beeped as it picked up the presence of a microchip. I left the reader in place for as long as I dared, hoping that it would secure the reading, then I raised my voice to the woman. "I'm coming."

Behind me, a branch on one of the tall gum trees cracked like a pistol, and abruptly crashed to the ground. There was a split second of silence, and then all three horses wheeled as one and took off at a fast canter, snorting and prancing, nostrils wide and eyes apprehensive. I was left standing with no cover, the microchip reader visible in my hand as I fumbled it back into my canvas bag. The case dropped to the ground, and I bent to retrieve it.

"Oh look, is that the trail riders coming back?" Josie's attempt to distract the woman failed. She flicked a glance at the returning riders, then directed her gaze back to me.

"Is that a microchip reader?" Her voice was flinty and hard, and her expression shuttered. "You mind telling me what you're doing?"

Was there any possible reason for being in the middle of a paddock with strange horses other than the actual one? I couldn't think of one, and neither, it seemed, could Josie. I'd never seen her lost for words before.

"It's not a... What did you call it?" she said.

The woman's gaze hardened. "I'm not a bloody idiot. Unless you're checkout chicks who for some bizarre reason have brought the supermarket barcode scanner on your riding holiday, that's a microchip reader. For reading microchips," she added, when we both continued to stare at her. "I can wait all day," she said, when neither of us answered.

I took a deep breath. "Is this horse called Flame, by any chance?"

She nodded, her face still mired with suspicion.

"And she's on agistment here?"

The woman folded her arms. "This is an agistment yard as well as a trail-riding place. What's it to you?"

Josie gave me a slight nod. I guess despite the antagonism coming from the woman, the fact that the horse was also on agistment put the yard in the same place that we were: potentially in deep shit.

"We're from outback Queensland," I said. "This is going to sound strange, but we have a horse that has been left with us for agistment, also called Flame. Our Flame is uncannily similar to your Flame. And both Flames bear a strong resemblance to a racehorse that's gone missing. Stolen. That horse is called—"

"Fiery Lights." The women's face relaxed somewhat. "Which one of you is Ripper?"

# CHAPTER 19

"I'm Ripper," I said. "Which means you must be Penny Dreadful."

"My user name." She uncrossed her arms and stuck out a hand. "I'm Pen."

"I'm Felix, and this is Josie. Ripper is the name of my friend's dog."

"I nearly didn't answer your message. The name sounded a bit serial killerish."

"He's a little ripper of a dog; that's how he got his name. It was the first thing that came to mind when I registered for the forum."

"Let's get out of the paddock before the owner here comes chasing. She doesn't like people roaming the paddocks. It really is an insurance thing."

With a final glance over my shoulder at Flame, now grazing peacefully again, I walked with the others back to the yard. Pen skirted the office and led us back around to our car.

"I think we need to talk, and I'd rather not be overheard. My ride was earlier; I was just hanging around the horses, so why don't we go and get a coffee? There's a teashop about five minutes away. My car's the blue one by the gate. Will you follow me?"

I nodded and Josie slid into the driver's seat of our car and opened the door for me.

We were silent as we followed Pen's car, and soon we pulled up outside a café built of bluestone. Pen paused to point out the path of last year's bushfire which had narrowly missed the community, only destroying two houses on the next ridge. Then we went inside and ordered mugs of coffee and scones.

Pen waited until the coffee arrived. Then, cradling her mug with both hands, she leant forwards.

"I think it's a bit of a leap of faith for us to trust each other. After all, we're strangers."

Josie and I nodded.

"You've already told me a bit of your interest in this, so I'll start." She sipped her coffee before continuing. "I live in one of Melbourne's outer suburbs, about fifteen minutes from here. I ride at Casey's place on the weekends—that's the yard we've just come from—and spend a fair bit of time there. Casey knows me well now, and I basically work in exchange for rides. I'm sure you know the drill: I help with the beginners, get horses ready, often ride as Tail-End Charlie at the back of a string of new riders. Casey has a dozen horses of her own, plus another eight or nine on agistment. Those horses aren't ridden by the trail riders, they're purely boarded for their owners. They tend to come and go. Flame came a few weeks ago. I don't know who her owner is. One day she was there, and Casey told me she was spelling."

I nodded. It was common to turn a competition horse out into a paddock for a few weeks to let it rest and put on weight.

"I didn't ask, as we often get horses for this, but I presumed she was a racehorse or maybe an ex-racehorse, now eventing or the like. Haven't seen the owner, but that's not unusual."

Beside me, Josie opened her mouth as if to ask a question, but then she shut it again. Pen glanced at her but continued.

"I didn't think anything of it until last week, when I saw an article in *The Age*. It talked about the missing racehorse, Fiery Lights, and how she had totally vanished. It compared her disappearance to that of Shergar, the Irish racehorse that disappeared in the 80s."

"That horse was kidnapped." Josie watched Pen carefully.

"So was Fiery Lights. Never proven, but she vanished from the one area of her paddock not covered by CCTV."

Exactly as I'd discovered.

"There was a photo of Fiery Lights in the paper. It struck me how similar to Flame she was. And the dates more or less matched. Flame arrived at Casey's place only a few days after she disappeared. So I hunted down more photos of Fiery Lights. And every photo I found made me more and more convinced that Flame was Fiery Lights. I became a little obsessed with it, and then made that offhand post on the trail riding forum—the post you saw—just to see if anyone bit."

"Did anyone bite apart from Felix?" Josie watched Pen over the rim of her mug.

"Yeah. Two other people told me about horses they had seen that were identical to Fiery Lights. One in New South Wales, not far from where she was stolen. The other is about two hours up the road in central Victoria."

The scones arrived at that moment, and we paused the conversation long enough for the waitress to put the plate down, long enough to spread the scones with butter and raspberry jam. Pen took a bite of her scone, swallowed and continued.

"Obviously, they can't all be Fiery Lights. That's four different horses, including yours."

"Five," I said. "There's one in Western Australia too."

"I was on the verge of going to the police," Pen continued, "but I wanted to be sure. Have more proof. I didn't want to drag my friend in. It's hard enough for her making a go of her yard as it is."

I nodded. That had been part of my thinking too. I could understand.

Pen spread more jam on her scone and added a dollop of cream. "When I found out there were more horses, to be honest, I thought I probably was seeing a crime where none existed. Obviously they can't all be Fiery Lights. It's probably just that she's in the media eye at present, and people are jumping to conclusions. Or wanting a bit of reflected glory." She paused to take another bite of scone. "When I was a kid, someone in my town thought they saw a UFO. The next thing, every low flying plane brought more reported UFO sightings. The herd mentality, I guess." She smiled slightly. "We're all horse people; we should know about that.

"But there's a couple of things that keep me thinking there might be something in all of this. The first is that Casey said to me last week, just before I made that post, that she thought Flame's owner was strange. Evasive. He booked Flame's agistment over the phone. As far as we know, he's never visited the yard. Flame arrived in a cattle truck with nothing with her. No tack, no rugs, no grooming kit, nothing except the halter used to tie her to the truck. She was in pretty poor condition. Now I don't know about you, but if I cared about my horse, I'd send her with a lot more than that. And if she is a racehorse, I'd take more care of her. Special feed. Rugs. And in the weeks that she's been here, no one has visited her."

"Do you think your Flame is Fiery Lights?" My coffee had cooled while Pen was talking. I took a big gulp.

"I don't know. Sometimes I'm sure she must be. The next minute, I think I'm an idiot and there's no way she is. But then what's with all the other horses?" Pen shrugged. "Well, the two of you arriving here from Queensland with a microchip reader means that I'm not the only one with suspicions. Do you also have a lookalike horse, or is that bullshit? Maybe you're reporters." She ran a hand through her short hair. "I guess I should have asked that first. You can tell I'm no good at espionage."

Somewhere in her story, I'd decided I trusted Pen. Her face, her gestures, her lack of subterfuge or evasion meant I believed her. I pushed down the little kernel of doubt that was reminding me I'd trusted Josie too.

"What we told you before is true. We have an identical horse who is also called Flame." I glanced at Josie, unsure how much of her involvement she wanted to relate.

Josie seemed to have no hesitation, and she quickly relayed to Pen the story of how she came to have Flame.

"Flame arrived at Jayboro—my place," I added. "I run a camping and trail riding place in outback Queensland. She, too, came in a truck with nothing except a torn rug and old halter. As if she'd come from some sale yard or something. A friend's brother picked the similarity between her and Fiery Lights. I didn't think anything of it, until…"

I hesitated. Until I'd begun to suspect Josie, until I'd wondered if she were truthful.

Pen didn't seem to notice my pause.

"But something made you suspect enough to read her microchip." She nodded at my bag on the floor at my feet.

"What did it say? I'm guessing your horse isn't Fiery Lights, but something made you investigate further. It must be major, if you've come all the way from Queensland."

Josie's gaze focussed on a picture on the opposite wall. Her face was fallen in lines of sadness. She had picked up on what I hadn't said, even if Pen hadn't. "Our Flame's microchip identifies her as Fiery Lights," she said. "But she can't be. Felix rode her. She's broken down."

"I think she's got a cardiac condition, almost certainly longstanding. She couldn't have won the Jackson Plate, not as she is. If our thinking is correct, your horse will have a microchip that identifies her as Flame—the real Flame, our horse, who supposedly is an ex-racehorse from South Australia. We think that your horse is the real Fiery Lights, misidentified as Flame. And that someone is going to enter her in a middling race sometime soon, where she will cavort home by many lengths."

"Betting fraud?" Pen bit her lip. "It makes sense. 'Flame' will have odds of two hundred to one or something, and people will bet big on her and clean up. But why go to the trouble of fabricating a microchip saying the real Flame is Fiery Lights? That's a huge amount of effort for something that seems pointless."

Josie's gaze came back from the wall and she said, "If someone challenged 'Flame's' win and made the connection with Fiery Lights, all they'd have to do is suddenly 'find' Fiery Lights at Jayboro with the correct microchip. It's possible."

"This is doing my head in." Pen drained her coffee. "So what we need to do is look up the chip you just read from my Flame in the database. If we're correct, then it should identify her as your Flame, ex-racehorse from South Australia."

"Yeah," said Josie.

"I think so," I said at the same moment.

"Don't suppose you have a laptop with you?" Pen looked from Josie to me, and we both shook our heads.

"I live about fifteen minutes away. Come with me, and we'll use my computer."

Josie was silent until we reached the car. She once again took the driver's seat.

"It seems you were right not to trust me." Her voice was low, defeated, and her gaze remained on the road. "I caught what you didn't tell Pen. You wouldn't have investigated Flame as much as you did if you'd thought I was trustworthy, someone to believe in. No wonder you pulled back from me."

I was silent. So often, words failed me around Josie in these situations. I couldn't tell her that she was wrong, because she was exactly right. But equally, her willingness to investigate this, even if it meant she would end up having some blame, put her in a better light.

"You don't have to answer." Josie changed down a gear with a crunch. "Your silence says it all. For what it's worth, I'm very sorry. It seemed so harmless at the start. After all, I thought we'd gain a superficial kind of friendship, and then Flame would be reclaimed, my job at the pub would end, and I'd be on the road again. I didn't expect to still be around. I didn't expect to love living in Worrindi or enjoy working at the pub. I certainly didn't expect to find somewhere like Jayboro." She paused while she overtook a slow moving ute. Pen's bright blue car remained just ahead as we accelerated onto the highway. "And I certainly didn't expect to fall for you."

She crunched the gearbox again. "Little white lies can be easier when you move around as I do. You tell a prospective employer that you plan on settling in the town when you know you'll be gone as soon as you've got enough money to move on. You tell them that yes, you've picked cherries, or tended vines, or worked bar, or done factory work, when you haven't a clue. But you tell them because you need the job, and menial jobs are easy to pick up. They never know you're new at it, or if they figure it out, they don't care because you're reliable and turn up for work on time and smile. At least until you decide it's time to go, when you get your final pay and then disappear. So the little white lies I told you, Felix? They were unimportant and meaningless, until suddenly they weren't." She flashed me a glance. "I guess if you hadn't been suspicious, we wouldn't be here now."

"Josie, you're not entirely right." A montage of the time I'd spent with Josie scrolled through my head: riding together, laughing, her helping me with the horses, even cleaning the amenities block. Her ease with my friends, her relaxed manner with the campers and her great ideas. Kissing her.

There the montage stuck, like a freeze-frame. Kissing Josie.

It really had been one of the best parts of my life in recent times.

"It's okay. I understand."

She had obviously taken my tongue-tied silence for discomfort. But then Pen turned left into a small residential street, and then right, and left again and pulled up outside a small '50s red brick house.

Josie parked behind her, and we got out and followed Pen to her front door. Her house was old and worn but eclectic and comfortable. There was a shabby lounge, draped in a batik cloth in front of an old-fashioned glass coffee table, and shelves of books covering one wall. A cat greeted us at the door, a chocolate Burmese. He meowed and wound himself around our ankles. When Josie bent to pet him, he purred and arched his back in pleasure, green eyes slitted shut.

"That's Milo," Pen said from the kitchen, which was around a wall of exposed brick. "Push him away if he's a pest."

Josie picked him up and he snuggled under her chin in ecstasy. "I like him. I miss having a cat."

I wondered when she'd been stable enough in her life to have a cat. I followed Pen into the kitchen.

"More coffee?" She indicated a space-age coffee machine on a cluttered bench.

"Yes, please."

Pen made three coffees and then we rejoined Josie in the living room. Pen sat at her desk and booted her computer.

"Do you want to do it?" she asked. "You've looked up the microchip database before."

I pulled the reader out of my bag and logged in to the database.

I was pretty sure of what I'd see. Flame's details. The real Flame, ex-racehorse Flame.

The microchip was registered to Fiery Lights.

# CHAPTER 20

LATE MORNING FOUND US SITTING around Pen's kitchen table, eating toasted cheese and chutney sandwiches.

My theory was shot to smithereens in tiny shards around our feet. Why would there be two identical horses with the same microchip? Obviously, they both couldn't be Fiery Lights. Now, I doubted that either was.

Josie and Pen were similarly clueless, and we figured the best use of our time was to fill our stomachs.

"It doesn't seem that hard to duplicate a microchip." Pen scooped a bit of melted cheese from her plate and licked her fingers. "The internet is full of stories about animals with the same chip. What is strange is what horse the chip is registered to."

"Could you ask Casey a bit more about her Flame?" suggested Josie.

"I honestly don't think she knows anything. I don't think she's knowingly involved."

Pen's certainty was absolute. She didn't believe for a second her friend could do that.

I glanced at Josie, who was staring at the crusts left on her plate. I reached out and took her hand, wrapping my fingers firmly around hers. "Neither is Josie."

Josie's head raised, and she stared at me with wide eyes. She didn't speak, but her fingers squeezed mine back. The room faded away, and Pen's chatter became muted background noise. What was important was Josie and me and our linked fingers and locked gazes.

It was true. I did believe her. And while I didn't feel wrong for distrusting her initially, the fact that I now believed—now *knew*—that it wasn't in her character to attempt this sort of fraud made me feel warm. Happy. The potential between us that had drifted away during the days of uncertainty could return, if we wanted it to.

I wanted it to.

If I hadn't come to this trust of Josie in my own time, if I had pursued something with her anyway, slept with her, fallen in love with her, built a life with her, this would always have been between us.

Now it was open and clear.

"Thank you," she whispered and looked down at the table, but not before I'd seen her shining eyes.

"—only two hours away. What do you think?"

Pen was speaking, and I hadn't heard a word of it. Going by Josie's blank look, she hadn't either.

"Sorry, Pen, what did you say?" I said.

Pen glanced from me to Josie and back again, then down at our linked hands. "Why do I feel I've just missed something big between you two?"

I smiled but didn't answer.

"I just said that another horse that is also supposedly like Flame is in central Victoria, in a tiny town called Walmering. The person who mentioned the horse on the forum didn't email me directly, but I've pieced it together from their supposed location and their previous posts about where they agist their horse. It's only a couple of hours away. What do you think? We could get there and back before dark."

Josie answered for both of us. "I think we should go."

We took the hire car, and with Josie driving, we set off. We didn't talk much. Josie concentrated on the road, and I looked at the landscape, so very different from where I lived. Here there were rolling hills, mainly still green and lush from winter rains. We passed through many small towns, the highway often running down the main street. The buildings were stone, all lowset. There were no highset Queenslander houses as I was used to. But Queensland's houses were highset to catch the breeze and to stay out of the floodwater when it came. Here in Victoria, flooding obviously wasn't as much of a problem, and the thick stone walls would keep out the heat in summer and trap the interior warmth in winter. There was history in these towns, and the overseas heritage was more evident, both in the style of building and the type of businesses. We passed a German bakehouse, an Italian restaurant, a South African biltong shop, a Korean barbecue restaurant, and a shop selling English smallgoods. There were also art galleries and plenty of cafés, community centres, and altogether more population in ten kilometres of road than there was in Worrindi and the communities scattered along the nearly four hundred kilometres of road to the Isa.

Pen pointed out a few things of interest but was otherwise silent.

When we reached Benalla, she pulled out her phone to get the address of the stables from the forum posts, then put it into the GPS. We turned down a smaller paved road.

Twenty minutes later, she said to pull over. We were away from any settlement, on a dirt road surrounded by paddocks.

"The yard should be a couple of kilometres further on," she said. "What are we going to do? It's not a trail-riding place, it's a private agistment yard, at least according to the poster."

"Can we not go and enquire about agistment? Maybe one of us could do that, while the other two wander around, pretending to look at the horses?"

"That might work. It depends on how busy they are. I have no idea if it's a big place or not. I'll do the asking." She glanced down at her breeches and shirt. "I'm dressed like someone who knows horses. You two can be my out-of-state friends that I've dragged along for the drive. That way, if anyone challenges you as to what you're doing in a paddock—" she flashed a grin "—you can pretend to be clueless."

The yard was rather run-down; a bare earth yard with half a dozen boxes on one side, badly in need of repair and paint. We exited the car, and I hitched my canvas bag with the microchip reader higher on my shoulder. There was no one around, but I could see three heads hanging over the stable doors. None of them were Fiery Lights. A quick glance into the other stables showed they were empty, although they were in need of mucking out.

"Go," Pen said. "I'll hang around here in case someone comes."

Josie and I walked behind the boxes to where paddocks stretched down to a line of trees that looked like a creek. The wire was sagging in places, and Josie cursed as she ducked underneath and got her shirt caught on a rusty barb. There were three horses grazing in the first paddock, but even at a distance, we could see that they were stocky ponies, not anything resembling a thoroughbred. An adjoining paddock looked more promising. There were several horses, and although they were too far away to see clearly, they looked larger than ponies. Keeping to the fence, we walked in that direction.

We'd just ducked under a second barbed wire fence when I heard the roar of a dirt bike behind us.

"Keep going," said Josie. "We're ignorant tourists from Brisbane. Never been bush in our lives."

We were halfway to the horses when the dirt bike caught up with us.

The helmetless rider swerved in front of us and screeched to a halt. "Where the fuck do you think you're going?"

"Hello." Josie smiled. "Do you live here? We're with our friend who's in your yard asking about somewhere to keep her horse, and we thought we'd go and look at yours. How many do you have?"

"You're trespassing." He folded his arms across his chest. "It's not safe. There's a bull in this paddock."

I hadn't seen as much as a heifer, but it was a good excuse. "Oh, we're not trespassing, as our friend is talking to the owner of the yard. I'm sure we won't be long."

"I'm the owner, so your friend can't be talking to me, can she? I don't have any room for more horses. Look around. No grass."

I dutifully looked around; compared to my own paddocks, these were in a luxurious state.

We seemed to have reached a stalemate. The bike rider wasn't keen to let us go further. We didn't want to leave without having a closer look at the horses.

"Please, can we at least see the ones over there?" Josie made one final attempt. "I have peppermints. My friend told me that horses love peppermints."

The man heaved an exasperated sigh. I could almost see the thoughts in his head: where on earth did these two idiots come from?

"Ladies, you're trespassing, and if you don't leave now, I'm calling the police. I don't want one of you falling in a rabbit hole, breaking an ankle, and suing me."

There was no option. We walked slowly back, and as soon as the man saw we were leaving, he roared off in a cloud of exhaust, probably to see what damage our friend was doing to his yard merely by walking around it.

We didn't talk on the way back. I tried to get a look at the horses we'd been stopped from approaching, but they were too far away. Out of calling distance as well.

Back at the yard, the man waited, holding the gate open for us to leave. Pen was already in the backseat of the car, so I guessed she'd got short shrift from the personable owner as well.

We waved brightly as we exited, and when I looked back, I saw the owner putting a chain around the gate.

"Any luck?" asked Pen. "He was barely civil to me, saying that he didn't take agistments anymore, hadn't for months, and where I had heard about him? I was vague, saying someone in Benalla, and I made up a name, but I don't think he believed me."

"No luck from us," I said. "Only ponies in the first paddock and we couldn't get close enough to the horses in the second to even see what colour they were. Then he ran us off his land."

Josie, who was once again driving, had been quiet, but she abruptly made a left turn down a dirt road marked as a no-through road. "We might get to see them." She changed down to second gear to manoeuvre over a washout. The undercarriage caught and ground alarmingly. "I saw a ute go past the other end of the paddock when we were talking to Mr Charming. If that's a public road off this lane, as I think it is, we might get a closer look."

There was a track, although it was too rough for the car. We left it at the end and walked and came up on the other side of the same paddock we'd been in earlier. Even better, the horses were clustered under a tree near the fence.

"Two chestnuts," said Pen.

But as we got closer, we could see they looked nothing like Flame. They were thoroughbreds, but one had a wide blaze and the other was a gelding.

They came over easily enough when I called. Figuring we'd come this far, and so we might as well check, I ran the chip reader down each of their necks. The gelding had no chip at all, but the mare had one, so I stored that to look up later.

Pen clicked a photo of each on her phone and we went back to the car.

"Wasted trip." I tipped my head back to the rest and stared out through the windscreen.

"Let's go and have a coffee or something before we head back," Josie said.

We found a small town with a coffee shop. Josie and I looked out of the window, watching life pass by in a small town. Even so, it was busier than Worrindi on a winter weekend. Pen was busy on her phone.

When we'd nearly finished our coffee and some rather good Anzac biscuits, she looked up. "Do you have flights booked back to Queensland? I've just logged in to a couple of forums, and one of them has an entire thread dedicated to horses that look like Fiery Lights. My Flame's listed as well as the yard that we've just come from. Your Flame isn't, but that's not surprising. But there's more. While most of the sightings are in New South Wales, with a couple in South Australia, there's another one near Beechworth, which is maybe an hour away from here." Pen put the phone on the table and looked at each of us in turn.

"Another wild goose chase? I don't even know really what we're hoping to prove," I said.

"We're looking for the real Fiery Lights. We're clearing my name. We're girl detectives on a jaunt. We're having fun." Josie grinned at me as she spoke.

I was having fun. This was a time out of my everyday life. I'd barely left Queensland before, and now I was racing around the country chasing stolen racehorses. By now, I honestly didn't expect anything to come of it, but it didn't matter. We were here. The hard work was done in getting here. I might as well enjoy it.

"We don't have flights booked," I said. "If we go off to look at this horse, it might mean another day down here."

"So?" Josie's eyes sparkled. "We wouldn't get back to Queensland tonight anyway. What about you, Pen? Do you need to be back anytime soon?"

"Not me. As long as I'm back for work on Monday, I'm free as a bird."

"We could go and check out this horse. Stay overnight somewhere. Drive back to Melbourne tomorrow." Josie wore an impish grin. She was enjoying this haring around the country, this derring-do.

"I'm game," I said. "But I should call Sue and Moni first and make sure a meteorite hasn't flattened them."

"Call now." Josie pushed the empty plates to one side and pulled her coffee closer. "Pen and I will check the route."

I walked outside and called Jayboro.

"Jayboro Outstation: real outback, right here. Moni speaking."

She sounded totally professional, but there was warmth in her voice as well.

"Real outback, right here?" The tagline—one that I had never used—was perfect.

"Felix! Where are you? Sue came up with that line."

"I'm in central Victoria. Town called Benalla. And I love the line. I hope she'll let me use it."

"She will. It's better than the first one she came up with: 'Come to Jayboro. If you can find it, it's free.' So what's in Benalla?"

"Chestnut horses."

"Oh?"

"Who aren't Fiery Lights. But there's another look-alike an hour away who might be. We're travelling with the woman from the trail-riding forum—Pen. She'd been suspicious of her Flame as well. We'll fill you in when we get back." I took a deep breath. "How's Jayboro?"

"No worries. Everything is fine here. There's a couple from Perth in the campground and a mother and daughter in one of the cabins. Sue and I took a short beginner's trail ride yesterday. Sue rode Patch and nearly got bucked off. I rode Budgie because it meant I wouldn't have far to fall. Take your time. We're good until Monday, and we might be able to stay until Wednesday if necessary."

"That could be good, if you really don't mind."

Warmth permeated her voice, even down the phone. "Felix, we love it here. It's no trouble. Really."

"Thank you. How's Tess doing? Are she and Ripper getting along okay?"

"Oh, Felix." Amused exasperation coloured Moni's voice. "That dog is such a cutie-pants. I just want to cuddle her and give her love. When we arrived, Tess barked and barked and barked from the veranda. Then she decided we were here to stay, and she must have felt that she should go. So she took off and dug herself a wallow along one side of the barn. Sue tempted her out and she hung around, all wary. We didn't want to drag her home and tie her up, but of course she couldn't stay out all night. I know she's lived rough, but that was in town. We were worried that if she wouldn't come into the house, the wild dogs and dingoes would get her."

"What about Ripper?"

"He was chilled. He's quite mature and sensible these days, and he trotted off and made friends with her, but she still wouldn't follow him back to the house. We figured that Tess must have thought the house was Ripper's now, not hers. So before dusk, Sue made a big show of putting Rip into the four-wheel drive, and then she was able to tempt Tess inside and feed her."

My heart melted for my dog, still so unsure of her place that another dog was able to usurp it without trying.

"But it's okay now. More than okay. We shut the two dogs in the house overnight together. Where does Tess normally sleep?"

"She has the run of the house, but she normally sleeps at the foot of my bed."

"That's okay, then. That's where Ripper usually sleeps—now that we've finally got him to stay on the floor—and so Tess came in to see where Ripper was, and the two of them snuggled up together on the rug at the foot of the bed. I'll send you a photo."

"Thank you for being so kind to Tess. I hope Ripper was okay."

"Rip was fine. He rolls with it. But you're in trouble now with Sue." The smile in Moni's voice told me it wasn't anything to worry about.

"Oh? Why?"

"Because I want to go to the animal refuge in the Isa and bring home a dog. A dog like Tess who needs another chance in life. Rip would like a friend. And *I* would love another dog. So would Sue, actually. She just wants to make sure Mrs T's okay with it."

The cheery update reassured me. Jayboro was home, and home was definitely where my heart was. But it would still be there in a few days. In the meantime, I would enjoy the moment.

"Thanks again, and my love to both of you."

"Bring back a bottle of decent Yarra Valley pinot noir, and Sue will love you forever."

"She already does, but I'll remember that."

"Oh, and Mrs T made you a cake. It's sticky pear and ginger. She made us promise not to eat it, but if you're not home by Wednesday, all bets are off."

"I'll be back. That's the incentive I need."

"Sue will be sorry she missed you. She's cleaning the amenities block. So far, she's evicted a bad tempered goanna and a baby magpie. If she hadn't intervened, one might have been breakfast for the other."

I said goodbye, and with the image of Sue and a goanna having a standoff, I hung up and went back inside the coffee shop. Josie and Pen had their heads together, looking at Pen's phone. They looked up as I sat.

"Beechworth. That's where we're going." Josie pointed to a dot on the screen. "It's to the east of here, on the edge of another wine region. It's historic and rather pretty. I picked grapes at one of the wineries there a few years ago."

Pen pointed to a green area on the map just to the south of the town. "This is where someone reckons Fiery Lights is hidden. She's in an agistment yard, but I found them on the net—they exist, and they're advertising space for horses, so we'll have a reason to go in."

I drove for a bit, now that we were on the country roads, and Josie occupied her time by singing along to the radio and keeping up a running commentary on the towns we passed through. It seemed she'd spent quite a bit of time here over the years, as she had a funny story about most of them.

Pen was quiet, and I wondered what her story was. She was probably thinking she was stuck in a car with two crazy women from the internet.

There was an accident about twenty minutes from Beechworth, and traffic came to a standstill. An ambulance screamed past on the hard shoulder. I turned the engine off and laid my head back on the rest.

Josie got out of the car and walked up the road, as if she had too much energy crackling inside her to stay in the car any longer. I fiddled with the radio to find a traffic report.

Pen sat forwards and rested her arms on the seats in front.

"I hope you don't mind me asking this," she said, "but are you and Josie a couple?"

Were we? A week ago, I would have said we were heading that way. Then I would have said we most definitely weren't. Now I was back to *maybe* again.

Pen must have taken my silence as unwillingness to answer, as she said, "It doesn't matter. I was only passing the time."

"No, it's not that." I turned sideways in the seat so I could see her face. "I was just wondering how to answer you. See, we were heading that way, but then this whole thing about Flame came up, and I backed off. Trust and honesty are important to me, and well, suddenly it seemed we had neither."

"And now?"

"I don't know, Pen. Maybe. I'd like to think so. But there's still the fact that I've spent my whole life in a remote part of the outback, and Josie, well, she's never lived anywhere for more than a few months at a time."

"That's not a reason to avoid a relationship. My last boyfriend was from Vietnam. Oh, the issues that initially kept us apart, including his family, including mine. Including Australian immigration and lack of money. But we got through that because we wanted to be together."

I wanted to ask if they were still together. Her house had the look of a single person living there, but it seemed nosy to mention that.

"He died two years ago. He was hit by a drunk driver. But I wouldn't have swapped our years together for anything, even though I wondered at the time if it was even worth trying to start something."

"I'm sorry."

Pen gave a half smile. "Thanks. I'm getting there. She looked at her watch. "If this traffic doesn't clear, we won't get to the yard before dark."

I took the change of subject. "What would you be doing tonight if you weren't here?"

"Not much. I have my books and the TV and a frozen dinner for one. I usually ride on Sundays. Casey and her yard saved my sanity after Hien passed. That's my motivation for this tour of country Victoria."

The car door opened, and Josie jumped back in. "The police are letting people past in one lane. We'll be moving soon."

"Story of your life?" I teased, and she grinned back.

"Maybe it was."

I noticed the past tense, and I was willing to bet that Pen did as well.

# CHAPTER 21

It was nearly dusk when we pulled into a quiet lane, lined with the green leaves and grey bark of gum trees. Josie, who was driving again, pulled up in front of a five-bar gate that led to a gravel driveway. The sign read *Ghost Gum Stables*.

She rested her elbows on the wheel and leant forwards to peer out the windscreen. "This is posh. This is the sort of place I would expect someone to put a valuable horse, not that last place—too run-down."

Pen got out and opened the gate for Josie to pass through. Pen latched it behind us, and we drove slowly along the drive, tyres crunching on the gravel.

The yard was beautiful. There wasn't a stray piece of hay, not a weed, not a piece of manure. The loosebox doors were painted blue, and there was even a weather vane on top of what looked like the tack shed. The entire yard looked like it belonged in the English countryside.

There didn't seem to be anyone about. Without discussion, we split up. Pen headed to the looseboxes to check the occupants, Josie headed left, and I headed right to where I could see some horses grazing behind post and rails. I got closer and could see they were fine horses. Breeding showed in their clean lines, and money showed in their thin coats, which were covered with monogrammed rugs. One was a chestnut, but the rug hung too low for me to see if it was a mare.

There didn't seem to be anyone about, so I ducked under the fence and walked over. It was a gelding, so without wasting time, I headed back.

A quiet whistle sounded. I looked over, and when Josie waved at me, I changed direction and headed towards her. She pointed to the paddock, where a light bobbed—someone walking over to see who we were and carrying a torch, I guessed.

"Here," Josie hissed as I came over. "Look at this one."

Another Flame. The mare was friendly, nudging Josie in the ribs. A thin white stripe ran down her chestnut face, and even in the dim light, I could see the white socks on her hind legs.

I fumbled in my bag for the reader, wishing I'd had the foresight to pull it out of its case and turn it on before getting out of the car.

"Hurry. They're getting closer." Josie stood next to me, as if by shrinking together in the shadows we could avoid being seen.

"Hello." Pen's voice came loud in the dusk. I glanced back and saw her wave to the bobbing torch. "Sorry to make you come across the paddock."

The torch changed direction slightly to head towards Pen.

"He hasn't seen us." Josie grabbed the edge of my bag and held it open so that I could more easily retrieve the chip reader.

I dropped the case but ignored it and moved over to the chestnut. She lipped at the end of my plait with her soft nose, then switched to nuzzle the beads in Josie's hair.

She had a chip. Of course she would. A horse as fine as this was obviously going to be chipped. I stored the reading and nodded at Josie. She picked up the case I'd dropped and dumped it in my bag. Then we walked back to where Pen was talking to a small, wiry man. From his build and stance, I guessed he was a jockey or an ex-jockey.

"Josie, Felix, meet David." Pen turned to us. "I was apologising that we were so late, but he knew about the accident that held us up."

"That's okay, ladies," David said, his voice soft. "I'm not sure what I can show you in this light, but I can tell you about the yard. We don't do many straightforward agistments, though. We're mainly in the business of training eventers, and most of the horses that come to us are being brought on for three-day events. Maybe you've heard of Shenanigans, the Olympic gold medallist?"

I hadn't, but I nodded anyway.

"That mare was trained here. Jessica, her rider, came here for pre-Olympic preparation."

Considering we were three rather scruffy-looking women with a small hire car, he was treating Pen's request for information about agistment with the utmost seriousness.

"Two of our horses used to be on the Australian show jumping team, but most of them are youngsters."

"Are those the horses out in the paddock there?" I indicated the paddock I'd just left.

"No, those are racehorses spelling—that is, having some time off before preparation starts again."

"They're beautiful. What are their names?"

"To be honest, I don't know. If you're looking for racing tips, I'm not the person to ask." David indicated his leg. "I'm not a fan of racehorses after one nearly put me in a wheelchair, so I don't have much to do with them."

I let the subject drop. It seemed too pointed to continue asking about them.

"Tell me about your horse," David said to Pen. "We've got a couple of spots in the yard at the moment, but Craig, the owner, is hoping to find a promising young horse he can work with."

"My horse, uh, Milo, isn't in that league at all. I mainly do amateur events, some dressage competitions, one-day events, that sort of thing. But Milo is important to me, and I want the best place I can find for him. I'm not sure if you would take a horse like that."

"I'm not sure either," David said with candour. "But with a name like Milo, I think we'd take a second look. Are you able to come back tomorrow? Then I can show you around properly."

Josie was slightly behind David, and she shook her head. It was a brief movement, but Pen caught it.

"To be honest, I think we might be wasting your time. I love my horse, but I think he would be outclassed here." Pen held out a hand.

David shook her hand. "It's no problem, really. Have you just moved to Beechworth? I can send you a couple of recommendations for yards, if you want." He fished out a business card from his shirt pocket and handed it to Pen.

"Thanks. I'll email you tomorrow, if that's okay?"

"No problem. I'll look forward to hearing from you."

He watched as we piled back into the hire car and drove off. We didn't speak until we were back on the road, heading for Beechworth. It was full-dark now, but there was plenty of traffic.

"Well?" demanded Pen. "You must have found something."

"A chestnut mare, white stripe, two white socks. Thoroughbred. Looks eerily like the horse Felix has and the horse in your yard. Has a microchip." Josie accelerated towards the distant lights of Beechworth. "I think this calls for a celebratory glass of wine."

We found a pub in a back street that had rooms on the first floor. They were old-style pub rooms, each with a narrow double bed and a ceiling fan. The bathroom was down the corridor, and there was no TV.

"Perfect!" Josie bounced on the bed. "My favourite sort of place to stay. Reminds me of Worrindi. My room in the pub there is similar."

We had three rooms in a row with doors that opened onto the wide veranda. From there, we could see up and down the street. Rather than eat in the pub, we walked into town to see what there was and picked a pasta place that occupied a stone building. Inside were several small rooms that made up the restaurant area. It was quiet, and we had a room to ourselves. The database was awkward to look up on the small screen of a mobile phone, but this time, we didn't have any choice. Using Pen's phone, which was faster and flasher than Josie's or mine, I logged in to the microchip database and looked up the chips I'd scanned earlier. The first one, the mare from the rundown place where we'd been escorted off as trespassers, was, as I'd thought, an ex-racehorse, nine years old. Not Fiery Lights.

The second was the mare we'd just left.

The chip was again registered to Fiery Lights.

I was silent as I twirled tagliatelle on my fork. Two horses I could explain. Three made no sense. I couldn't think of any reason why someone would go to the trouble of finding three

221

nearly identical horses and implanting microchips with the same information in all of them.

Pen voiced what we were probably all thinking.

"We have to go to the police. This isn't just a caper for us anymore. It has to be criminal, even if we can't figure out what or why."

Josie and I nodded.

"I hope that Casey isn't involved. I'm sure she's not, but I suppose I better not mention it to her. Perverting the course of justice and all that. What about you two?"

I looked at Josie, and she looked at me. I reached across the table and grasped her hand. "Neither of us has done anything wrong, but that, of course, will have to be proven. But we'll face it together." Josie's hand squeezed mine so tightly my fingers went white. "But I would like to be back home when we call the police. I don't think a day or two will make a difference, but it's my home, my business, my horses, they will investigate. It's not fair to expect Sue and Moni to deal with that."

"Fair enough." Pen speared a piece of gnocchi. "When will you get back?"

"Assuming we can get back to Tullamarine in time for a flight tomorrow, it would still be the next day. I doubt we'll be able to drive home from Townsville without an overnight stop. That means it will be sometime Monday."

"How about we call our respective police around four on Monday? If you're not back by then, you can email me."

"That's reasonable to me. Josie?"

"Yeah. We have to." Her gaze moved from our linked hands back to my face. "I'm sorry, Felix. I've dragged you into something you really shouldn't be involved in. I shouldn't have listened to Barney in the first place. I shouldn't have agreed to take Flame. And I shouldn't have brought her to Jayboro." Her mouth twisted wryly. "It's your fault, of course. If you hadn't been so gorgeous, so obviously lesbian, so attractive, and so *nice*, I would have taken her somewhere else. Flame was my excuse to see you."

Our gazes met and clung. The restaurant faded from my vision. The noise from the other rooms, the buzz of conversation, the scrape of Pen's fork on her plate all muted as if we were underwater. There was only Josie and only our linked hands, her gaze meeting mine and the promise and heat in her expression. I dragged out shallow breaths as I turned her hand over so that it was on top of mine and encompassed it with my other hand. Her skin was cool in the air-conditioned room, her hands rough from her physical work, but to me, it was all heat and promise. It was spark and sex.

Pen put down her fork. "I can't keep staring at my plate any longer. Do you two want me to leave?"

The spell was broken, and I released Josie's hand.

"No, of course not. We're in this together. The three of us." I reached out with my other hand to grasp Pen's, and the three of us clasped hands over the table.

"You could have saved the cost of a room, though," Pen said as she released our hands. "I doubt you'll use both."

Despite the promise and the knowledge of how the evening would end, we didn't rush. We lingered over tiramisu and coffee, and then went back to the pub where we were staying and bought a bottle of wine to take upstairs to the veranda. There were three chairs, and we drank the red wine and chatted there. Pen was between Josie and me, and if I would rather have been next to Josie to hold her hand and more easily watch her face and the curve of her lips, Pen's presence between us heightened the anticipation and yet also made the evening a pleasant one between friends. It wouldn't be right to rush off and leave Pen alone.

So we talked about our lives and inconsequential things, an easy banter. We learned that Pen did something techy and esoteric on the internet for work, something to do with websites and apps. She had a master plan to pay off her mortgage as soon as possible and then travel for a while, maybe living overseas. She could work from anywhere, she said; she didn't have to be in an outer suburb of Melbourne, living for the weekends when she went riding. She talked of Casey, the yard owner, fondly, and I wondered if she was leaning in that direction. But then the conversation shifted to her last partner who'd died, and if Pen was attracted to Casey, she had a long way to go before her heart would be free to give to someone else.

Around ten, Pen rose. "I'm off to bed. Don't stay up too late, children." She bent and kissed each of us on the cheek, and then she was gone. The door of her bedroom closed behind her with a thud.

Josie rose as well and I thought she would also suggest we go to bed, with all the promise in those words, but she shifted to Pen's vacated chair. She reached for my hand across the gap and for a few minutes, we were silent, hands joined, as we finished the wine.

There was the occasional drift of conversation from the bar below, but otherwise the night was quiet. Although it was well into spring, it was cooler than back home, and I hadn't thought to bring jeans.

Josie's skin was extra golden in the dim lights overhead. I wanted to rest my palm on her inner thigh, feel the softness, the weight of muscle, but the distance between the chairs was too great.

I thought of all she still hadn't told me. I thought of the evasions since I'd known her. I thought of Pen's assumption that we'd sleep together tonight and her quiet urging that I seize the moment.

Things weren't completely right between me and Josie, but would they ever be? Could I live with myself if I slept with Josie and it turned out there were still more evasions and half-truths to come out into the daylight?

Could I live with myself if I didn't sleep with her?

We hadn't kissed since the day I'd found out about Fiery Lights. Yes, I now believed her about Flame and her part in it, and yes, I thought I was doing the right thing, but my mother's words ran through my head: "There's no love without trust, Felicity. How can there be?" My parents' deep love for one another had been the bedrock of our lives. Could I settle, even on a temporary basis, for less than that?

I stood and held out my hand to Josie. One kiss, that would tell me. One kiss would decide if the risk was worth it, if I could live with myself, whatever the outcome.

Josie stood too. I tugged at her hand so that she took a pace forwards. Her curly hair tickled my cheek, and the beads in her hair tapped lightly on my face as she moved.

She settled her arms around my waist. She was physically tough from all the manual work, and the wiry strength in those arms was enough that I would find it hard to break away if she wanted to stop me. If I wanted to escape in the first place.

"Kiss me," she said. Her voice was laced with laughter, lighthearted. It skipped over all seriousness. "You know you want to."

225

I bent my head and touched my lips to hers, just waiting. What would she do? There was enough hesitation in my body, enough tension, that she must sense it. She didn't let me pull away. Her mouth opened under mine, her lips parted, and her tongue stroked the corners of my mouth. There was garlic and red wine on her breath, but there was sweetness underlying that. She gave me her lips and her kisses, and although I wasn't an active participant, she didn't seem to mind.

Her tongue touched mine in a soft press, and her fingers tightened on my waist. My hands hovered in the air, then came to rest on her shoulders, not to push her away but to grasp them and pull her closer.

Her breasts pressed against my chest, and when one of her thighs nudged at mine, I softened my stance so she could push between.

She knew the moment I stopped resisting the roadblocks in my head. Maybe it was when I locked my thigh around hers. Maybe it was when I framed her face with my palms and kissed her long and deeply. Maybe it was when I pressed down on her thigh so that the crotch of my shorts was a ridge that pressed on the side of my clit. Maybe it was all of those things, or maybe she knew all along that it would come to this tonight.

When we broke apart, the longing caught in my throat with such force I could hardly breathe around it. She took my hand. "Your place or mine?"

"Does it matter? I'm not sure there's any difference."

We walked to the nearest door, which opened to my room. There was only my bag on the floor by the bed.

Josie turned from me to bolt the door closed and pull the curtains across. There was a sliver of light shafting in where the curtains didn't meet the frame, but otherwise, the room was dark. She fumbled her way to the other door, the one out to the corridor, and found the switch. A harsh glare flooded the room. After the quiet night and the peace of the small town, it seemed intrusive and sharp, too bright. Right now, I wanted those shadows and muted colours. They echoed the uncertainties between us.

Maybe Josie thought the same as she turned on the bedside lamp and turned off the overhead light.

She was uncharacteristically solemn as she pulled her T-shirt over her head and dropped it onto the floor. Her bra followed, and I saw her breasts, firm, lush, and oh, so perfect.

I followed her lead, and my silent disrobing was as stately as hers. I unbuttoned my shirt. My bra was old and frayed, but she didn't seem to mind. In the space between heartbeats, I shed my bra and unzipped my shorts before I could talk myself out of it. She did the same, and clad only in our undies, we stared at each other across the bed.

Her lightheartedness had deserted her. There was no smile on her face, just those deep, watchful eyes following my movements. I flicked my plait behind me and hooked my fingers into the edge of my briefs. They were functional rather than seductive, the comfortable full granny knickers that I preferred. Her own briefs were plain cotton bikinis, faded from many washings.

She knelt on the bed and held out both hands to me. I took her fingers and knelt too, and we kissed again. This time, there was no hesitation, and the kiss built to a sweet crescendo of stolen breath. Josie slanted her mouth over mine, and our tongues danced and our breaths mingled.

She pulled back and moved her fingers to the sides of my undies and tugged. It took a bit to get them down; they bunched at my hips. But despite the comical clumsiness of less-than-seductive underwear, there was still that seriousness on her face. When they were low on my thighs and my pussy was revealed to her gaze, then she took my hands and moved them to her own underwear. The cotton panties were easier to push down. She trimmed, I noticed, and her bush was clipped so that it was minus the luxuriant curls that I'd expected.

Abruptly, the seriousness was gone, and still hobbled by her briefs, she toppled over onto her side on the bed. The bed bounced, but she removed her underwear in one swift movement.

"Your turn." She grinned, and it sent the impish light back into her eyes, as if she'd decided that this moment was becoming too serious for what we were doing.

My own fall was less graceful than hers, and my knickers caught on my toes, bending them back as I tried to free the material. But it didn't matter. We were both naked, and we were together.

Josie moved closer, so that our bellies touched and our thighs entwined.

My nipples shot tiny shocks down low in my belly as her breasts brushed over them. The ache was building, the low thrum of desire, the sweet, heavy throb.

I slid my palm up her side until I could curve it around to cover her breast. Her nipple stiffened against my fingers, and I scissored it, holding it in place so that I could bend and touch my tongue to the point. Her involuntary shudder and indrawn breath drew a flicker down to my clit, as surely as if she'd touched me there. Her hand clasped my plait, and she wound its length around her fist, anchoring me to her.

I increased the pressure of my fingers on her nipple and touched again with my tongue. Her deep groan and the tug on my hair told me it was welcome.

I kissed her nipples, one, then the other, using mouth and tongue and a gentle scrape of teeth. When I released her breast, and moved up so that I could look her in the eye, she released my plait, and her fingers danced their way down my spine. They cupped a buttock briefly before curving over my hip to rest on my belly, just above my pubes.

"I knew I wanted you, Felix," she said. "I just didn't realise how damn *much* I wanted you."

My breath caught in my throat. I wasn't good at this, at sex. My opportunities had been limited, my partners few. Sue was my last lover, and that was over three years ago, before she and Moni got together. Since then, nothing. Just me and my fingers. Not even a buzzing toy, as I was too nervous of it being discovered in the post office where Narelle checked the senders on the mail.

I didn't have the skills that people in the city seemed to acquire so effortlessly. But here, with Josie, none of that mattered. She was into *me*, if her sounds of appreciation were anything to go by, and I was oh so very definitely into her.

I encouraged her onto her back and pushed her knees apart, spreading her wide to my gaze. Her sex was puffy, wet with desire. I touched her with a finger, then another, mimicking the scissoring action on her breast by repeating it on her clit. Gently, though. As my fingers circled slowly on her clit, she pushed her hips towards me.

"Tell me what you want," I said. "Don't make me guess."

"You. Inside me."

Her hand feathered through my pubes, enough of a distraction that desire built hard and sharp and fast. But I tamped down my own needs so that I could push a finger inside her. Her internal muscles shivered around my finger, and she clamped down hard. I added a second finger and moved them back and forth slowly. She was wet as a monsoon, and there was no friction, just the sweet slickness of her and the warm smell of sex.

"Felix. Oh, Felix." She chanted my name, and the urgency of her words, the staccato beat of them, like galloping hoofbeats, urged me to move faster, harder, until her inner muscles clenched and spasmed around my fingers.

I withdrew slowly, trailing my damp fingers over her mound.

She looked at me with wide eyes. "That was incredible." My water bottle was on the nightstand, and she reached for it, gulping huge swallows.

My breathing hitched in my throat as she focussed back on me. "Lie down." The order was accompanied by a wicked grin. When I'd complied, she said, "Put your hands above your head. Stretch." My hands hit the wall behind my head, so I shuffled down until I could do so. I bent my knees up so they remained on the bed.

Josie rolled off the bed and stood at the foot, looking down at me. "You probably have no idea how amazing you look right now—all long and clean lines, lean with muscle, like a thoroughbred." She knelt on the bed, between my knees, and dropped forwards onto all fours. She kissed my mouth, slantways, just a kiss. I arched up, trying to deepen it, but she moved down, and settled her lips on my neck. A kiss, a nip, a slow slide, and she moved downwards, always downwards.

She nibbled along my collarbone, and when I thought she would drop lower again and kiss my breast, she dropped her tongue into the dip at the bottom of my neck and continued her trailing soft kisses along the other collarbone.

"Josie..." My hands came down to twist in her riot of curls.

She lifted her mouth long enough to bark, "Hands up!" Only when I'd obeyed did she continue her long, slow nibbling kisses.

And then she finally moved down, and her mouth closed over a nipple. She was hot and wet, and her tongue did amazing things, teasing the tip and sucking gently. When my other breast received the same treatment, I closed my eyes to better focus on the sensations, on the desires she was causing.

When she moved yet even lower, I learnt an advantage to my position. With my hands above my head, my small breasts stood up proudly, and Josie was lured into kissing their undersides. I'd never realised how sensitive the skin was there, but under Josie's lips, it became a whole new erogenous zone.

She shifted lower again, this time backing down to the floor on her knees, her upper body between my legs. I lowered my arms, as I wanted to touch her. Needed to touch her. I twined my fingers in her hair as she rested her head on my belly and pressed a kiss just above my navel.

For a few moments, we stayed like this, our breath moving in time, but there was more to come. When her lips started their tortuous, slow descent once more, I was almost sobbing with the need to push her head where I wanted it most. But then she was there, her breath hot on my sex, her fingers circling my clit. When her tongue touched where her fingers were and flickered, it was almost too much. So much for the slow ascent to climax that I'd been working towards; instantly she brought me to the foothills. Once, twice, three times she passed over my clit, and my hips raised off the bed. I came under her flickering tongue and clenched around the finger she'd pushed inside me at the last instant.

When she was sure I was done, she moved up the bed and rested her head on my shoulder.

I curled an arm around hers and brought her closer still. We lay in silence for a few minutes, and then she said, "What are you thinking?"

I pressed a kiss to the top of her head. "That I'm comfortable. How amazing that was. That you're incredible. That it's very warm in here."

I felt her smile curve against my skin. "That's what I'm thinking too. All of that. I'll turn the ceiling fan on."

I missed the touch of her skin in the thirty seconds it took her to get out of bed and flick the switch, but the movement of air from the fan instantly felt better.

"I wish we could stay here longer," she said, "take a few days together. Explore Victoria. Eat yum cha in Melbourne. See the ocean."

I wanted that too. "We can't. We have to get back so that we're at Jayboro when the police come."

"I know. I'm just wishing." That soft kiss on my shoulder again. "I'm wishing a lot of things right now."

# CHAPTER 22

PEN DIDN'T SAY ANYTHING THE next morning, but her warm smile as we met in the dining room for breakfast said that she knew exactly how we had spent the night. She probably did know exactly. The interior walls were a single skin of panelling.

It was Sunday, and the pub didn't open until noon, but they'd set out a simple breakfast for us: coffee, toast and Vegemite, and some muffins.

I borrowed Pen's phone and checked the flights back to Townsville. "There's one at three," I said, "but it's very expensive. Twice the price of what we paid to fly down." I checked another airline. It was the same. "How long will it take us to get to the airport?"

"Three hours, if there's no hold-ups." Pen sipped her coffee. "This instant stuff is pretty awful."

"I've had worse." Josie drank her own. "At least it's hot."

"Would we make a midday flight?"

Pen considered. "Yes. If we leave as soon as we can."

For a moment, we were silent. It seemed a shame to end our jaunt together in a mad dash for the airport. But equally, it was vital that we got back as soon as possible.

"I think we better go for it," I said. "I'll book the flight if you wouldn't mind packing the car?"

Josie exhaled, a long, soft breath. "Back to reality."

I booked the noon flight while the others packed. I hoped I'd have no unexpected bills in the next few weeks; my credit card must have been close to maxed. Josie didn't have one, so I'd paid for both of us.

Pen had obviously checked the route. "You have to return the car to the airport?" she asked.

I nodded.

"I'm not sure we'll have time to go via my place," she said. "Melbourne traffic is insane, even on Sundays, but you can drop me at a friend's place on the way."

"Are you sure?" It seemed a bit mean to dump Pen and run. She hadn't known us before yesterday, but she'd come along for the ride and had been a good companion.

"Absolutely."

"I hope we see you again." Josie found Pen's hand and squeezed. "Somewhere. Not sure where, but I hope we do."

"You can count on it. Maybe I'll holiday in outback Queensland. I've heard of these lovely little cabins in the middle of nowhere with trail riding."

"You don't need to book a cabin," I said. "You can stay with me anytime."

Then we flung the bags in the boot, and Josie slid behind the wheel once more and took off as if the hounds of hell were after us.

The traffic was light, and we made good time, the little Victorian towns and the rolling landscape sliding past. We stopped at a winery, and Josie rushed in and bought a bottle of pinot noir for Sue and Moni. But other than that, we kept going. We detoured slightly to drop Pen at her friend's place in

Seymour, a little out of Melbourne. Her friend would drive her home, she said.

Josie and I hugged Pen, and then Pen encompassed us both in a three-way hug. "Look after each other," she said.

I nodded, and the mood might have got sentimental except that Pen stuck to practicalities. "So you'll call me when you're home, sometime tomorrow, and then we'll call our respective police?"

"Yeah. We won't be able to get home from Townsville tonight, not without risking it by driving in the dark."

"Call." Pen kissed us both on the cheek again, and then with a wave of her hand, she swung away up the drive of the neat brick house.

It was back to me and Josie again. Bonnie and Clyde. Thelma and Louise. Except neither of those had ended well, if I remembered rightly.

The flight back was nearly full, and because we had booked late, we had to sit separately. I was crammed between two bulky men who glared at me every time I tried to turn a page of the in-flight magazine. Josie fared better. She entertained a young child she was seated next to by pulling faces while his mother enjoyed some quiet time.

Thanks to the time difference, it was mid-afternoon when we arrived in Townsville and retrieved the ute.

Josie and I hadn't had much time to talk. Not about things that mattered. Not about Flame. Not about us. I hadn't wanted to raise the subject of us with Pen around. Then we'd had to race to return the hire car, and the rush and stress of airport security and boarding hadn't left much time for a heart-to-heart. But the journey back to Jayboro stretched ahead of us—long hours, the two of us in the car. It was inevitable we would talk, not just about us, about her and me together, but also about Flame and what was likely to happen there. In particular, there was Josie's involvement to discuss and, to a lesser extent, mine.

Josie caught my hand as I opened the ute. "Hey," she said. Her smile was a little out of kilter, a little hesitant, compared to her normal exuberant confidence. "You okay?"

I was okay. I'd swung like a pendulum over who and what to believe, and knew that I might change my mind again, but right now, I was okay. It was still just me and Josie, with no outside world to intrude.

"Yeah. I'm good." I turned from the ute and wrapped my arms around her shoulders. She pulled me tight, her own arms encircling my waist.

"Any regrets?" Her voice was muffled by my shoulder.

"No." I thought they might come later, but right now, I had none. Last night and the memories of lovemaking still thrummed in my blood.

"Good." She lifted her head to regard me with a steady gaze. "Me neither."

I bent down, and she reached up, and I don't know which of us had moved towards the other first, but then we were kissing, and that was the thing that mattered.

We eased apart.

"Want me to drive?" She grinned as she said it, and I knew she knew I would turn her down.

"I'm fine. I'm more used to these roads."

We didn't discuss it, but we drove without stopping. I knew it was unlikely, but if there was any chance of making Jayboro safely tonight, then I wanted to take it. But even though I pushed the speed limit and we only stopped once for fuel, a coffee, and a sandwich eaten as we drove, when dusk fell, we were still five hours away.

I slowed as we passed through a small town. There was a motel, and the pub offered accommodation.

"What do you think?" I asked. "We can keep going, driving slowly, and we'll get to Jayboro in the middle of the night. Or we can stop here and leave early."

As I said the words, I knew what I wanted. Real life, drama and discussions would take place tomorrow. Any thought of Josie and me together would have to wait, and with the future uncertain, I wasn't sure if we would even regain what we had. I wasn't sure if I would want to. But now, it was still just us, in the darkness of a small town.

"We told Pen we'd be back tomorrow. And Sue and Moni are fine at Jayboro." She turned so her back rested against the door, and she shrugged. "I know what I want. But it's not entirely up to me."

I slowed down even more. The motel was small, and the sign said *vacancy*. "It's dangerous to drive at night. Kangaroos. Cattle. Road trains. I try and avoid it; there are too many accidents, too many people killed."

"I'm not arguing loudly."

I pulled to a stop outside the motel.

"Or at all."

"Let's see what rooms they have." I rotated my shoulders after the long drive. "If they have a queen room with air con and it's not too expensive, then let's stay."

The ute door slammed as Josie leapt out without another word. I turned off the engine and sighed. Random thoughts rolled through my head: I had to call Sue. How were Tess and Ripper doing? How many bookings did I have? The daily thoughts that had been pushed aside while we were in Victoria came crowding back. Already, the caper was over. Already, I was thinking of home. With an effort, I pushed the thoughts away, at least until tomorrow.

Josie came back within five minutes, waved a key, and pointed to the row of units. I started the ute and followed her to the end one. When I joined her inside, she gave me a tour as if she owned the place.

"King bed. Flat screen TV. All the fancy toiletries you could want. Kettle, coffee, biccies, and there's a discount voucher for brekky at a café in town." She named the price and it was extremely reasonable.

She darted back to the ute, dragged in our bags, and dumped them on the bench before falling backwards on the bed.

I sat next to her, and she rolled over so that her cheek rested on my lap. I stroked her hair, twisting her windswept curls around my fingers.

"I should call Sue and Moni. Let them know what's going on and when we'll be back."

She nodded against my leg. "I think I'll take a shower. I'm all sweaty from the journey."

She bounced to her feet like a jumping jack and disappeared into the bathroom. Her head popped back around the door. "Scented soap and body lotion. You better hope I leave you some."

I called Jayboro and Sue answered on the first ring. "Jayboro Outstation, this is Sue."

"What happened to 'real outback, right here'?" I asked. "I liked that phrase."

"Felix! Thank goodness." Sue's tone was harried for such a laid-back person. "Did you get my messages?"

'No.' I looked at the display on my basic phone and only then saw the two text messages and a missed call. "They must have come in when we were out of range."

"Never mind now. Where are you?"

"Small town about five hours west of Townsville. We'll be back before lunch tomorrow."

"Good. Moni's down at the barn at the moment. We've brought Flame in for the night. Someone appeared here yesterday in a rattly old cattle truck. The driver said he had authorisation to take Flame."

Worry settled in the pit of my stomach. "What did you do?"

"I can spout legal bullshit with the best of them." The smile in Sue's voice came clearly across the line. "I asked him for the authorisation to take the horse signed by the owner, the owner being Josie. He said Josie wasn't the owner, to which I said that Josie had brought the horse here and had been paying the bills. As far as I was concerned, I said, Josie was the owner. He got a little nasty, said that was crap, and that he would take the horse. I told him if he did, the charges would be trespass and stealing. He left empty-handed. However, we don't trust him not to come back, so Flame's in the barn where he can't get to her as easily. What happened down in Victoria?"

"Short version is we found two more look-alike horses, both with a microchip saying they were Fiery Lights."

Sue was silent for a moment. "You have to go to the police, Felix."

"I know. Pen is waiting until she hears we're back, and then we'll go to the police at the same time. I want to be back at Jayboro when they arrive."

"I don't think you've got that long. I think you have to call them now."

She was right. "I'll call Pen first. Have her check if her Flame is still there."

"Call me back if there's anything you need to tell us. Otherwise, we'll see you tomorrow." There was a noise in the background, and then Moni's American twang came down the line. "Josie's horse—well, *someone's* horse—is fine. Happy as a pig in shit in the barn."

I ended the call and moved to rest against the headboard. The sound of the shower had stopped, and Josie appeared, wrapped in a towel. She took one look at me and moved to sit on the edge of the bed. "I guess now isn't the time to seduce you."

I rested my hand on her leg, just below the towel. "Wait until later. We have to call Pen." I filled her in on what Sue had said.

"It seems like me and my horse are a lot of trouble." Her head bowed, and she picked at the edge of the towel where it lay on her thigh.

"Yeah. You are." Her head shot up until she could see the twist of a smile on my face. "But we've come this far now. We'll sort it out."

She moved to rest against the headboard next to me, and I dialled Pen's number and put the phone on speaker.

"Hi, Felix." Pen must have programmed my number into her phone. "Where are you?"

"Not home yet. There's a problem. Sue says that someone came with a truck and tried to take our Flame. Have you been out to Casey's yard?"

She was silent for a moment. "Not today."

240

"Any chance you could go out? Or call Casey?"

"I'll go out. Casey would wonder why I'd called to ask about Flame. I'll call you back." She ended the call.

I looked at Josie. Her face was back to business, the edge of flirty playfulness gone. "This isn't the happy caper anymore."

"No." I picked up her hand, played with her fingers for a second, then put her hand down with a sigh. "I'll have a shower, and then maybe we should get something to eat. Pen won't call for a while."

Pen called while we were eating dinner in the pub.

"She's gone," she said without preamble. "I rang Casey when I realised and gave her the excuse that I'd left my book at the yard, gone back to retrieve it, and noticed that Flame was missing. She said that she went late this afternoon. Her owner came to collect her. Casey sounded puzzled; she said they gave no advance notice, just arrived at the gate with the truck and called to get in."

"That sounds like what happened to our Flame."

"I'm calling the police." Pen was businesslike, as if she expected me to argue. "Then I'll call Casey. Assuming the police will come out tonight, I'll hang around."

"I'll call the police too. But hopefully, they won't come until tomorrow morning when we'll be back."

"I'll do it now. I'll let you know what happens. Talk soon." And she was gone.

I relayed to Josie what she'd said. "We better do our bit too."

Josie ate the last of her lasagne and finished her beer. "I'm ready. Let's call from the motel. It will be quieter." A burst of noise from the public bar backed up her words.

We didn't dilly-dally on the way back to the motel but walked fast and in silence. I wasn't thinking about the call we had to make. I was thinking of the woman at my side and what would happen to her. Would she face charges? I didn't think so, but what did I know about such things? My only dealings with the police had been a speeding ticket and the time they'd come to get me out of school when Dad died. I wished I'd thought to ask Sue, but it was too late for that now.

Josie didn't appear troubled, but then with her float-through-life attitude, she probably assumed it would all come out in the wash. Or maybe, if it all went wrong, she was planning on doing a disappearing act. I pushed down that thought and concentrated on getting back to the motel as quickly as we could.

"Do you want to call or shall I?" I kicked off my boots, sat on the bed, and dug out my old phone. "Which would be better? Maybe you should. Flame was supposed to be your horse. If you call, you can explain how you came to have her. That might make it clearer that you didn't know what you were getting into."

"I don't know." Josie sat too, and her knee jiggled fast. "Maybe you should call as the business owner with suspicions."

"Let's both call," I suggested. "We can put the phone on speaker and say we're both here."

"Okay." She gave a decisive nod. "Let's do it."

My finger hovered over the buttons. "I guess we call Crime Stoppers, not 000. It's not an emergency. I could call the police station in Worrindi, but it's not just a local matter." I caught her hand. "Josie, Crime Stoppers is anonymous, if you want it to be."

Her gaze was steady. "Thank you. But really, what would be the point of that? They'll come out to Jayboro. They'll look at Flame. They'll talk to you as the owner and Sue and Moni who were there when they came to retrieve Flame. You won't be able to keep me out of it—and I don't want to be. I want to clear my name as much as I can." Her fingers twitched in mine. "I know I lied to you before, Felix. I know I was evasive. But that part is finished. I want you to know that."

I shifted so that my back was against the headboard. She moved next to me. "Ready?"

She nodded again, and I called the number. A female voice answered.

"My name is Felicity Jameson, and I'm here with Josie Beccari. We think we may have some information on the missing racehorse, Fiery Lights."

The responder was efficient and first took down our details before asking us what we knew.

Josie glanced at me, and her voice shook as she started to tell the first part of the story, about working in a motel in Longreach cleaning rooms and the man who asked her to find somewhere for his horse. "I didn't think it was strange, after all. I've been offered weirder things in pubs. We'd been talking about horses; he knew I rode, and he seemed pleasant."

"Can you describe him to me?" The responder's voice was calm, detached, but non-judgmental. I was grateful for that. I had expected blame, censure, and while that might well come in time, right now it was a relief not to have to deal with that as well.

Josie bit her lip. "Forties, maybe. Full head of brown hair on the shaggy side. Clean-shaven. Dressed in tourist clothes, the sort you see on any city person holidaying in the outback—those lightweight travel shorts with zips everywhere, T-shirts—that sort of thing. He said his name was Barney."

"Do you know his last name?"

"No. I guess the motel would have details, though—it was the Outback Oasis, and he was there, oh, sometime around the end of May this year."

"So what happened then?"

"I gave him my mobile number and email and said that I'd be in Worrindi in a couple of weeks. He said that was fine and asked if I could find somewhere before July. He said he needed to move his horse—he called her Flame—by then.

"In June, I was working in the Commercial, a pub in Worrindi. I'd met Felix—Felicity—and had been out to her property for a trail ride. Felix knew her stuff and cared about her horses. I thought Jayboro would be the perfect place for Flame. I didn't say anything to Felix immediately. I hadn't heard any more from Barney, and I was starting to assume it had been the usual bullshit. But then I got a call from him, asking if I was in Worrindi yet and if I'd found anywhere for Flame. Of course, I told him about Jayboro. He said it sounded perfect. I asked him for his details so that I could give them to Felix, but he said, 'No. The deal is that you find somewhere for the horse, not me. You do this in your name.'"

Josie shot me a glance and her thigh was as rigid as a fencepost beside me. "I admit it sounded strange. I hesitated, and I was about to ask why when he said, 'I'll contact you in a week when the horse will arrive,' and he hung up. I figured that was the last I'd hear of it, but the next day, I received money sent via PayPal to my email address. It was three months' agistment money. To me, it was a huge sum. I knew I could pay Felix half of it and she would be happy, and I would be happy. I did wonder, of course, but I brushed it aside, told myself he was probably a stupid city businessman with more money than sense. If he didn't know the going rate for agistment, well, it wasn't my problem. So I went to Felix with the proposition. She accepted, and I called Barney again and gave him Jayboro's details."

"Go on." The responder's voice was encouraging. It must be strange, I thought, working for a hotline like Crime Stoppers, never knowing who would call. Doubtlessly, there would be a lot of crank calls, a lot of vindictive people trying to dob in an enemy on some made up reason. But occasionally, there'd something interesting.

"Felix, you better take over." Josie nudged my knee.

I described Flame's arrival in the cattle truck, out of condition and without any of the paraphernalia you would expect for such a horse.

"I was suspicious," I said, "but I pushed it to one side. And Josie gave me explanations for that." I drew a deep breath, wondering where to continue the narrative. "I had some friends visiting from the UK, and one of them took a photo of herself with Flame and sent it to her brother. He fancies himself as a gambler and immediately picked the likeness between Flame and Fiery Lights. We all laughed it off." I was rambling and needed to cut to the chase. "To cut a long story short, I borrowed a microchip reader from a friend. Flame has a microchip that identifies her as Fiery Lights. But she can't be Fiery Lights. I rode her, and she has some sort of chronic condition, most probably her heart. She can't possibly be the racehorse that won the Jackson Plate a few months back. We went online and hooked up with other people who have also seen horses similar enough to Fiery Lights to raise their suspicions. We've just been down to Victoria. There are two horses there, both similar enough to pass for Fiery Lights, and both with microchips that identify them as being that horse."

"Wait." The responder's voice sharpened. "So you're saying that your horse, Flame, is not Fiery Lights, even though the microchip says she is, and furthermore, you've found two other horses with the same microchip?"

"Yeah." I slid down the headboard a bit and wished hard for a beer, or a wine. Something to take the edge off this difficult conversation. "That's exactly what I'm saying."

After that, it was all rapid question and answer as the responder quizzed us. Josie and I answered what we could, but there was a lot we couldn't, especially when we were asked about the horses in Victoria. I told her that our friend there had also called Crime Stoppers and she might have more information.

Eventually, the call ended. I dropped the phone on the bed and slid down so that I was lying flat. Josie slid down next to me and reached for my hand, threading her fingers through mine.

"I'm glad that call is over," I said. "I didn't enjoy that. I've never done anything wrong before, not that warranted that sort of inquisition." I glanced across at Josie. "What about you?"

She was silent for a moment, then said, "Got caught shoplifting when I was fifteen. My dad had pissed off again—he often did that, but normally he'd return before the food ran out. I couldn't ask anyone for help; if they knew I was alone in the house, they would have told the authorities and I'd have ended up in care. I'd heard stories about kids in foster homes and what happened to them, especially the girls. In hindsight, those tales probably weren't true, but at the time, I believed them. My dad told them to me, probably as a way of keeping me around. I was useful. I did the housework and the cooking, so I was too scared and too proud to ask for help. I stole a tin of tuna and a couple of packet of spaghetti from the supermarket instead. They caught me and called the police. I was let off with a caution, and they said they'd call my father. Luckily, Dad arrived home the next day and took the call. He swore a blue streak to them about me being a wayward kid, and then he swore a bigger streak at me for being stupid enough to get caught. Then he took off again, but this time, he left twenty bucks. After that, I stole the five-dollar notes from his wallet and hid them under my mattress so I'd never be caught out again." She heaved a sigh. "That's my only run-in with the police."

I thought of my own upbringing. My two parents, who had loved each other—and me—above all. We'd been a close-knit family, bound tight by love. When Dad died suddenly, Mum and I clung tighter to each other. As I'd grown up, there was never any question of me leaving home. Jayboro was my home, and I'd never considered living anywhere else. When Mum sickened, I'd juggled her nursing care with horse breaking and trail rides, and when she was confined to a wheelchair, I'd spent most of our small savings on making the house wheelchair accessible for her, even though I knew she likely had less than a year to live. I hadn't thought twice about spending the money.

No, my childhood was light years away from Josie's. I guessed hers had shaped her personality much as mine had. She had an easy way with people. She put them at their ease, encouraging them to talk about themselves while skipping lightly over any probing questions that came her way.

I turned on my side to face her and placed my fingertips on her cheek. I walked them down across the slant of her cheekbone, around the curves and whorls of her ear, and into her hair, twisting one of those wild curls around. I tugged, and she rolled onto her side, facing me. I wanted to kiss her. There were still so many murky layers between us, of doubt and the unknown, but right now, I wasn't thinking about them. I was thinking about Josie the woman, and how well we fitted together. Our lovemaking. Desire pulsed in my blood.

I tightened my grip on her hair, and she took the hint and moved closer. One of her hands settled on my hip, and she rested her lips on my forehead. They were hot and dry.

"Are you going to kiss me properly?" I said against her throat.

I felt her swallow, and then her lips moved down and claimed mine, coaxing them apart for a long, leisurely kiss, as if we had all the time in the world. Her tongue flicked on my lips, then delved into my mouth, and we started an advance and retreat of tongues, dancing across each other in slow exploration.

Josie sighed into my mouth. "Don't talk. Let's just make love."

I tried to push aside the buzz of worry in my head, the tangled skeins of conversations with the police, with Pen, with Sue. What would happen when the police came to Jayboro— would they take Flame? What would they do? Would Josie be in trouble? Would they arrive before we got home?

*Enough.*

I wound those thoughts into a knot and shoved them into a corner of my mind to be dealt with later.

Josie. I would think only of Josie, of Josie and me together.

I reached for the buttons of her shirt, flicked them from the holes, and pushed the shirt back. Her bra was plain white nylon, and her nipples pebbled against the thin material. In turn, Josie pushed up my T-shirt, ran a hand down my stomach, and undid my shorts so that she could stroke down to the top of my undies.

"I love your belly," she said. "So flat, so hard."

"All work and no chocolate," I teased, although my leanness was as much hereditary as it was hard work.

I sat up, pulled my T-shirt over my head, and unsnapped my bra. Josie raised up too and removed her shirt and bra and then stood and dropped her shorts to her feet. She kicked them away.

I wasn't as graceful as her and chose instead to wiggle out of the rest of my clothes on the bed. I slid under the covers, then kicked the sheets and blankets back.

I held out a hand to her. She took it and lay with me. Then there were no more words, only the soft sound of lovemaking.

# CHAPTER 23

We arrived back to Jayboro just before noon. Tess and Ripper met the ute halfway down the drive. They bounded along together like best mates. I opened the ute door, and Tess leapt up without hesitation. For a moment, I had a large dusty dog in my lap, as she licked my face, seeming to remember me, before continuing over the gearstick to greet Josie in the same way. Ripper put his paws on the sill, polite enough to need an invitation. I patted my lap, and he leapt up and we drove the final couple of hundred metres to the house, getting smashed in the face by waving tails.

Sue must have heard the engine, as she came out to greet us. We stopped the ute, and the dogs tumbled out and ran onto the veranda to flop on the boards.

"The police called," Sue said. "I told them I expected you home about now. They're coming out from the Isa." She hugged me, and then turned to Josie and hugged her as well. "Welcome home."

We followed her into the office. Her laptop sat on my desk and there were a few legal looking papers spread around. She bundled them and pushed them to one side. "Sorry for the mess. I had a bit of work to do. Moni's down at the campground. One of the cabins was booked last night, and she's down there cleaning and getting it ready for tonight. Both cabins are booked."

"That's great," I said. "Thank you so much. I didn't think you'd have this much to do. We'll have to work out how I can repay you."

Sue flapped a hand. "Don't worry about it. It will do Moni good to get her hands dirty."

I thought of all the times I'd seen Moni covered in dust and dirt from head to toe. Neither of my friends was one to shirk from manual work, despite their professional careers.

I went out to put the kettle on, and when I came back to the office with a tray of mugs, Moni had arrived. I went back for a fourth mug, and the four of us sat around my desk catching up on what we had missed. Between us, Josie and I related what had gone on down in Victoria and our call to Crime Stoppers. Sue and Moni filled in the details of the man who had attempted to remove Flame.

"Flame's still in the barn," said Moni. She blew on her mug of tea. "Poor lady's getting antsy, she wants to be outside with the others, but we felt she was safer inside."

"Sue, what does this mean for us? Not so much me, but Josie. Do you think there'll be anything to pin on her?" I didn't look at Josie, sitting next to me, sipping on her tea, but the tension instantly radiated off her.

Sue took off her reading glasses and rubbed her eyes. "I don't know, to be honest. Not yet anyway. It depends on what the police turn up, what angle they take." She directed her next words to Josie. "It's highly likely they'll want to question you. They might not be too polite. But if they take you in, don't talk to them until your legal representation is present. Don't let them bully you."

"I can't afford legal representation," Josie said, and she would have said more, but Sue interrupted.

"You do have representation. Me. I'm not the greatest criminal lawyer in Queensland, Josie, but I'm your lawyer if you want me. *Pro Bono.*"

"You don't have to do this." Even as Josie said the words, the relief shone in her eyes.

Sue shrugged. "Yes I do. Felix is my friend. Now you're my friend. And it'll stand me in good stead with the Queensland Law Society. I've been a bit lax with *pro bono* work lately."

I knew that was a lie; Sue often worked for free for those who couldn't afford to pay her, but I kept my mouth shut. Josie might need a lawyer, and for all her modesty, I knew Sue was good.

"Thank you. I'm not going to turn you down."

Sue nodded, and handed Josie a business card. "Call me anytime, and make sure you call immediately if you're hauled in for questioning. It will take me a few hours to get to Worrindi or the Isa, but be sure I'll come, and don't say anything until I arrive unless it's 'Where's the toilet?' or 'Can I have a cup of tea?'"

I looked over at Josie. She hunched in the chair, looking smaller than ever. Her face was grey, lined with worry. I hadn't seen her look like that before, I'd only seen the carefree face she presented to the world. It seemed Josie was more nervous about this than she'd let on. I wanted to reach over and take her hand, but the gap between our chairs was too great.

Just then, Tess lifted her head, and she and Ripper leapt off the veranda and took off down the driveway at warp speed, barking like mad things.

Moni stood and looked out. "Cops."

Together, the four of us walked onto the veranda and stood in a line, awaiting the police. Tess and Ripper arrived back, panting, before the police had exited their car, put their caps on, and hitched up their pants.

There were two cops, and I didn't recognise either of them. They weren't the local police from Worrindi.

"Afternoon," one of them said. "Which of you are Felicity Jameson and Josephine Beccari?"

Sue stepped forwards. "Can we see some ID first?"

They fished out their cards. Federal Police, not the Queensland Police.

"I'm Felix, and this is Josie," I said.

The taller of the two, whose ID proclaimed him as Sergeant Tarrant, nodded. He ignored Sue and Moni and directed his words at Josie and me. "Can we talk privately?"

Sue stepped forwards so that she was nose to nose with Tarrant. She was only an inch or so shorter. "I'm the legal representative for both of these women. I will need to be present for both interviews. Right now, it seems an informal chat with all of us present would suit us all better."

The officers exchanged a glance. "That will be fine." Tarrant managed an approximation of a grin obviously designed to put us at our ease, but it only succeeded in putting me into a state of low-key alert. Tess obviously agreed, as she rested her nose on her paws and growled low in her throat.

"Why don't we start by taking a look at the horse?" suggested the other policeman, whose ID had identified him as Lopez.

"No worries. She's in the barn."

The six of us walked out of the house and down to the barn. Flame was pacing around restlessly in the end stall. We stretched out in a line and leaned on the bar that separated her stall from the aisle. Inside, Flame twirled, digging up the bedding with her hooves. She looked magnificent, every inch the racehorse. Good fodder had filled her out, and she was no longer the too-ribby horse who had arrived all those months ago. Her ears pricked, and her coat gleamed. She lacked in muscle tone, but I doubted the police would pick up on that. To the untrained eye, she looked a champion.

Without asking, Lopez pulled out a microchip reader from his belt and ducked under the railing. From his bristling manner, I could tell he wasn't used to horses and wasn't very comfortable. Flame agreed. The whites of her eyes showed, and she snaked her head around him and moved away to the other side of the stall.

Lopez followed her, the reader held in front of him, as if he were in a standoff. Again, Flame whipped around him.

I glanced at Josie. This could go on all day. She ducked into the stall. "Would you like me to try?" she said. There was a neutral politeness in her voice. "She's used to me."

Lopez ignored her and once more approached Flame. She shook her head, and her forelegs pranced. The bedding churned underneath her hooves. Josie waited until Flame had once again avoided Lopez, and then she walked slowly up to the horse, her hand held palm up, and spoke softly until Flame steadied and allowed Josie to approach. Josie petted her, speaking gently all the while.

"If you come slowly from the side," Josie said to Lopez, "you should be all right. Not from the rear; that's a horse's blind spot."

At first, it seemed as if Lopez would ignore her and blunder in from behind, but he hesitated long enough that Flame turned sideways, and when he did move closer, it was okay. It wasn't

254

what I would call a sensitive approach, but it worked, and he ran the chip reader down her neck.

Josie opened her mouth and closed it again. I guessed she had been about to tell him where to find the chip and had thought better of it. Beside me, Sue gave a short nod of approval at Josie's silence.

Josie waited until Lopez had exited the stall before giving Flame a final pat and coming out to join us in the aisle.

"What other horses do you have here?" Tarrant directed his words to Josie, but she deflected him to me.

"My own six and Flame." I listed them. "They're all stockhorses or ponies, though. No thoroughbreds."

"Can we see them?"

"Sure." I turned to walk out of the barn.

"They're down in the long paddock," Moni said.

I glanced back at her. She wore a sweetly innocent expression, one that made her look like a slightly ditsy woman, nothing like the sharp-minded doctor she was. She shrugged. "It's a long walk. Sorry, Felix, I turned them out there as I thought there was more grass."

My lips twitched. There was barely a blade of grass anywhere on Jayboro, thanks to the drought, and Moni knew that very well. There was only saltbush and red earth, and it was a lot easier to cart hay to the paddock nearer the barn. Whether the horses were in the long paddock or not, Moni obviously intended to make it hard for the cops.

Tarrant gave a half smile. "Maybe we can drive?"

"Sure. I'll get the ute. You can follow."

The four of us piled into the cab of my ute. Moni, squashed on the outside, asked, "Can they book us for not wearing

255

seatbelts? Even if this had seating for four up here, I couldn't get to the belt as Sue's bony hip is sticking in my stomach."

"Private land," Sue replied. "They can't touch us for that. And if you hadn't eaten so much last night, you might be more comfortable."

She turned, and the two of them shared a look of amused affection. My fingers paused before turning the ignition key. The ease and warmth between them was palpable. My friends had a solid and loving relationship. Would I ever have that? With Josie, maybe? I swallowed. Right now, it was looking less and less likely.

There were five gates between the barn and the long paddock. As per outback custom, Moni jumped out to open each one and left it for the following car to close. I saw Lopez stomp out of the police vehicle to close each gate.

After the third gate, Moni said, "I've made my point." This time, she waited for them to drive through after us and then she closed it.

My horses were indeed in the long paddock, grouped together under the gum trees by the creek.

Lopez got out with the microchip reader. Maybe he'd had a lecture from his partner during the drive, as he said to Josie, "Would you occupy the front end again while I check the chips?"

"Of course." Josie's quick smile was equally as swiftly hidden.

"None of them are chipped except Patchwork," I said. "She's the piebald."

Tarrant ambled over to stand next to me. "She's a fine looking mare. Did you barrel race her?"

I wondered if he'd done his research on me—photos of me and Patch at the Isa rodeo were in the newspaper archives—or if he genuinely had an eye for horses.

"Yeah," I said. "It was years ago now. Some barrel racing, some camp drafts. She's a good lady." I kept my eyes on Josie, moving from horse to horse to allow Lopez to sweep his chip reader. Greedy Jetta tried to get her nose in Lopez's pockets, searching for food, but otherwise there was no drama.

We bounced back across the paddocks to the house, and this time Sue, who was on the outside, opened and closed all the gates.

Inside the house, I offered coffee. The boys were only doing their job, and it would be easier for all of us if it were pleasant.

"Thanks, that would be good." Tarrant's words were accompanied by a smile. He, at least, was trying to be polite.

"I'll make it." Moni disappeared to the kitchen.

The officers stood while I sat behind my desk. It gave me a sense of security. This was my house, my office, my horses. I hadn't done anything wrong—at least, I didn't think I had—and the familiar chair gave me comfort. Josie sat next to me, and Sue chose to stand over by the window. Her demeanour was one of casual nonchalance, but I knew my friend and her legal reputation well. She was listening intently and was ready to pounce if need be.

The questions were all fairly standard. A verification of personal details. Josie gave her address as the Commercial, and a quick calculation on her date of birth told me she was thirty-one. So she was older than she looked.

"Previous addresses?" Lopez looked at me first.

"None. I've always lived here."

He wrote something in his notebook and glanced at Josie.

She smiled slightly. "How far back do I have to go?"

"Three years should do it."

"I'll try and remember."

She was still listing addresses and approximate dates when Moni arrived back with a jug of coffee, mugs and a stack of sandwiches. "Only cheese and pickle," she said.

My stomach gurgled. Josie and I hadn't stopped to eat in our haste to return to Jayboro. Josie must have agreed, as she paused in her recital to grab a sandwich before continuing. Her previous addresses included a lot of pubs, some fruit farms, and a couple of private houses where she'd apparently been a nanny or a house sitter. The addresses were in South Australia, New South Wales, and Queensland. Josie had lived in more places than I'd visited in a lifetime.

Sadness swelled. Someone like her would never be happy living in one place, with one person. That sort of restlessness was totally alien to my experience. The confirmation that Josie and I had no future was listed right there in that multitude of addresses covering half of Australia.

With a start, I realised that Tarrant was addressing a question to me. "What is your relationship to Josephine?" he asked.

I hesitated. What indeed? How could I answer a question when I wasn't sure myself? Out of the corner of my eye, I saw Sue frown, and I knew I couldn't hesitate any longer.

"We're friends," I said. Sue's frown grew more pronounced. "With benefits," I added. Sue's face was expressionless once more. I dared not look at Josie.

Tarrant swung around to Josie. "Would you agree with that?"

"Sure," Josie said. "What else could we be, when I'll be moving on soon?"

The little crease was back between Sue's eyes, and Moni set her mug down carefully, as if afraid it might spill. Neither would look at me.

"I must ask you both not to go anywhere at the present time," Tarrant said. "We will almost certainly need to talk to you again. Josephine, will you be at your address in Worrindi?"

Josie nodded. "There or here."

Lopez looked down at his notebook as if the words *with benefits* were written in flaming script. "Right. Do you have a passport?"

When Josie nodded, he said, "You'll need to surrender that for the time being."

"It's in Worrindi."

"You can surrender it to the local police there."

"What about Felix?" Sue asked.

"I don't have a passport," I said. "I won't be going anywhere."

After that, the questions were about Flame and our trip to Victoria.

Eventually, they took their leave. "We will need you both to give statements." Lopez, who'd softened during the interview, was back to being an officious dick. "If you remember anything else, or if you find you need to change what you have already said—" his eyes rested on Josie "—then you must call us immediately." He handed cards to myself, Josie, and Sue. "Josephine must surrender her passport within twenty-four hours. Her details will be passed on to border security, effective immediately."

They left, and the four of us watched the dust trail as they departed.

"That was unpleasant." The tension that had held me rigid left my body.

"Actually, it wasn't that bad." Sue came over to perch on the edge of my desk. "I've heard a lot harder lines of questioning for a lot less of an offence. That Lopez was an idiot, but considering the potential seriousness of the offence, they were decent."

"Offence?" Josie's voice was expressionless. She could have been asking what was for lunch.

"Horse stealing. Blackmail. I don't know exactly. Lopez asked if I knew whether either of you had money problems. I gave him my best blank stare—" Sue demonstrated "—and told him he'd have to ask you both. As he didn't, you can assume they will be checking."

"He'll find nothing on me," I said, "except a loan for the cabins and a small amount in the bank."

"What about you?" Sue tilted her head in Josie's direction.

"A little money in the bank. My wages, saved up from the pub, plus the payments from Flame's owner. Or the person I thought was her owner," she amended. "I was saving up to move on, of course." She didn't look at me as she said it. "One bad mark from a few years back when I had a credit card that I didn't pay. No more credit cards for me. But nothing else."

There was a silence. I studied the timber grain on my desk. Really, the pattern was mesmerizing. It stopped me thinking about Josie's words, but I heard Moni say quietly, "Were you, Josie? Were you really thinking about moving on? I thought you liked it here?"

Josie's reply was bright and brittle. "Victoria was pleasant. I haven't spent too much time there lately. I might see what work I can find."

I looked up and caught the glances that Sue and Moni exchanged. They seemed surprised at Josie's words. But why would that be? It seemed that her earlier talk about wanting to settle down in one place, maybe in Worrindi as she liked it so much, had been part of the yarn she spun to me, just as she'd said she did to potential employers. Josie, it seemed, had a restless heart. And mine was bound to Jayboro.

# CHAPTER 24

It was too late for Sue and Moni to get back to Mungabilly Creek by dark, so they stayed another night.

"What about you, Josie?" Sue asked. "When are they expecting you back at the pub?"

"I'm not sure." Josie picked up her coffee mug, turned it around, and set it back down again. "I should call them."

I stood and gestured to the phone. "Go ahead. Of course you can stay if you don't have to be back tonight." I didn't want to think too hard about what would happen if she stayed over.

I left the office to give her privacy, and Sue and Moni followed me to the kitchen.

"I don't believe her," Moni said, as soon as we were out of earshot of the office.

I opened the fridge. "Beer?"

"Yes, please." Sue perched on a stool. "I agree with Moni. I don't believe her either."

I handed both of them a beer, took a third for myself, and left another on the counter for Josie. "What, about Flame?"

Sue frowned. "Flame? No, I'm positive Josie is being dead straight about the horse. I'm talking about the important things here." She leant forwards, put her hand on mine where it rested on the counter. "I'm talking about you and Josie. Your relationship."

"You heard me. We're friends with benefits."

"So you say." Moni moved to sit next to Sue. With both of them drilling into me, it felt more confrontational than the police had earlier. "But did you see Josie's face when you said that? She's got a very expressive face, but when you said 'friends', it shut right down."

"What else can we be?" It was my turn to keep my face blank, although with two pairs of eyes analysing my every twitch, it was hard. "You heard her. She's lived in more places in the last three years than I will ever live in the next three lifetimes. She's looking to move on."

"Is she?" Sue sat back and folded her arms. "Seems to me she only said that after you'd described her as a friend with benefits."

"How was I supposed to describe her? I saw your expression when I called her a friend."

"Yeah. Because if you call her a friend and the police find out you're lovers, they will think you're being evasive, even if you don't mean to be."

"You could have called her your girlfriend." Moni's smile was more sympathetic. "After all, isn't she? You spend a lot of time together. I got the impression you're fond of her, Felix."

I picked at the label on my beer, scoring it with a fingernail. "There's no future in that. She'll be moving on."

"I think you're missing the point." Sue took a swig of her beer before continuing. "Josie only talked about moving on when you demoted her from 'girlfriend' to 'friend with benefits'. Before that, her talk had been about how much she loved it here. I think she was salvaging her pride."

Moni nodded. "And if so, and if you want her to stay, you need to ask her."

Behind their heads, I saw Josie appear in the doorway. "Hi, did you get through to the pub?" I asked.

Sue and Moni straightened from their inquisitorial positions and turned too. "Beer?" Sue picked up the fourth bottle and held it out.

Josie accepted it and twisted the top off. "Thanks. Yes, I got through, and no, I don't have to be back tonight. Is it okay if I stay?"

"Of course. I was hoping you would." And I was. I didn't quite believe Sue and Moni's assessment. To me, the patterns of a lifetime wouldn't be dropped that easily. But whatever the future brought for us, right now, I wanted her to stay.

"Are you working tomorrow?" Sue asked. "If it's not until later, maybe the four of us could go for an early morning ride— if that's okay with you, Felix? As long as Moni and I leave by lunchtime, we'll be right."

"I'd like that. Three days without being on horseback seems like a lifetime."

"Three days of being *on* horseback seems like a lifetime to my thighs," groaned Moni. "I want to ride Budgie tomorrow. He's the most comfortable."

"I'll rub your thighs for you. Later." Sue picked up Moni's hand and pressed a kiss to it. "Even though I know you're joking. Your thighs are fine."

"Thank you, lover. Yours aren't bad either."

Again, the warmth was palpable between my two friends.

Sue stirred herself. "If you want, I'm happy to cook tonight, Felix. I was in the Isa a few days back, and I've got some chicken schnitzels and salad. There's also a jar of Mrs T's homemade tomato sauce that she said to give to you as well as the cake she made. If you want, I can use all of that to make chicken parmie and salad, with the cake for dessert, if that's not too dull."

"Sounds fabulous, if you really don't mind."

"Not at all." She started rummaging in the fridge, pulling out ingredients. "You just keep the cook supplied with beer."

"Or red wine." Moni winked. "I think there's one more bottle left that we brought with us."

Josie had been silent throughout the exchange. As the others started making a mess in my kitchen, I went over to her. "Everything all right with Madge and Chris? When do you have to be back?"

"Yeah. I spoke to Madge. I have to be back by tomorrow arvo."

"Good-oh. So you'll be able to come riding with us."

She mustered a smile. "That sounds fantastic." She raised her voice so the others could hear. "If Moni's riding Budgie, then I'll ride Jetta."

"I'd ride her, but my feet would sweep the dirt." Sue turned. "How about avocado on top of the parmies as well as cheese and tomato?"

"Sounds great," I said. "Sue, you want to fight me over Patch and Ben?"

"What about Josie riding Flame?" Moni tilted her head. "The poor lady's restless as anything cooped up in the barn. She would like to get out. And Flame is Josie's horse."

"She's not." Josie set her beer down. "But I'd like her to be."

"She's as much yours as anyone's," I said. "But it would have to be a very gentle ride. Flame can't go fast."

"Sounds good to me and my thighs," said Moni.

Josie's eyes sparkled, the first happy expression I'd seen in them in the last few hours. "I would love to ride her." She turned to me. "As long as you don't think it would harm her?"

"I don't think so. Not if we just walk, maybe a short trot. No more than that, though."

"I'll be as gentle and as slow as the continental drift."

I was looking forward to seeing Josie ride Flame. And Moni was right. Flame, it seemed, was nobody's horse. What would happen to her if Josie moved on? *When* Josie moved on, I amended. Flame was useless for most purposes. What would happen to a horse like her?

There was a crash, and I was jerked back to the present. Moni's beer had gone flying. Moni grabbed a cloth and dropped to her knees to wipe it up.

"Sorry, Felix. I'm such a klutz at times."

"No worries. The floorboards have had far worse."

"You wouldn't think this woman is the neatest stitcher-upper of people this side of the Barcoo, would you, Josie? Not when she's dropping beer bottles." Sue stood at the stove where she pan-fried the schnitzels.

"I'm a neat doctor, just clumsy with bottles."

"Don't worry about it." Indeed, the beer hadn't soaked into the polished boards.

"Dinner won't be long." Sue turned from the stove. "This is just about ready for the oven. We'll be eating in twenty minutes, in case anyone wants a shower first."

The dinner conversation didn't mention the police visit. It seemed we had all said what we needed to about Flame, and now it was a case of wait-and-see. See what the police came back with. See if they wanted to interview us further, take the statements they had mentioned. See if they charged Josie with anything. See if they took Flame away.

I paused at that last and spiralled back to my earlier thoughts. Take her where? I'd miss Flame, gentle lady that she was. I'd miss her way of lipping at the buttons of my shirt and how she would walk companionably with me across the paddock when I got the other horses.

The four of us went outside on the veranda to eat. The evening was hot, and the cicadas sang loudly enough to drown out the noise of the fan overhead.

"I heard from Nora and Ger while you were away," Sue said. "They send their love. Nora said to tell you she's cooking crocodile tonight—Thai green curry crocodile."

Moni grinned. "Amazing what you can buy in London these days."

"The Melbourne Cup is coming up, and Young Seánie is still convinced that Fiery Lights will run," said Sue. "You can bet on anything in London, no matter how outrageous, and he's put fifty quid on Fiery Lights to come in the first three in the Melbourne Cup."

"What odds did he get?" Josie sliced into her parmie and loaded her fork. "This is great, Sue."

"Thanks. He got a thousand to one! I think the bookie saw him coming."

"Nora and Ger told him that it was all a joke and that there was no way the horse in the photo with Ger was Fiery Lights. Young Seánie just said he'd take the chance with his fifty quid." Sue didn't look too worried about that.

"I wonder where the real Fiery Lights is." My gaze was on my plate. "And I wonder if Pen knows anything more. We haven't heard from her since we found out her Flame was gone."

"I was thinking that too." The beads in Josie's hair gleamed under the overhead light. "She shouldn't be in any sort of trouble, but she may be looking out for the owner of the yard. She seemed quite protective of her."

"Yeah, I noticed that too."

"Are they lovers?" Sue asked.

"I don't think so. Pen mentioned a boyfriend in the past and I didn't get any sort of queer vibe from her. I think she's just a friend. But if Casey is getting the heavy word from the police, that might explain why Pen is quiet."

Then the conversation spun away into a catch-up on outback life and the people we knew. Sue found the last bottle of red wine and poured four glasses. Moni said how the doctor she'd taken on as a part-timer was romancing with one of the station owners. "I don't know what will happen if it turns serious. Bellarine Station is most of 150 kilometres from Mungabilly Creek. I'd hate to lose Ellen—she's a great doctor, and the patients love her. Many of them love her more than they love me. She's a great listener."

"So are you." Sue reached over the dirty dishes to squeeze her hand. "But you cut through the bullshit better than Ellen does."

Moni squeezed back. "Maybe. But if she moves out there to be with Keith, it will be hard for her to keep working. I don't think she'd want to stop doctoring, though. I don't know what she'd do."

"Maybe she could stay in Mungabilly a couple of nights a week?" suggested Josie. "Surely someone would rent her a room on that basis."

"Yeah. That's an option. Mrs T's friend, Rosalie, might be up for that. She's got a big old house all to herself."

"Funny that Rosalie never moved in with Mrs T." I cupped my wine glass and peered into it. It was nearly empty. "Those two are such good friends and both live by themselves in large houses."

"They both like their own space too." Sue grinned. "I suggested that to Mrs T once, and she nearly bit my head off. They seem to like living apart, but they see each other every day. That's what works best for them. Rosalie's a great help in the office. She's taught herself to audio type, and now I use a Dictaphone like a real lawyer, and she types my file notes. Very handy on the off-chance someone else ever looks at my files. Now they'll be able to read them."

Moni emptied the last of the bottle into our glasses. "'Fraid there's no more, not unless you've got a bottle hidden away, Felix?"

I shook my head. "Only beer. Sorry."

But after the rich red wine, none of us wanted more beer. We moved to sit in a row, our feet on the veranda railing. Outside, the moonlight painted the ground silver, and it was as bright as day. One of the horses snorted, and the sound carried in the clear night. Tess raised her head from where she was lying with Ripper, and the two of them bounded down the steps barking at some imagined night creature. She returned and put her head on my knee, staring up with soulful eyes, as I petted her. For Tess, at least, life was now set.

For me and Josie, though, it was anything but.

Sue and Moni went off to bed a short while later, leaving Josie and me on the veranda. The others moved around for a bit, and then there was once again only the silence of an outback night.

"Bed?" I stood and held out a hand to Josie.

She stared at it, then up at my face. "Am I sleeping with you?"

I paused. I'd been assuming she was—after all, we'd slept together the past few nights during our time away. We were lovers. But now, back at Jayboro, Josie was obviously unsure enough about my feelings to ask.

"If you want to," I said.

She remained seated. "But what do you *want*, Felix?"

I knew what I wanted: Josie. Certainly for tonight. Past that, well, I was conflicted. But it seemed silly to ask her to sleep on the couch—Sue and Moni were in my only spare room, and her tent was in Worrindi.

"Sleep with me, Josie. I'd like that, if you would."

It was hardly a romantic declaration, but it must have been enough for her, as she rose and placed her hand in mine, and I led her to my bed.

# CHAPTER 25

WE WERE GETTING READY TO ride the next morning when Tess and Ripper both pricked up their ears and raced off. A vehicle was coming up the driveway.

"Probably someone for the campground. If one of you could get Ben ready for me, I'll see to them."

"I'll do it." Moni popped her head over the partition. "After all, there isn't much of Budgie to groom."

"But there's a lot of Ben." Sue, who'd won the toss to ride Patch, called from the piebald's stall.

It wasn't a camper. It was Alain, the vet. Guiltily, I remembered I still had his microchip reader. I met him in the driveway. "Alain, I'm sorry, I was going to return your reader today."

He waved aside my apology. "That's not why I'm here. The Federal Police asked me to do a veterinary inspection on Flame."

"Oh." I gathered my thoughts. Really, this wasn't unexpected. We'd alleged that the horse couldn't be an active racehorse due to a chronic condition. Of course the police wouldn't take our word. "Sure. She's in the barn. Actually, we were just about to go for a ride, and Josie was going to ride her. Just a very slow walk, nothing faster."

"That's fine. I can watch her being ridden, if you don't mind riding in the paddock for a bit."

I got into the passenger seat of his vehicle for the short ride to the barn.

"Flame, she's the horse you asked me about before, with the possible heart disease?" asked Alain. I nodded, and he continued, "And that's why you wanted the microchip reader?"

I nodded again.

"This could be a short inspection in that case. I trust your judgement, Felix. You know horses. But I still have to do this. The feds want an official report."

Flame was already bridled, and Josie was helping Moni with Ben.

I explained why Alain was here.

Sue came up beside me. "Do you mind if I observe? I'm the legal representative for Felix and Josie. I doubt it's necessary, but that way I can be satisfied everything is done correctly."

"Of course not." Alain looked uncomfortable, but his manner was brisk and competent.

He dragged a couple of heavy cases from his car. "I'm going to take an ECG, blood samples and swabs."

We watched in silence as he set up his equipment and checked Flame over physically. Josie held her as he slid the needle into the vein. Good horse that she was, she didn't even flinch.

Moni moved around as he placed the ECG leads, so that she could see the screen, but made no comment.

Alain frowned. "Can one of you mount and ride her around in a circle?" He removed the ECG leads but left the pads in place.

Josie stepped forwards, and I gave her a leg up onto Flame's back. Flame's ears flickered back and forth as Josie settled. For a moment, Josie simply sat, speaking softly, letting Flame become accustomed to her. Then she shortened her reins and squeezed her calves, urging the horse to walk forward.

For a few moments, Alain watched Flame circle around him. "Can you go faster?" he asked.

In answer, Josie urged Flame faster. She sprang willingly into a bouncy trot, and they circled Alain. Flame's ears pricked, and Josie had to work hard to keep her contained.

"Canter if you want." Alain didn't take his eyes from Flame, turning in smaller circles to track her larger ones. Josie changed the rein and went in the opposite direction, pushing Flame into a canter. She started with a light-hearted buck that tipped Josie forwards, but with a push back from Flame's neck, she regained her seat and urged her faster. For a few moments, woman and horse flowed as one across the ground. Dirt and dust puffed from Flame's hooves until they were moving in the haze of a red cloud. For a few moments, they were beautiful.

And then they weren't.

In the space of a minute, Flame went from a horse that could win the Melbourne Cup to a broken-down old nag. Her neck dropped. Her sides laboured. She stumbled. Josie pulled her up without waiting for Alain's command. She slid to the ground, speaking gently to her, waiting as Flame laboured to draw breath. Sweat foamed on her neck.

Alain approached, dragging his portable ECG machine, and reconnected the pads.

"I've seen enough. This horse could no more have won the Jackson Plate than I could have qualified for the Olympics in the one hundred metres." He pressed a button and a ribbon of paper spooled out. "When she's able, walk her back slowly."

Josie nodded, took the reins over Flame's head, and led her back to the barn. The rest of us followed.

"Can you tell us what's wrong?" I asked Alain, as he packed away his equipment.

"Not officially. It's to go in my report for the police. But unofficially, your best guess was a good one." He looked uncomfortable. "I have to get back to Worrindi, Felix. I'd like to stay and chat, but I can't. Look after yourself."

"No worries. Send my love to Narelle." I remembered the microchip reader. "Wait a moment."

By the time I returned with the reader, Alain had driven around to the front of the house. He gave me a slight smile and drove away.

I walked back to the barn to find the others leaning over Flame's stall. Flame had recovered, enough to pick at the hay someone had given her.

"I don't know about anyone else, but I don't feel like a ride now." Moni's eyes remained fixed on Flame. "Which is a pity as I just wore my arms out brushing that tank called Ben."

"Ben thanks you for it." I too gazed at Flame. "I wonder what will happen to this beauty now? She's not a racehorse, not now, anyway. She's not microchipped in any meaningful way. I doubt anyone will come rushing to claim her—she's pretty much useless as a riding horse."

"Broodmare?" Sue's gaze rested on Flame. "You said she was young."

"She would breed such pretty foals. I'd love a youngster from her to bring along." I sighed. "Like I have the land for that, the time, or the money to pay stud fees."

Sue turned around. "I hate to break up the party, but Moni and I should leave. If we go now, we can go via Worrindi—

Moni wants to pick up something from the GP there—and still be back at Mungabilly Creek before dark."

We walked back to the house, the dogs following in our wake in a mini-dust cloud. Sue and Moni went off to throw their things in the car. Josie went out on to the veranda.

The others came back up to say goodbye. Sue hugged me and then Josie. "Don't forget. If the police want to take you in for an official interview, questioning, or to give a statement, you call me first. Don't go in alone. It's probably unnecessary but far easier to have me there in the start than to try and untangle the mess later. *Pro Bono*. You got that, both of you? No arguments."

I nodded. "Thank you."

Josie nodded too. "That's really good of you, Sue. After all, you don't know me that well."

"Don't think anything of it." Sue's voice was gruff as if the words made her uncomfortable. "I worked *pro bono* to get Mrs T's sister's stepson's uncle's niece's best friend out of the lockup. Because there's nothing closer than family. Believe me, after that, my friend's girlfriend is a cinch."

I wondered if her word choice was deliberate.

Moni hugged both of us. "Thanks for everything. We had a great time. If you want to get away again for a short break, call us first. We're toilet cleaners, horse groomers, firewood collectors, spider removers, laundresses extraordinaire. And we're cheap." She winked. "Seriously, we enjoyed it."

"Thank you," I said. "Both of you. For everything."

The conversation was starting to sound like a wake.

Sue called Ripper, only to find he was already in the passenger seat. Tess sat on the ground by the open door looking disconsolate.

Moni shooed Rip into the back. "Don't worry, darling," she said to Tess. "You'll see Ripper again soon."

With a human-sounding sigh, Tess padded back to flop down between Josie and me.

It was just us again. I gripped the railing and stared out over my land. There was the campground, with the guests in the cabins packing their cars for departure. There was the amenities block that I would have to clean later. Smoke and Diesel were out in the paddock, lipping at the dirt. And in the barn, a horse neighed. It reminded me that I needed to turn out the horses that would now not be ridden today.

But I stayed by the railing. Josie stood next to me, equally quiet. She, too, would leave today, back to Worrindi and her pub job. Would I still see her now that there wasn't Flame as a reason? But Flame was still here, and what would happen to her? Her agistment had been paid up until the end of the month. After that, I didn't know.

I was in no hurry to dive into the chores. I turned to Josie. "Fancy a cup of coffee?"

"Sure. If you don't mind."

Her stilted reply gave me pause. Maybe I wasn't the only one wondering about us and how we navigated our relationship, such as it was, from here.

I made instant coffee and brought it out to the veranda. Josie hadn't moved. She still stood, staring out over the landscape. I set the mugs down on the table and sat. Tess pawed at my leg. I gave her the dog treat I'd brought out for her, and she leant against me. I pulled her ears and was rewarded with a lazy, wet lick on my hand.

The silence stretched. I wanted to ask Josie questions, but not about the horse, about her, Josie, the woman. How much of it was real, and how much of it was as false as her story about Flame? But I didn't know where to start.

But I wanted to know about Josie.

I cradled my mug in both hands and took a sip to gather my thoughts.

Josie beat me to it. "I want to tell you that I never thought of you as just a convenient place to park Flame. I liked you that very first day in the pub, when I turned around and caught you checking out my arse. I came out to Jayboro because I wanted to, because of you. Because of finding somewhere to ride. Because I enjoyed living in Worrindi, and having you nearby was a bonus. Yeah, later it came together as a place for Flame, but you came first.

"I've enjoyed getting to know you, Felix. You and Jayboro. I think I fell in love with Jayboro first. The silence, the land, the horses. I love what you're building for yourself out here."

She fell in love with Jayboro first. *First.* The implication rolled around my head. What was second? Flame? Me? No. If it were me she fell in love with, why would she talk about moving on? *Unless she thinks I don't want her*, a little voice whispered. But that couldn't be right.

"You're going," I said. "Down to Victoria."

She shrugged, a tiny movement that conveyed nothing I could read. "Things are different now. I don't know that I can stay around."

"Would you?"

"I don't know, Felix. I would have, yes. I liked it here. But Flame's not mine, and I'm not sure I have a job anymore. Madge is pretty pissed off with me. I took off to Victoria on short notice and didn't tell them when I'd be back. When I called yesterday, she was curt with me. Told me to come and pack up my things this afternoon and be gone by tomorrow."

"Why didn't you say something earlier?"

"What difference would it make? I didn't want to say anything in front of Sue and Moni—they're so nice they would probably have made up a job for me. I don't want charity."

"They know a lot of people. And there's a busy pub in Mungabilly Creek. They might know of something. I can call and ask—"

"No. Thank you, but no. I'll find something myself. I always do. I don't hang around where I'm not wanted." Her lips twisted. "Maybe I'll find a job at a horse place. I'd like that. Riding with you has been a special pleasure."

"If you find you are out of a job, you can stay here for a while."

"Charity again?"

"I'd offer a bed to any friend who needed it." I swallowed hard. Did she now think so little of me that she wouldn't even accept that?

She nodded, a jerky movement. "I guess that was an overreaction. Thanks, Felix. You're a good friend."

"With benefits." I tried to make it sound like a joke, but the words were flat. Josie was a friend. There were benefits. So why did I feel as if I were selling her out?

We both fell silent and sipped our coffees as we looked out to the land. There was a heaviness in the air that wasn't entirely due to our conversation. Maybe it would rain.

Josie tipped the dregs of her coffee over the rail. "I better be going. I don't want to be late. Maybe I can still talk Madge into keeping my job. After all, it's not that easy to get bar staff out here."

"Good luck."

I waited on the couch while she went back inside. She returned with her battered daypack over one shoulder.

"Well, goodbye then."

"You'll let me know if you need a place to stay?" I stood and went over to her.

She shifted her pack to the other shoulder. "Yeah. Thanks."

She exuded a wariness, a stand-offish manner that I'd never felt from her before. I grasped her free hand and bent to kiss her on the mouth. She tilted her head, and my kiss landed on the corner of her mouth and slid off her cheek.

I stepped back. I wasn't sure what had changed in the last twenty-four hours, but it felt wrong. I forced a smile. "See you soon."

"Yeah." And then she was gone, bounding down the steps to her red car.

# CHAPTER 26

I DIDN'T SLEEP WELL THAT night. I hadn't heard from Josie as to whether she still had a job in the pub. I'd hung around the house, hoping for a call, and whenever I'd gone down to see to anything in the campground, or the horses, the first thing I'd looked for on my return was the blinking red light on the answer machine.

"What do you reckon, Tess?" I said to the dog at my heels. "Should we call the pub and ask?"

Tess wagged her tail. Since my return—and Ripper's departure—she had barely left my side. Tess knew that the people she loved often left, and she seemed determined not to let me out of her sight.

The campground was empty. It was now well into the hottest time of year, the ground baked, and there was a definite promise of rain in the air. I checked the Bureau of Meteorology's rain radar on the internet as I sipped my morning coffee. There was rain to the west of Jayboro, over in the Territory. I wasn't sure if it would swing this way, but I could hope.

I stood and moved towards the kitchen to make another coffee. I'd barely gone two paces when the phone rang, and I nearly tripped over my boots racing to answer it.

"Jayboro Outstation, this is Felix."

"Hi Felix, it's Pen." Her voice came clearly down the line. Coffee forgotten, I sat again, cradling the phone between my shoulder and my ear. "Pen! Nice to hear from you. We were wondering when we didn't hear anything. Any news?"

"Yes. You obviously haven't seen the papers. Check the headlines in *The Age*."

I hooked my boots on the base of the chair and rolled it back to the computer, bringing up the Melbourne paper. "Oh!"

"Oh, indeed. It's all there. Is Josie with you?"

"No. She had to go back to Worrindi."

"I'll let you call her."

"Actually, Pen, would you mind letting her know? I'm barely going to have time to read this before I have to get the horses ready for a trail ride." I crossed my fingers against the lie. Josie hadn't called. Despite the urgency I'd felt last night to hear her voice, suddenly I didn't know how to deal with her.

"Sure." If Pen thought that was odd, it didn't show in her voice. "Felix, I'm sorry I didn't call sooner. I know you must have been wondering. But the feds told me not to contact you. I guess they wanted to rule out any possibility of collusion."

"I didn't call you either. But I intended to sometime today. We weren't told not to contact you, but so far, our only contact with the feds has been fairly informal."

"Not me." Amusement hummed in Pen's voice. "I was hauled in for questioning, official taped interview, then a written statement. The works. Casey too." She paused. "I'll let you go. I'm sure you're dying to read the paper. I'll call Josie. Should I call the pub or her mobile?"

"Her mobile probably at this hour." I didn't mention the possibility that Josie may not have a job.

"We'll talk soon, I'm sure. Bye, Felix."

It wasn't hard to find Flame in the paper. It was front page news. *Fiery Lights Found!* blared the headline, along with a picture of Fiery Lights passing the post to win the Jackson Plate. *The Age* wasn't a sensational paper, so the reporting was factual. Fiery Lights had been found, and the Federal Police had busted a complex scheme to secrete the immensely valuable horse out of the country. Details about the scheme were sketchy, and it mentioned several lookalike mares without going into much detail, and I guessed that was because the case was ongoing. The article mentioned that three people had been arrested in connection with the theft of the horse.

The feds had found the real Fiery Lights in Darwin, her white socks dyed to match her coat, and her mane and tail coloured black to make her a bay mare, not a chestnut. The article said that as a result of multiple tip-offs, all horse movement out of the country had been under scrutiny, and that was when Fiery Lights had been found. She was apparently bound for a Middle East racehorse breeding program.

I rose and went to look out of the window. I could see the horses in the paddock, nose to tail, flicking flies from each other's faces. Flame was paired with Smoke. Their grey and chestnut tails were swishing away. I wondered again where she had come from.

The phone rang, and my first thought was that it was Josie. I waited a moment before picking it up. It might be a potential booking; it might be Pen. But it was Mario, the local policeman from Worrindi.

After the pleasantries were exchanged, Mario got down to business. "It's about the horse you have out there. Flame. Have you seen today's news?"

"Yes. They found Fiery Lights."

"They did. However, I'm calling about the horse you have. Do you have any idea where she might have come from?"

"None. She apparently came from South Australia, but that might have been part of the deception."

"I'm asking you to hold onto her for the time being. We're trying to trace her owner, but it's difficult. No horses like her have been reported stolen in the last few months—well, apart from an old nag called Fiery Lights." Amusement coloured Mario's voice. "It's unlikely we'll be able to find where she came from—or indeed, if she was purchased, the previous owner may not want her back. Would you mind keeping her there for a bit? I know it's a big ask, what with the drought and lack of fodder and all, but I'll see if I can do anything for you in that regard."

"I'll do that. Don't worry too much at this stage. I have another couple of weeks paid on her agistment. After that, we can see."

"She may be with you for a lot longer than a couple of weeks," warned Mario. "Is that a problem? We want to keep tabs on all the lookalike mares for the moment."

"That's okay."

"Thanks, Felix. That's all I wanted." There was a pause, while he talked to someone in the background. "One other thing: your friend, Josie. Is she with you?"

"No. I'm not sure where she is. She left yesterday to go back to the Commercial. You might try there."

"Been there already. Madge says she no longer works for them. If you see her, can you tell her to call Worrindi Police Station? We don't want to lose track of her either. She needs to be where we can reach her. She hasn't surrendered her passport yet, although she still has the rest of the day to do that."

"I'll tell her if I see her."

The call ended, and I sat back in my chair. When would I learn that my initial assessments of people were more often than not spot on? I'd thought Josie was a drifter, one who would float away like morning mist when it suited her to no longer be around. And with no job, she had even less reason to stay around Worrindi.

I should be happy. I should take the memories of our nights together, wrap them in the pleasure of her easy company, the help she'd given me around the stables and campground, and file them away under the heading *Good Friend Gone*. I should keep the good things in my head, as memories of a happy time, and let the rest go. Josie wasn't a bad person. I should remember that.

But it was hard to let her go that easily. For a moment, I sipped my cooling coffee and remembered the laughter and the good times riding with her in the brush of an early dawn, our horses' hooves thudding hollowly on the baked ground, the touch of her hand as she pointed out a flock of budgies wheeling across the blue sky. Her company had made life lighter and brighter, and her presence in my bed had sent me to the stars and back.

I missed her.

I rose from the desk and chucked the rest of the coffee over the veranda railing.

Followed by my faithful shadow, Tess, I went down to the stables. Even Tess reminded me of Josie—her face when she'd given Tess to me: wistful, open, giving. Wanting me to be happy with the dog. Wanting Tess to have a forever home.

On an impulse, I grabbed a bridle and went across the paddock to where Flame grazed. I bridled her and vaulted up bareback. I relaxed as I eased her into a walk, feeling her muscles move under my legs, the warm smell of dusty horse in my nose. Flame flickered her ears back and forth, probably wondering what was up. I stayed relaxed and encouraged her into her free-swinging walk over to the gate and out to the long paddock. Keeping to a walk, we rode along the creek, Tess panting at our heels. She crisscrossed our path, nose to the dirt, taking in new and exciting smells.

I patted Flame. At this pace, she was the perfect ride. Gentle, easy, comfortable.

"You like it here, don't you, girl?" I said to her. "Relaxed life with your friends. No stress."

Her ear flickered back to listen to my words.

I turned her back along the fence line. Twenty minutes walking was enough for her. I didn't want a repeat of our previous time.

While the ride had cleared my head, it hadn't made the decisions I faced any easier. I wondered if Pen had spoken with Josie and what she had said.

I exhaled slowly.

Josie had been gone less than a day, and already I missed her in my life.

The day passed and then another. I hadn't heard from Josie, and I wondered if she was still in Worrindi or if she'd moved on. Twice I picked up the phone and started to dial her mobile, but twice I clicked off before the call could connect. I wanted to call her, but pride held me back. After all, she had said she was thinking of moving to Victoria, and now that she had lost her job in the pub, as soon as the police lifted their travel restriction, there was nothing to stop her. Once, I had hoped that she might want to stay around, but her silence, her lack of contact, made me curl up into a big insecure ball, afraid to put myself out there. I thought of driving into Worrindi, but really, I had no other reason to go, and quite simply, I was too busy.

Even though it was now the first week of November and the heat was already blistering, I had a bunch of tourists staying. There were six four-wheel drives, each with a couple or a family on board, all members of a touring club from Victoria who planned on staying three nights while they explored the area. They were a jolly bunch and had ranged their tents over the campground. My amenities block was stretched to the limit. Many of them also used the camp kitchen rather than their own vehicle-based set ups. Both cabins were also occupied, and so many people wanted to ride that I was taking a morning and an evening ride each day. It was great for my finances, and also kept me busy enough that I didn't have much time to dwell on Josie and what might have been.

I borrowed a saddle that fit Flame's narrow back from the main Jayboro Station and was able to use Flame for the guests a couple of times, although she wasn't the easiest horse to match to a rider. Too large for children, too feisty for an inexperienced rider, and of course the experienced riders wanted to go faster than Flame could manage. But I had one family where the mother was knowledgeable enough to manage her, but wanted to stay with her beginner children. Flame was perfect for that.

The four-wheel drivers had a roaring campfire every night and didn't need me to lay on entertainment. I brought out the damper anyway—it wasn't a novelty for this bunch as it had been for the others, but they enjoyed it nonetheless. And the guests in the cabins also came over to join the fun. But I missed Josie. I missed her relaxed company, her friendly manner that could draw out the most introverted guests and get them talking about themselves. Josie's easy knack of including everyone, her light-hearted nature... I missed it.

I missed her.

The Melbourne Cup came and went and was won by a horse from New Zealand. I got an email from Ger saying how pissed off Young Seánie was that Fiery Lights hadn't entered at the last minute, but as he had picked the winner, he was still quite happy.

Then I received a call from the feds, asking me to come in and give an official statement about Flame and my involvement.

"Where do I have to go?" I asked, thinking of my overflowing campground and mountains of work.

"We're using the Worrindi Police Station," said the efficient sounding voice on the other end. "Can you be there at ten tomorrow?"

I'd arranged a ride at eight for some of the campers. I wouldn't be able to do that and get to Worrindi in time. Then I remembered Sue's instructions for times like this. "I'll need to check with my lawyer," I said. "If she can make that time, then I'll be there."

"That's fine. Just let us know."

I hesitated. "Can you tell me if Josephine Beccari will be giving her statement at the same time?"

"I can't tell you that." There was no inflection in the voice. Nothing to give me any clues as to whether Josie would be there as well.

"No worries. I'll get back to you."

I hung up, and called Sue. She answered on the third ring.

"Whitely and Brent Law. This is Sue."

"Still no receptionist," I teased.

"Not unless there's a multiple vehicle pileup of wanna-be divorced criminals with outstanding debts who were all just about to purchase a house in Mungabilly Creek. That's the only way I need a receptionist. Although Mrs T's friend, Rosalie, has been hinting she'd like more work."

"Maybe I should come and work for you. It might be an easier life right now."

"Everything okay, Felix?" Sue's voice was carefully neutral, but I knew from past experience that she'd be there for me if I needed to talk.

"Yeah. I'm fine. But thanks for asking."

"You always say you're fine. You can whinge, you know. It's only Moni who's not allowed to complain around here."

"I don't think I've ever heard Moni whinge about anything."

"She does." Laughter in Sue's voice. "Trust me, she does. But anyway, I'm sure you didn't call about my office staff or Moni's complaints."

"You're right." I sat at the desk and moved three dirty coffee cups from one side to the other. "I got a call from the feds. They want me to give a statement. They told me ten tomorrow, but I said I had to call you."

"Okay. I'm sorta free tomorrow, but it will be hard to make it by ten given the distance. I can do noon. Would that suit you?"

"Much better than ten. I've got a trail ride at eight."

"Perfect. Can you call them back and say... No. I'll call them. It will sound better coming from me. If they can't do noon, are you okay for later?"

"Yeah. And of course you can stay over if that's easier for you."

"Thanks. If it's late, I'll take you up on that, but otherwise, I'll get home to Moni if I can. I was in Worrindi two days ago, actually, when Josie had to give her statement. I would have called you, but I honestly didn't have time to see you. It was hard enough to squeeze Josie in as it was."

"That's okay." I shuffled the coffee mugs into a line, all the handles pointing at the same forty-five-degree angle. "Was Josie's statement okay?"

"Yeah. I think she'll be right, but the feds aren't letting her off the hook just yet." Sue hesitated, then said, "I asked if she'd seen you, but she said she hadn't and changed the subject. What's happening, Felix?"

I didn't try to pretend I didn't know what she meant. "I don't know. You heard her; she wants to move on. She went back to Worrindi to see if she could save her job, but apparently they don't want her back. I haven't heard anything since. I guess now that she hasn't got Flame as the drawcard, she has no reason to come out here."

Sue heaved a gusty sigh. "That makes no sense. You make no sense. I don't know why Josie hasn't come to see you, but what's stopping you going to see her? She's still in town—she hasn't been told she can leave yet. My guess is *she* thinks *you* don't want to see her. You haven't been particularly open to her since you got back from Victoria."

"We slept together the last night you were here."

"Yeah, and did you say anything about wanting to see her again?"

"She didn't say anything either."

Sue was silent for a moment. "Felix, she's on your turf. Your house, your barn, your horses. Plus she was the one who was less than truthful with you. If I were in Josie's place, I think I would wait for the invitation too."

I swallowed, the thickness in my throat choking my words. When I could speak, I said, "Maybe I'll see her tomorrow. We'll be in Worrindi, after all. Maybe we'll bump into her—it's hardly the metropolis of Sydney."

"Maybe." Sue's voice was noncommittal. "Anyway, I'll meet you tomorrow in Worrindi. If they don't agree to the change of time, I'll call you. Otherwise, let's say 11.45am in The Drover's Rest coffee shop. If you're there first, I'll have a long black, double strength, with hot milk on the side."

"No worries. See you then." I hung up.

There were thumping feet on the veranda, and one of the campers stuck their head around the door. "Hi. I just wanted to let you know there's no hot water in the showers."

"Sorry about that." I gave him an apologetic smile. "The gas must have run out. I'll come down and switch the cylinder." At least I was going to Worrindi tomorrow; I could get a replacement then.

It took me longer than usual to do the rounds that morning. Every camper wanted to talk—either to ask about trail rides, or tourist attractions in the area, or simply to whinge about their cold shower. The showers were a mess, and all the rubbish bins were overflowing. The cabins had to be turned over, and the new guests for them arrived before I was finished. I suggested they take a walk around the campground or down to the horses while they waited, but they unloaded all their bags onto the cabin's tiny veranda and sat waiting, making it very difficult for me to get around them. To cap it off, when I went to catch the horses for the evening trail ride, Smoke was hobbling, barely able to put her near foreleg to the ground. It turned out to be a stone wedged in her hoof, but even when I removed it, the poor lady was still tender with a bruised sole.

I went back to the house for a late lunch. The light was blinking on the voicemail. I sat and pressed the button, but it was someone wanting to book a cabin. The disappointment was crushing.

I picked up the phone again. I wanted to call Josie. I should call Josie, but as my finger hovered over the button, I remembered once again the lightness in her voice when she talked about moving on. I remembered, too, the lies she had told me. I knew her reasons, and to an extent, I understood them. But she had still lied to me. My family had valued truth, and I always found the casual white lies that people told very hard to accept as normal.

"You call a spade a bloody shovel," Narelle often said to me. And she was right.

So once again, I put the phone down, jammed my hat on my head and went to groom the horses.

Sue was waiting the next morning when I arrived at The Drover's Rest. A coffee and a cheese and ham toastie were beside her, and a second coffee sat in front of the vacant chair opposite. She was reading a sheaf of papers, something dense with black ink, and making occasional marks with a red pen. I sat opposite and picked up the coffee. She peered at me over her specs, and set down the papers.

"Glad you could make it!" She grinned and tapped the side of her mug with her pen.

"I'm only five minutes late," I protested. I took a swig of the cooling coffee and set it down again.

"Your coffee would have been hotter if you were here on time. Anyway," she changed the subject swiftly, putting on her serious lawyer face. "You're going to give a statement. I'm not going to tell you what you can and can't say—indeed, I can't give you that advice. You must obviously tell the truth, without embellishment or exaggeration, and equally without deliberate omission. They may ask you questions. It's okay to answer them, but if I put a hand on your arm, you stop talking *immediately*. Got that? I'll only do it if I think they're trying to steer you in one direction or to trap you. I doubt it will happen, but if I do that, you stop. In midsentence."

I nodded and picked up my coffee again. "Did you have to do it with Josie?"

"No. Which is why I doubt they'll try and trip you up. Josie was always more in the firing line than you."

"Do you know if she's still in Worrindi?" I couldn't meet Sue's eyes as I asked the question. It felt wrong, asking my friend where my lover was, but my guts were still tied in knots. The coffee hit my stomach, and suddenly I felt queasy.

Sue took her specs off to see me better. "You haven't called her. Felix, you are bonkers. Utterly bonkers. She's so perfectly right for you, and you're sitting here asking me where she is." She took a bite of her toastie. "Do you know where she's staying in Worrindi?"

I shook my head. "No idea. Not at the pub though. You must know though, if you were there when they took her statement."

Sue was shaking her head before I'd finished the sentence. "Can't tell you that." She put her hand on my arm. "Sorry, Felix, but I can't. But it's really easy: you call her. You can even use my phone, which is better than your old thing." She pushed her mobile closer. "But after you've given your statement. Not now. Finish your coffee and we'll go."

I'd been nervous about giving the statement, worried that I would inadvertently say something that would make it worse for Josie. But the policewoman who took my statement set me at my ease from the start, and her questions were easy and unthreatening. I related how I'd come to have Flame, how Josie had told me about her, and how she'd arrived in the beat up cattle truck with no accompanying tack or kit. I answered questions as to when I first became suspicious and what led Josie and me to take the trip to Victoria. Throughout the questioning, Sue remained quiet. When the policewoman asked why I didn't call Crime Stoppers when I found Flame's microchip identified her as Fiery Lights, Sue's hand hovered briefly over my arm. But my answer must have been okay, as she withdrew her hand.

It was nearly two hours later that we left the police station. Although I'd been fine during the interview, my knees were wobbly as Sue and I walked out to the street. I wanted nothing more than to flop down somewhere and stare upwards.

"Got time for a beer?" I said to Sue.

"If it's a quick one. I'll have to leave soon if I'm to get back to Mungabilly Creek before dusk."

We went into the Commercial. My eyes instinctively searched behind the bar for a familiar curly head, but the bar person was a young girl with an indeterminate European accent who fumbled her way through our order for two pots. Madge watched her with steely eyes from one end of the counter. She was probably regretting letting Josie go.

We drank our beers, and gradually the tension of the past few hours seeped out of me.

Sue pulled her mobile out of her pocket and shunted it across the table to me. "So call her."

The phone lay face up. I stared at Moni's face on the screensaver and wished I had someone I loved, someone whose face would be on my phone.

"I'll go away if you want privacy," Sue added. "Her number's in my contacts."

I picked up the phone. "No, it's fine. You can stay."

I found Josie's number and pressed the call button. On the third ring her voicemail kicked in with a simple, "Hi, this is Josie, please leave a message."

I hung up. I didn't know what to say. What I could say in a one minute message? I pushed the phone back to Sue. She took it without saying a word.

"I know," I said. "You think I'm chickening out."

She quirked an eyebrow.

"Okay, I am chickening out."

"At least you know it."

She didn't say any more. She didn't have to.

# CHAPTER 27

THE MISSED OPPORTUNITY WEIGHED ON me during the drive back to Jayboro. I was behaving like an idiot.

I checked my email and found one from Pen. She included a link to an article on Fiery Lights. More details had been released, and for the first time, I read about the purpose of the lookalike horses. It seemed that the gang had purchased several chestnut thoroughbred mares which, to the casual observer, were identical to Fiery Lights. Calling each horse Flame and implanting each horse with a fake microchip identifying them as Fiery Lights, they placed them with unsuspecting horse yards around the country. Apart from our Flame and the two horses in Victoria, there were two in New South Wales, one in Western Australia, and another in Queensland. The gang members posted to various horse forums, using false names and dropping mention of a horse they knew that looked like Fiery Lights. The idea was to create a quiet buzz about the fake horses and ideally get the feds on alert, watching the imposters. Then, at the same time that someone tried to take our Flame, each lookalike horse was removed from their agistment, given fake papers, and taken to different seaports where they were bound for various destinations: New Zealand, southeast Asia, even America. With the feds already on alert, the gang hoped to create enough confusion to tie up border security at various seaports with the lookalike horses. They hoped that as each horse was checked and found to have a microchip identifying them as Fiery Lights, it would create enough confusion that the real Fiery Lights—disguised and implanted with a microchip identifying her as an ex-racehorse, would pass through unnoticed. By the time the feds had waded through the confusion, Fiery Lights would be out of Australian waters, on her way to the Middle East.

It was a long article, and I got to the end of it, sat back, and rubbed my eyes. It was an ingenious plan, which very nearly worked. Australia's borders were notoriously understaffed, and with multiple reports of Fiery Lights being shipped out of the country coming in at once, the real horse would have slipped out easily.

I wondered what would happen now. With this information now public knowledge, would Josie be allowed to leave Worrindi? Maybe she had already left, and that was why she hadn't answered her phone.

I thought about my life as I did a final check on the horses, a last walk around the campground that evening. My life alone. Josie was doubtlessly making plans to move to Victoria. The question was: did I want her to stay? Was I prepared to put our past history behind us and commit to her wholeheartedly? Was I prepared to put myself out there and ask her to stay with me?

I pondered the question as I ate my solitary dinner, and it was still rattling around my brain when I sat on the veranda with a beer. Tess came over and put her head on my knee, and I petted her.

"What do you think, Tess? Should I ask Josie to stay? One bark for yes, two barks for no."

Tess barked once, and I smiled. "Clever dog." But then she leapt away from me and raced to the other end of the veranda, barking furiously at the bobbing torch light going down the driveway. It must be a camper taking a late-night stroll.

Memories of Josie were everywhere. I took a shower and pictured her form, made blurry by water and indistinct behind the glass of the partition. And when I got into bed, the space on the other side was empty. Her space. I lay on my back and put my hands behind my head, staring up at the ceiling. Moonlight made light and shade in the room, and the night was warm. I got up again and turned on the ceiling fan, but it was still uncomfortably hot. I threw the sheet off, and lay naked to the movement of air. I turned from side to side. Tess, too, seemed restless. She paced around the bed, claws clicking on the wooden boards. Then her head appeared, resting on the mattress, right in my face.

"Come on then." I sat up and patted the foot of the bed. Tess jumped straight up. She'd never slept on my bed before; she was a big dog and I liked to sprawl in my sleep. Just this once, I reasoned. But if Josie didn't come back, then Tess may be my only bed companion.

Tess settled once she was at my feet, but I was still restless. I looked at my watch, glowing faintly in the moonlight. Just gone eleven. There was no way I was going to sleep anytime soon. I got out of bed, pulled on a T-shirt and undies, and went into the kitchen. Tess padded behind me—she probably thought she was in for a late night treat.

I found a tin of hot chocolate at the back of the cupboard, made myself a mug, and took it outside. Moonlight cast silver shadows over the ground. There was the click of a night bird, and over in the campground a small fire glowed brightly.

Thoughts of my parents slid into my head. They had lived together at Jayboro for nearly forty years. In that time, they had had their ups and downs, but they had faced them together. When I was young, when other kids' parents were splitting up and getting back together or getting new partners, I'd never doubted my parents' love for each other or for me.

They had always been the yardstick I'd held up to any potential partner. But they had taken a risk in the start: the station hand and the rodeo girl from far away. They had made it work. They had been happy. But somewhere, back in the mists of doubt at the start of their relationship, one of them must have taken a chance and laid themselves bare to the other. One of them must have set their heart on the line, open for rejection, if that was what was meant to be.

And here was I. Thirty-eight years old. Living in a place I loved, but living here alone. Maybe I didn't have to be.

*But what*, a voice whispered in my head, *what if Josie doesn't want you? What if she doesn't want to live here? What if she wants you, but not Jayboro? Would you leave Jayboro for her?*

That question was unanswerable. My life was here and, more lately, my business. I couldn't just walk out.

I pictured Sue and Moni. Their relationship hadn't been a stroll in the bush. Not only was Moni an American, but when she'd got together with Sue she'd been living nearly four hundred kilometres away in the Isa. But they had made it work, because they had wanted to.

Even if Josie didn't want to live at Jayboro, at least we could try. At least then, I'd know I'd given it a shot, rather than wondering what if, what if, what if.

I got up from the couch and went into the office and picked up the phone. Josie's number was written on a sticky note stuck on my computer monitor. Maybe Sue had put it there. I called the number. Once again, it went to voicemail, but this time, I left a message.

"Hi Josie. It's me, Felix. I'm wondering how you're going, whether you're still in Worrindi. I miss you. It would be nice to hear from you." I hesitated. "I love you."

I hung up, heart pounding. Had I really said that?

When I went back to bed, sleep still didn't come easily. Even Tess deserted me, jumping down away from my restless legs and twitching feet to sleep in her normal position at the foot of the bed.

I was finally drifting off to sleep when the phone rang. I sat bolt upright as if someone had jammed a fencepost up my arse. For a minute, I was disorientated. The phone shrilled again. I leapt out of bed and ran barefoot through the house to the office. I stubbed my toe on the leg of a chair, cursed, and half ran, half hopped the rest of the way. Tess followed at my heels, barking joyfully as if this were some new game.

I lunged for the phone in the dark, missed, and sent it and the base crashing to the floor. The phone stopped ringing.

"Shit. Fuck. Bugger." I went back and turned on the light. Not only had I knocked the phone from the desk, I'd also sent a half-drunk cup of cold coffee flying. There was a spreading stain on the rug. Leaving the cup where it was, I picked up the phone and set it and its base back on the desk.

It rang again.

I picked it up before the echo of the first ring died away. "Hello."

"Felix."

I knew the voice. How could I not. I'd heard it in my head as I'd stalked around the campground for the past couple of days, and I'd visualised the owner riding alongside me across my land.

"Hi, Josie."

I waited. I'd been the one to call her, so I should speak, but my throat was locked tight. Tentative coils of hope unfurled. She had called me. There must be a reason.

"I got your message," she said, and the line fell silent. A quiet sigh, then she spoke again. "I'm doing okay. I couldn't talk Madge into giving me my job back. She said she'd found a backpacker from Finland who works for half what I was getting. It's illegal, of course, but that's the way it is."

The inept person I'd seen behind the bar. Madge would regret that choice, that was for sure.

"The police say I can leave town. They've given me my passport back, and I'm officially not a suspect. They found Barney and arrested him. During questioning, he verified my story. Not to clear my name, of course. I'm sure he couldn't give a rat's arse about me. But he gave them enough information while trying to save his own skin that he confirmed my innocence. The police ask that I keep in contact, as I'll be a witness at some point, but I'm off the hook for being thrown in jail. At least for now."

"That's good." Indeed, it was. Until Josie said it, I hadn't realised how a little nugget of worry had sat heavily in my chest. Not for myself, but for Josie.

"I'm still in Worrindi," she said, "but I'm leaving tomorrow. I've got a job as a cook on a station about seven hundred kilometres to the south. The last cook left in a hurry, and they're desperate." She gave a short, humourless laugh. "They must be desperate to hire me. Madge gave me a good enough reference, it's not that, but my cooking is a bit haphazard. I hope they like burnt chops and mashed potatoes. It's my speciality. Maybe I'll get to Victoria eventually, but I'm not in a position to pass up a job offer after this length of time without work."

She was going. Leaving Worrindi, just as she'd said she would. For a moment, I considered the bright and breezy approach, the one that protected my pride, if not my heart. The one that would have me saying, *That's great, Josie, I'm sure you'll do well. See you around.* But words not spoken, mine, hers, had already brought us to this point. I had to throw my heart out there, even if she threw it straight back. And the hardest words had already been spoken.

"Is that what you want, Josie? A new place, a new start?" I was still taking the easy way out. I was still making her come to me.

I could visualise the shrug of her tanned shoulder. "Well, I need a job. And there's one going on Glenoak Station. It's the only offer I have."

"Do you want to stay on Jayboro? With me?" My mouth was dry, and in the moments of silence that followed, I felt light-headed with that queasy feeling that tightens your guts as you wait for something. I'd last had that unbearable freeze-time of anticipation when I was in the hospital at the Isa, waiting for the doctor to tell me Mum's test results.

Josie sighed. "What are you offering, Felix? We've already had so many layers of misunderstanding between us; I don't want another one."

"I love you." I said the words and waited with pounding heart.

"Thank you." Her voice was quiet and I had to strain to hear. "But I'm still not sure what that means to us right now. Maybe you need to consider exactly what you are offering me.

If I stay with you, I need to know how we stand. It's easy to say words."

"It isn't for me. I've never said them before to a woman."

She was silent for a moment. "I'll have to leave at seven tomorrow morning at the absolute latest if I'm to get to Glenoak Station by dusk. If you mean what you've said, if you are sure about what you're offering me, then come and say it in person. So that I can look in your eyes, and you can look at me, and we can work out what we mean to each other. If you're not here, then I'll leave. No hard feelings if you reconsider in the meantime."

My chest was tight. How would I get to Worrindi by seven with everything I had to do in the morning? "Where are you staying?"

"I'm at Alain and Narelle's. They offered me a bed while I looked for work."

I hadn't even known she knew them that well.

"Bye, Felix. Maybe I'll see you in the morning."

A click as she hung up. I put the phone back on the rest and pressed the heels of my hands into my eye sockets, trying to rub away the confusion. It would be difficult to be there by seven. I had horses to look after, a campsite to run, office work to do. My life.

But Josie might also be a part of that life, and if I let her walk away, for no better reason than I was too busy to get to town, how would I feel then?

I'd feel as if I'd missed a huge chance. There were no guarantees in life, and certainly not in love, but that was no reason to let opportunities slide by.

I had to go to her. I looked at the clock glowing on the far side of the room. It was just gone one in the morning. I would have to be up in three hours. Josie had said she was leaving at seven. That meant I had to be there at six at the latest if we were to have any chance of resolving anything before she had to drive away. I could leave at five and be there by half-past.

Or I could leave now.

"What do you think, Tess?" I said to my dog. "Fancy a drive in the dark?"

It was something I only did in the direst of emergencies. Outback roads were lethal between dusk and dawn. Kangaroos were unpredictable and were responsible for many single vehicle crashes. Cattle were hard to see in the dark and, on the unfenced roads, were like moveable brick walls. Even the smaller wildlife was a hazard. But this was an emergency; I would drive slowly.

I grabbed the keys to the ute, turned off the lights, and went outside. Tess bounded joyfully at my side, ready for the adventure.

I drove a lot slower than usual, eyes peeled for wildlife. I saw a couple of big red 'roos, but they didn't move from their position by the side of the road. Forty-five minutes later, I cut the engine outside of Alain and Narelle's house. The night was a bright one. A half-moon glazed the sky with light, and the stars blazed silver. The gate creaked, and I walked up the path. I knew where the spare room was; I'd stayed there myself in the past. I went down the side of the house counting the windows until I came to the right one. Although the house was single storey, it was raised on stilts out of any floodwaters from Birragum Creek. I bent and picked up some gravel from the path and threw it at the window. Most of it missed and tapped quietly on the timber wall, but some fell in through the open portion of the window. I got another handful and aimed again, and this time it clattered against the glass.

I waited for a minute, but there was no movement inside. I crouched to grab a third handful of stones, and as I straightened, Tess barked once, her happy welcome bark, and Josie appeared at the window.

"Don't throw more," she said in a low voice, mindful of the sleeping people around. "I don't want a face full of gravel. Wait a moment; I'll come out."

I went around to the front of the house. In a couple of minutes, Josie appeared, wearing shorts and an old T-shirt. Her hair was snarled around her face. She let herself out of the front door and came down the steps to where I stood. Tess greeted her enthusiastically, pushing her head into Josie's hand and trying to lick her face when Josie bent to pat her.

Josie straightened and looked at me. Even in the moonlight, her gaze pierced through me and her eyes glittered. "Shall we walk?" She gestured to the empty street.

I nodded and, with Tess running ahead, we went out of the gate and turned away from the town so that we were heading for the open bush. For the first few minutes, we didn't say anything. As I paced alongside Josie, I wondered how to begin. For this was my call. I had made the offer. I now had to follow it up.

As we passed the last house, I slowed our pace. Now we ambled along the bitumen road that led to Caldine and further west. The landscape was silvered from the moon and, apart from the chuck of a night bird, it was silent.

"I love you, Josie." The words, once said again, lodged themselves a little more firmly into who I was. They were a truth that was part of me, and the repetition burrowed them in a little deeper, made them more real, entwined them around my heart. "Maybe you've said those words to a lover before, but

I haven't. It's the truth. But I know I've made it hard for you to believe what I'm now saying. For me, love is trust, and we didn't have that trust between us."

"I know." She stared ahead at the silvered road leading straight as an arrow over the land. "That's my fault. At first, I thought it wouldn't matter because I would be moving on before there would be anything serious between us. Then I realised I was wrong, but it was too late. I'd already deceived you."

I dared to take her hand. "We're both at fault. And now I'm the one who held us back. You made it clear you wanted to make amends. I found that hard to accept. But for a long time, I couldn't reconcile the feelings I had for you with the distrust. Even when I believed you about Flame, I couldn't shift that belief across to *us*."

"And can you now?" She halted and swung around to face me. Our linked hands were still between us. "Or will I stay with you and find there's always that element of worry? Will it gnaw at you until you doubt every word I say?"

I thought of her actions when we were in Victoria. Then, she had done what she felt was right, both to set things straight between us, and to try and solve a crime, even if it potentially put her under suspicion. Those were the actions of an honest person.

I started to shake my head, but she dropped my hand and grasped my shoulders. "You can't know that. Now you think you love me. But do you love me enough to trust me in your life? You still haven't said what you're offering. There's no work for me in Worrindi. Oh, maybe in time, something would open up, but I don't have any security to fall back on. I need to work."

"I can't offer you a job, not one with a roster and decent wages paid every week."

"I didn't think you could. But I'm not going to live with you and sponge off you, Felix. That's not my way."

"I know that." The offer I wanted to make hovered on my tongue. But I didn't know how Josie felt about me, and I didn't want to ask. But I was damned either way. If she said she loved me, would I think it was to get something from me? But if I offered to share my life with her, and she didn't love me, then I stood to lose a lot. My life as I knew it. My security.

I trusted Josie. I loved her. I had to go through with this, or else I would always wonder.

"I was thinking of a partnership. Move in with me. Work with me in the campground, with the horses. Initially, I'd pay you board and some money every week. It wouldn't be what you're worth or what you could earn at Glenoaks, though—I simply can't afford that. But together, we could work to build the business. If it works out for us, then we'll make it an official partnership."

She was silent, and her eyes searched my face. Then she set her face towards the road again and resumed walking. "And us? What will our relationship be?"

I was surprised. Did she think that I was only offering a business partnership? I'd said I loved her. My instinctive response was to throw her question back to her: *what do you want it to be?* But I realised she knew what she wanted; she was making sure I wanted the same thing.

"I love you," I said again. "I was thinking of a partnership in every sense. Live and love together. Share a room. Share a bank account. Share work and good times. Build our business together."

"How do you know I won't wait two years until the relationship is recognised in law and then take off, demanding half of everything?" She didn't look at me but simply kept walking, her steps steady.

"You won't," I said. "I know you won't. If you agree, I'll know it's because you love me as well and want to build a life with me, even if you haven't said the words."

"How can you know that?" Her voice was hard.

"I know you. Now I do." I stopped. "I realised I believed you about Flame when we were in Victoria. And I know I hurt you when I said you were only a friend with benefits. I'm sorry. I should have said you were my girlfriend, my lover, my partner. But if those things are not what you want, well, I guess we'll have to try and find time to meet up halfway between Glenoaks and Jayboro."

"And if it doesn't work?"

"We'll meet that if it happens. That's a risk you take in any relationship."

She sighed and patted Tess's head absently. Then she stopped again and swung around, back towards Worrindi.

"Let's get back. I have to finish packing."

Packing to go to Glenoaks. Then she would drive away in that battered red car of hers. Sure, I'd said we could meet halfway, but the reality was it was unlikely to happen often. A station cook worked hard, and my life was busy dawn to dusk. The long slide into misery started here.

I turned too. "I'll help." There would be no sleep for me that night. I might as well make the most of the time I had with her.

She slanted a glance at me. "I should hope so." She took my hand again. "If I'm moving to Jayboro, the least you can do is help me pack." Standing on tiptoes, she brushed her lips across mine. "We can do this, Felix. You and me. I love you too. I have done for a while now. Thank you for trusting me."

And then, as joy swept through me like a sunrise spreading over the landscape, I caught her to me and kissed her, really kissed her. Tess pressed herself against our legs, and we kept on kissing on the long moonlit road until we didn't have breath. Then we drew apart. I smiled at her, my heart bursting with hope and all that was now between us.

"Let's go home to Jayboro."

# ABOUT CHEYENNE BLUE

Cheyenne Blue's fiction has been included in over ninety erotic anthologies since 2000, including *Best Lesbian Erotica*; *Best Women's Erotica*; *All You Can Eat: A Buffet of Lesbian Romance & Erotica; Sweat*; *Bossy*; and *Wild Girls, Wild Nights*. She is the editor of *Forbidden Fruit: stories of unwise lesbian desire*, a 2015 finalist for both the Lambda Literary Award and Golden Crown Literary Award, and of *First: Sensual Lesbian Stories of New Beginnings*.

Her collected lesbian short fiction is published as *Blue Woman Stories*, volumes 1-3, with more to come. Under her own name, she has written travel books and articles and edited anthologies of local writing in Ireland. She has lived in the U.K., Ireland, the United States, and Switzerland, but now writes, runs, makes bread and cheese, and drinks wine by the beach in Queensland, Australia.

### CONNECT WITH CHEYENNE:
Website/Blog: www.cheyenneblue.com
Twitter:@IamCheyenneBlue

# OTHER BOOKS FROM YLVA PUBLISHING

www.ylva-publishing.com

# NEVER-TIED NORA

*(Girl Meets Girl Series—Book #1)*

**Cheyenne Blue**

ISBN: 978-3-95533-451-2
Length: 131 pages (38,000 words)

Nora Kelly's London Irish family have only one rule when it comes to dating: Nora can date any woman she wants—as long as she's not a Flannery. The Kellys and the Flannerys have been feuding for generations, and time has not lessened the hatred. But footloose Nora has just met the woman of her dreams, and suddenly commitment isn't a dirty word. Trouble is, Geraldine is a Flannery.

# FLINGING IT

**G Benson**

ISBN: 978-3-95533-682-0
Length: 376 pages (113,000 words)

Midwife Frazer and social worker Cora have always grated on each other's nerves, but they have to work together to start up a programme for at-risk parents. Soon, the unexpected happens: they tumble into an affair. However, Cora is married to their boss, and both know it needs to end. But what they have might turn out to be much more than just a little distraction.

# WHERE THE LIGHT PLAYS

C. Fonseca

ISBN: 978-3-95533-421-5
Length: 285 pages (97,000 words)

Dr. Caitlin Quinn is a sophisticated, self-assured Irish art historian visiting Australia on sabbatical. That doesn't mean she can't enjoy the local scenery—especially sun-kissed Surf Coast artist Andi Rey. Their attraction is unstoppable, but their lives are moving in opposite directions. Andi doesn't need distractions, and a woman that eschews commitment spells trouble, with a capital "T".

# TIMES OF OUR LIVES

Jane Waterton

ISBN: 978-3-95533-417-8
Length: 244 pages (60,500 words)

For the residents of OWL's Haven, Australia's first exclusively lesbian retirement community, life is about not being afraid to take chances. Together, Meg, Allie and their spirited group of friends share their lives, hopes and dreams, proving that whatever the setbacks, hearts that love are always young.

# COMING FROM YLVA
# PUBLISHING

www.ylva-publishing.com

# YOU'RE FIRED
## Shaya Crabtree

When an inappropriate Secret Santa gift backfires, Rose needs her smarts to save her job and Vivian, her sexy boss, needs her smarts to save the business. Can they stop bickering enough to do a deal?

# HOLD MY HAND
## AC Oswald

When Bethany and Savannah split up Bethany is heartbroken. But a year later they meet again and their feelings are as strong as ever. So why did Savannah leave her?

Bethany is devastated by the answer and realises she will lose Savannah again – to cancer.

In a world where time is fleeting but love lasts forever, Savannah and Bethany can only hold each other and live their dreams.

*Fenced-In Felix*
© 2016 by Cheyenne Blue

ISBN: 978-3-95533-706-3

Also available as e-book.

Published by Ylva Publishing, legal entity of Ylva Verlag, e.Kfr.

Ylva Verlag, e.Kfr.
Owner: Astrid Ohletz
Am Kirschgarten 2
65830 Kriftel
Germany

www.ylva-publishing.com

First edition: 2016

Credits
Edited by Jove Belle & Michelle Aguilar
Proofread by Zee Ahmad
Cover Design & Print Layout by Streetlight Graphics